ABOUT THE AUTHOR

Braja Sorensen hails from the beaches of Australia but has lived in on the banks of the Ganges in West Bengal since the turn of the century. She is the author of *Lost & Found in India* (Hay House Publishing, 2013), *Mad & Divine: Collected Writings* (2015), and her first novellas, *Kavita: Search for Transcendence,* and *Short Lives: Growing Up to Die,* were both bestseller e-books on Amazon in 2016. Sorensen has other published works in the Vaishnava genre, including the well-received *India & Beyond: Plane Reading for Part-time Babajis* (Amazon, 2012). She worked for a few years on *Nava-vraja-mahima* (Lal Publishing, 2013), authored by Sivarama Swami: a four-thousand-page, nine-volume treatise on the sacred sites of India through the Vaishnava perspective of philosophy, pilgrimage and pastime (lila). Find all her books at amazon.com/author/brajasorensen.

BRAJA SORENSEN

JAICO PUBLISHING HOUSE

Ahmedabad Bangalore Bhopal Bhubaneswar Chennai
Delhi Hyderabad Kolkata Lucknow Mumbai

D I S C L A I M E R

This is a work of fiction. Names, characters, businesses, places, events and incidents are either the products of the author's imagination or used in a fictitious manner.

Published by Jaico Publishing House
A-2 Jash Chambers, 7-A Sir Phirozshah Mehta Road
Fort, Mumbai - 400 001
jaicopub@jaicobooks.com
www.jaicobooks.com

OF NOBLE BLOOD
ISBN 978-93-86867-40-7

First Jaico Impression: 2018

Page design and layout: Special Effects, Mumbai

Printed by
Snehesh Printers
320-A, Shah & Nahar Ind. Est. A-1
Lower Parel, Mumbai - 400 013

To my mother, Betty, whose 90th year began the same month as *Of Noble Blood* appeared and whose influence and grace are woven throughout these pages, as they are with me.

And to A.C. Bhaktivedanta Swami, a saint from another time and place, who was solely responsible for introducing the culture and philosophy written of in these pages to the whole world, whose influence and grace are woven throughout these pages, as I pray they may one day be with me.

PART ONE

1

Rajendra Gupta

Delhi

RAJ wondered if it would always be this way, these moments of morning that were his own: inhaling the first quiet breath before dawn, the aroma of faraway years that crept from the walls of the house, so still and silent he could almost hear the stories of love doused with pain seeping from the thick stone, feel the sadness and joy of a thousand lives coursing through the carved walls. There was a comfort in knowing that this was where his days had always begun, perhaps would always begin, secure like a Saturday afternoon matinee: muted, dusty, black and white. Quiet and satisfying. The end already written.

The distant sound of a metal cup dropped on the marble floor in the downstairs kitchen drew him into the day. Rising from his bed and switching on a small lamp,

Raj walked sleepily to the balcony. Stepping through the curtained doorway, his eyes wandered across Delhi's pre-dawn skyline, a series of black, blue, and grey shapes and shadows resting one upon the other. He wished it were always this quiet, but soon the sounds would begin. At least the November sun would hide its face for another hour; like a mindful attendant it lurked behind the dawn, keeping neighbours indoors and the sounds of morning at bay, preserving the sanctity of the early hour. While most waited for the sun to rise to pay their respects, Raj bowed his head and thanked it for remaining hidden... at least for now.

Taking a woollen wrap from the chair and draping it around his shoulders, Raj walked through his rooms to the open central courtyard of the house. Leaning over the railing he quietly called down to the kitchen, "O Meenu!" He heard the sound of scuffing slippers on the floor as Meenu appeared from the rear of the house and stopped in the archway of the courtyard. "Haan, Rajji?" Her tone was soft and familiar; Meenu had been with their family since she was born almost forty years ago, and her mother before her, and so it went.

Raj's face softened as he looked down at Meenu; she was like a mother to him, an unchanging part of his life. He asked her to bring tea, which he would take to Dadaji. It was a morning ritual Raj shared with his grandfather; he loved the scent of the steaming hot mix of herbs and honey that Dadaji's father had taught Meenu's grandmother to prepare decades before.

Raj turned and walked to the end of the landing, trailing his fingers along the smooth wooden balustrade atop the iron rail. The house was quiet, but as he neared Dadaji's room, he heard the bell softly ringing behind the heavy door, the sound of quietly uttered mantras drifting through the wood. No one was sure what time Dadaji woke, but it wasn't too far past midnight; he took rest early and needed less sleep as he grew older. He was in his early nineties, and Raj knew that soon would be Dadaji's end of days.

Raj rested his forehead on the door; for some months now he had waited awhile before entering, savouring the sounds and scents of Dadaji's devotion, embedding them in his heart and mind. He knew that soon they would live only there, no longer sending their welcoming notes to him each morning. He stopped himself from thinking of Dadaji's imminent quietus. So much was timeless in the morning of this house.

The bell stopped. Raj gently pushed the door; it was always unlocked, closed only in consideration of Mammi and Bapa, and his sister, Archana – before she had married – that the sounds of morning within the room would not wake them. "Namaste, Dadaji," Raj said quietly as he entered, greeting his grandfather with both respect and affection.

The light was soft, the cool weather granting Dadaji the indulgence of his beloved ghee lamps. A luxury only because of the rarity of their use, he sorely missed them during the months of the year when ceiling fans turned overhead. Now they lent a gentle warmth to the room and their flames danced as the air swept in with Raj. Shadows flickered with the movement of the tiny flames, flitting across the book shelves that lined the walls. Raj saw on the small table near the altar the *Puranas* and the *Upanishads* that Dadaji was reading, always one volume or another, their pages turned steadily throughout the day and night.

Dadaji was, in Raj's eyes, the ideal man: dignified, kind, loving, cultured, intelligent, deeply religious yet pragmatic in his approach to life, people... everything. He had never known Dadaji to respond to a person or situation with anything but grace, regardless of the circumstances. He possessed every quality Raj considered worthy of aspiring to. He was, in short, Raj's hero.

Pressing his palms together, Raj bowed his head to the deities on Dadaji's altar, inhaling the incense smoke that curled towards the ceiling and filled the room with a scented haze. Wordsworth crept into his thoughts, as often happened upon entering Dadaji's room...

while incense from the altar breathes
rich fragrance in embodied wreaths,
or, flung from swinging censer, shrouds
the taper-lights, and curls in clouds...

Dadaji, too, savoured the time spent each morning with Raj, and greeted him lovingly. "Rajendra, *mera pota,* my dear grandson. Your name, Rajendra, means 'best of kings.' Come, come. Sit, my little emperor..." Dadaji always began their mornings together with a touch of the sweet humour that was so much a part of his nature, more often than not making references to the meaning of Raj's name. After many years, it had failed to grow old. He smiled with love at his dear grandfather and, first bending down to respectfully touch Dadaji's feet, sat next to him on the divan.

"So, *pota,* what is it that is troubling you? I saw you

speaking to that nice British lady in the garden, and since then you have been preoccupied. Tell me what is going on in that head of yours, na?"

Raj was not surprised: Dadaji knew everything, despite leaving his room only twice a day for a walk around the garden and for the one meal he shared with the family. Yet he knew where everyone was at any given time, knew the comings and goings of family, friends, staff, and guests, knew the reason for the troubled brow of his loved ones and, best of all, how to smoothen it.

Dadaji's and Raj's rooms were mirror images, facing each other from the landings on opposite sides of the first floor, reaching from the front of the house to the back. On the upstairs floor, Mammi and Bapa's room on one side and Archana's old room on the other were the same. A large window at the rear of the room looked out to the markets in the laneway below, which, despite being busy all day, was still a back lane and rather subdued.

Sultanpur was an oasis in Delhi, far from the madness of the centre of town, its streets still more like India than the high-rise malls around the city. Beneath Dadaji's street window were grocers, fruit- and vegetable-walahs, and old-fashioned stores with wood-shuttered doors that were chained at night, with one counter and one man serving the customers. Everything could be found in that street; there was no need, Dadaji would say, to venture any further to the modern, multi-storeyed shopping complexes with neon signs and mirrored facades that graced the landscape down the road at Vasant Kunj.

The front window of the room looked out over the gardens and the peaceful, tree-filled suburb. It was a quiet area; the gardens were spacious, the houses a pleasing distance apart, and the families who occupied them were grateful for the seclusion and quiet, and they endeavoured to preserve it. Dadaji had seen Raj from his window two mornings earlier, speaking to the lady he had mentioned. It was true. Since then, Raj's thoughts had been unsettled, his mind distracted. He wondered if there was anything he could hide from Dadaji...

* * * *

Raj had been in the garden, reading on the lawns not far from Dadaji's window, when he'd met "that nice British lady." He loved winter, the only time of year it was possible to sit in the sun and enjoy its warmth, want it, drink deeply of it and swallow it into the bones, recharging the body and sprinkling vitality through the blood. Poor Surya, the sun god: loved by all in winter, dodged and cursed through summer...

He sat in a low-slung garden chair, his back to the midday sun, the warmth seeping through the canvas, through his woollen wrap, and into his skin. The lawns were wide, surrounded by blooming flower beds and trees that filtered the sun in summer, and sheltered the garden and house from the view of neighbouring properties. At the end of the garden, a large weeping-willow-graced side, small ponds and a trickling fountain at its base. To the right was the guesthouse. Although only a few years old, it had been built to complement the family home and its design: a graceful, old stone mansion adorned with balconies, beautifully carved walls, and elegant chuttris, small domes.

The guesthouse was his parents' retirement plan. Now in their late fifties, they didn't consider their future welfare should be the burden of Raj and his younger sister, Archana; they wanted their children to grow into successful and happy adults, able to be where they wanted to be, do what they wanted to do, not anchored to ageing parents with endless demands for attention and care.

After spending their lives in the family business – the Guptas were cloth wholesalers who had operated out of Sultanpur for generations – they saw the changes happening in India in the 1990s, and knew that, as their children were beginning school, by the time they finished, the world would be different. Technology, opportunities for travelling abroad, university degrees – these things could not be achieved while tied to a family business in which neither child had showed any real interest. Archana was married with a baby son, Marcus; her husband, Vijay, was already advancing through the upper ranks of the military, and so her interests and time and focus were directed towards a different life than that of a cloth merchant's daughter.

Raj's parents had thus sold their business shares to cousins and invested their life savings in the design and construction of the boutique guesthouse on the family property. The grounds and the home had been Dadaji's, and before that, his father's; for so many generations it had stood in that place. Raj's father, Paresh, was an only child and had been born in the house; when he had married Madhuri, there had never been a question of them not living with his parents. It was still Dadaji's house, in every sense. But when Raj's grandmother had died fifteen years ago, Dadaji had passed the ownership over to his son and lived like a retired dignitary, watching the next generations take over, happy to observe and always willing to guide.

Raj loved Sultanpur. Nestled in Mehrauli at the end of the Aravalli Ranges, it was a prosperous area surrounded by farms with manor houses set in acres of land, and home to a number of gated colonies where each residence was private and secure, with high walls and expansive gardens. Their family home was large and spacious, a beautiful, palace-like, stone mansion with large rooms on three levels to house the family of five, and Meenu and her mother.

Life was good, yet the restlessness in Raj persisted. He loved his parents and knew he was fortunate that, while they possessed a deeply rooted love of culture and tradition, they saw a future where imposing rituals on their children would not help but only hinder them. In all respects, he and Archana had been free to find their way in life. His friends were not graced with the same freedom: the restrictions, rules, demands, regulations, pressure to succeed, Raj could see it all as a tremendous weight on their backs that found its release in exactly those things from which the parents were so determined to protect their children.

Raj had excelled at school and had gone on to study language, history, literature and culture at university. Despite completing his studies with honours, he had not a clue as to where he was headed in life. During the past year, so many questions had entered his mind and had lingered unanswered. He had always been more drawn to and charmed by Dadaji's talks of life as he had known it, before the Internet, before Hollywood had found its way in, before the idea of the global village the world seemed to think it had become. Raj couldn't quite determine if these things were passing trends or permanent adjustments to the country's social and cultural landscape; consequently, he seemed to be treading water while the jury was out.

He would be twenty three soon; old enough to start moving forward into adulthood but still young to know what decisions to make that would form his future; mistakes were easily made but sometimes hard to undo. Archana's life also made him somewhat restless: her husband, Vijay, was Raj's closest friend, yet his own path led him away from Raj, not in mind or thought, but in a practical sense. Thus, Archana and Vijay, whose lives were already carving inroads into a seemingly predictable, secure future, unsettled him, the older brother, and made him wonder if he was wasting time.

The laughter and chatter from the rear gate of the property interrupted Raj's thoughts, as the heavy metal service door that opened onto the market lane clanged shut. He turned in his chair and saw one of the guests with Mr. Singh, the caretaker and manager of the guesthouse and his parents' long-time live-in employee, who was like an uncle to Raj. He was helping the woman with her bags, carrying them up the few steps into the guesthouse dining room that faced the lawn where Raj sat in the morning sun.

The woman caught his eye and gave a small wave. Raj nodded and smiled, and settling back in his chair, continued reading. He sensed her approach, though, her shadow reaching him like ink spilled on a page, followed by the delicate rustle of footsteps on the grass. "Morning..." the voice said.

Raj looked up and smiled. "Good morning," he replied.

Realising that the woman wasn't just passing by, he stood, offering her his chair. "Oh…no, that's not necessary," the woman replied. "It's fine, really."

Raj raised his hand and signalled to Mr. Singh to bring another chair, at the same time reassuring the woman, "No, I insist. Please, join me…"

As he moved aside, the woman reached out with her hand, "I'm Diane… Diane Ellington. Pleased to meet you. I've seen you coming in and out of the house a couple of times."

Raj shook her hand and smiled. "Raj Gupta, and the pleasure is mine. Please, make yourself comfortable. It is beautiful in the sun at this time of year."

Diane relaxed into the chair as Mr. Singh appeared with another, and Raj sat. He quickly took in Diane's accent, appearance, age, and other details that others often took time to notice and absorb, but which Raj had a talent of doing in a matter of seconds. His friends jokingly called him "The Profiler," ribbing his talent to accurately assess people swiftly and precisely.

Diane was British, single, in her late forties – he'd wager forty eight, but sometimes it was hard to tell with western women; they dressed differently from Indian women, aged differently, wore their hair, clothes, stature, gait, and energy differently. Raj remembered walking behind a western tourist last year: a slim blonde girl in loose-fitting jeans, white shirt, and Nikes, with a small bag slung over her shoulder. He had noticed how her shirt seemed freshly ironed, how neat and shiny her hair, tied with a blue band. And he remembered his surprise when she turned, and he saw it was a woman of around sixty. It was sometimes impossible to tell. His mother was that age, and while she was a classically beautiful woman and quite youthful in spirit and body, he could still not imagine mistaking her for a young girl, from any angle.

"I hope I'm not intruding..." Diane began. Raj shook his head. "Not at all. I was just reading," and held up the book in his hand.

"Ahh, such a wonderful book!" Diane said. Raj was surprised: the book was *The Romantics,* by Pankaj Mishra. It spoke, as Indian books often did, in a voice tainted with melancholy; deep, quiet, and heartfelt, a graceful slowness filling its pages and unravelling slowly, binding the reader in its words until the very last. Raj had spoken to guests occasionally about books, and they often said they found Indian writing slow, sometimes even boring, not gripping. Raj had read some of the foreign-authored, blockbuster bestsellers that tourists tended to leave behind in the guesthouse, and knew that the genre of classic Indian writing was a universe away from those; he understood the attraction towards action and pace, and found those books highly entertaining. Yet Indian authors often wrote with a pathos that could touch and move only those whose hearts danced to the rhythm of the same melody.

"You have read Mishra?" he asked Diane.

"Yes, I love his writing. This book particularly; I found it the first time I came to India some years ago; I have it at home and reread it every few years. I don't know any English or European authors who can write like this; maybe D.H. Lawrence? I don't know, perhaps Lawrence's fans would shoot me down for saying that," she laughed, and Raj found himself enjoying her chatter and laughed with her. "But there's a tragic kind of reality in the books I read in India, you know? And certainly Lawrence had that. Others too, a style that made them classics... does that make sense?" Raj nodded, and Diane continued, "Sometimes I think there is too much of a safe pattern with English authors, and I say 'English' meaning, you know, outside of India, not just British. But there is a beginning, a build up, the middle, and then usually an exciting and often unfortunately predictable end, do you know what I mean?"

Raj smiled and said, "I agree. I've read the classics, but not so many modern foreign authors, just a few; I like to read them to see why others read them," he laughed and Diane joined him. "But yes, I think you're perhaps right about the differences in the nationalities of the authors."

Diane said, "With Indian authors, I see a fearless kind of, well, 'unplanned willingness,' I suppose you could say, to simply let the book explore itself and produce what it wants. I wish I knew how to explain it better; I'm sure the authors put a lot of planning into it, but somehow it seems to flow in a way that appears to be just... natural. Free. Uncharted. Maybe it's just the Indian in them..." she laughed uncertainly.

Raj was curious; he tilted his head a little to the side and said, "That's an interesting turn of phrase. What do you think it is about Indian authors that makes them different from foreign authors?"

Diane thought for a moment. "You know, it's a fascinating thing, a contradiction almost, but I would say it's almost conversely the somewhat impenetrable and immovable foundation of their culture and tradition that gives them such a grounded platform, one that allows them the freedom to express. Not that the culture is confining or restrictive, but it is solid, it supports, it has strength and age and completeness – it gives such depth to a person, doesn't it? And Indian people have that depth. They all do. Well... most, I think. Or rather, I haven't met one yet who doesn't, be it a villager or a government ambassador or businessman – I don't know if I'm making sense..." she trailed off.

Raj was intrigued. He leaned forward a little, the book was closed, placed on the grass, his attention on Diane's words. "You're making sense to me at least," and Diane laughed a little.

She continued, "When a person already has that depth and foundation, they don't have to explore it or discover it or find a way to explain it in order to express in the realm in which they want to write. Does that make sense?"

Raj nodded. "It does. So you like the Indian culture and traditions?" he asked.

Diane was quick to respond, "Oh absolutely. I love it," she said, nodding. "Don't you?"

They both laughed. Raj considered it a curious irony, that a foreigner was expressing the same views on his heritage that he held, but which he found lacking in his friends. They seemed to always be fighting against the current of tradition that swept them through life's events from birth to marriage to death and all the rites of passage in between.

He answered Diane, "I do, actually, yes. I love it very much. And I think what you say is true. It is the very solidness and secure nature of that culture that gives one the strength and freedom to be themselves. I like that description."

Diane smiled. "Well, I'm touched that you do. I confess, I'm a bit embarrassed by foreign tourists sometimes, of how little understanding they seem to have of the country and its culture, or how they might only focus on the bad things going on, or the negative aspects." She paused. "You're so fortunate; so very fortunate. I wish all Indians could know how fortunate they are. But so many seem to want to know about other countries, or want to go to other countries, want to be like them. I guess it's natural, to want to do that: I'm here, after all, aren't I?" she laughed. "Perhaps it is the nature of the soul to want to explore?"

Diane seemed to have a fascinating view of life and people in general. Dadaji was always talking of the soul's nature, its propensities and desires. Raj hadn't heard a foreigner speak like this, though, and it intrigued him.

"So this is why you come to India?" he asked her. "To satisfy the yearning of your soul?"

Diane thought for some moments, then said quietly, "Well… yes, actually, I think it is."

Raj said, "Can you not find that in your own country?"

Diane was quiet again. "Perhaps. Yes, I'm sure I could. But I find it here. What is the harm in that?" she smiled a little.

There was a silence between them as the exchange shifted subtly. Their meeting had been unplanned, brief, and yet they had said so much, connected so swiftly on the same intellectual platform that Raj was simultaneously fascinated, moved, and pensive. That someone came to India to seek something for which their soul longed: this woke in him again the questions that had fluttered unceasingly around his mind, demanding attention, exploration, answers.

He needed to allow them, as Diane had said, their freedom; freedom to find their feet, grow wings and soar into the realm of possibilities that was the world, both this and the next, the one of which Dadaji so often spoke.

He looked at Diane and smiled. Reaching down to pick up his book, he said, "Your words will feed my thoughts throughout the day and night and no doubt for many more to come, and I shall relish their taste." He rose from his chair and, bowing his head slightly, took his leave from Diane, wishing her well for the remainder of her journey in India.

For the rest of that day and the next, Raj thought of his conversation with Diane. That this woman had touched on something so very prominent in his mind and heart was not, he thought, a coincidence: providence had entered his garden, sat in the chair opposite, and spoken.

For so long he had troubled over his life's purpose, finding no desire to join his single friends in their reckless decadence and indulgence in the things that his parents had never really had to contend with, or at least not on the level of availability at which they now existed: nightclubs, liquor, new cars, fashion, girls, movies, this band, these sunglasses, that restaurant, and on it went. Influenced by the movies they saw and desperate to imitate the lifestyles depicted, his friends seemed to be chasing life as though it were a Hollywood script. Raj was tired of defending both his disinterest in their pursuits and his pull towards Dadaji's strength of character that he knew was a result of meaningful, conscious life choices – even though, while it had been not so difficult for his parents, for Dadaji, it had been even easier. Perhaps it wasn't Dadaji's only choice, but still the natural one.

But for Raj, it was a different time. Over fifty years ago a door in India had opened to the world, and through it had come so many people seeking life's meaning in temples and mosques, on the sacred riverbanks of his homeland, and in the practices of his country's traditions like yoga and Ayurveda. They seemed to come to India with arms open, ready to embrace what to them was a far more appealing and attractive alternative to their own bland upbringings and traditions.

His older relatives and some of his friends' parents often spoke of the West as a bad place: corrupt, sinful, drenched in illusion, devoid of meaning, religion, and culture. It seemed to Raj that their talk stemmed a little from fear: fear of being challenged that their own life choices would be exposed as having no meaning, no real result, just something they did because it was tradition, not even really a life choice at all. Diane was right about the freedom that a strong culture gave, but he wasn't sure if she was right in saying that most Indians had that strength. Maybe some didn't: they simply lived according to how they'd been raised and never questioned why.

Yet that was one of the symptoms of the strength of which she spoke – to not feel the need to question or challenge or rage against the inevitable, to rebel without a clue or cause, but rather to accept, to live simply. Yes. There was definitely a deep inner strength inherent in that kind of life...

While his friends were always talking about them, Raj knew that American movies weren't a realistic portrayal of life in the West; he wasn't fooled by that. Still, he could not he believe it was all bad, either. So many European countries had such strong, ancient cultures. Surely there was depth in their traditions? Dadaji said this was true, but that they had abandoned so much of it, "modernised." Yet he saw that happening in India, too, the rush to shake off culture and tradition like they were soiled clothes.

Consequently, Raj often felt alone, stranded between those who thought the West was all bad, and his friends who wanted to drag him into the endless possibilities they believed it held. While he and Vijay were close, Vijay's career often took him away. Since the military was not a career path Raj would ever choose, it created some physical distance between them. Consequently, he saw more of his single friends, yet was becoming increasingly distant from them.

And here was Diane, a foreigner, leaving her country and coming to India, to find what it was for which her soul yearned, certain that she could, accepting that she hadn't or perhaps couldn't in her own land. But that so many foreigners were looking must surely mean they were good people, Raj thought; that they, like him, were not satisfied with the direction their countries or their lives were headed; that they weren't content to be carried on the waves of popular choice, to let life wash over them.

They, like him, were searching...

* * * *

Trust Dadaji to sense the effect that conversation had had on him; to see his unrest, to draw it from him. Raj told Dadaji of the exchange with Diane and how it had left him with more questions, not answers. "I don't want to chase that life, Dadaji, yet it can't be all bad. If those people are coming here, looking for so many answers, then they, too, must have had some strong foundation to know what is right and what is wrong, *na*? To know that something is missing. It can't be all bad, then, can it Dadaji?" Raj asked his grandfather.

Dadaji moved his head with that unique Indian vagary, and said, "*Kabhi haan, kabhi na*. Sometimes yes, sometimes no. India is the same, don't you think? Nothing of this world is all good, or all bad. It is all temporary," he said, laughing a little. "Indian people pouring out of their motherland and into America, thinking life would be better there; the whole country taking on this foreign culture and influence, thinking it would make things better; everyone dressing and talking and behaving like they are in Hollywood movies, thinking it would make *them* better. That much is wrong. But whose fault is it, *pota*?"

Raj waited; Dadaji had never been anti-anything or anyone. He wasn't given to ranting, it wasn't his nature. Raj knew Dadaji as the most compassionate and patient person in the world, a compassion that lent its own form of softness and beauty to his eyes, his features. He was a tall man, over six feet, handsome in his youth, refined in his elder years, soft and sweet in his old age.

"While India is rushing to be somewhere else in the world, just see what the world is doing: it is looking at India, it is coming to India, millions of people every year from all over the world, so many foreigners, want to come to India, they fly so far to come to India, searching for something. Spiritual this and that, yoga, religion, all kinds of visitors, some of them just tourists. But why India? Because it has so much history. So much of it."

"What kind of history do these visitors want to find here, Dadaji?" Raj asked.

"All of it. India's dharma serves every purpose. Just see, we have so much to offer, so much culture in every tradition – Muslims, Hindus, Jains, all of them Marwaris, Rajasthanis, Bengalis, in every part of the country, villages, cities, all have so much, so much. Art, music, poetry, literature. And all of it connected to God. It doesn't matter what we call him: Allah, Krishna, Buddha, Lord, this, that, everything," Dadaji laughed quietly. "Every tradition is rich, filled with the kind of wealth that only a godly culture can create and maintain. That is what people are looking for when they come to India."

Dadaji laughed at his own words. "Coming to India? *Arre*, even India is looking for this!" He shook his head and chuckled, then he became thoughtful, serious. "'*People praise the rich and variegated plumage of the peacock, and he is himself blushing at the sight of his ugly feet.*' You know this, your studies... Saadi, he wrote this. So much beauty and wisdom in Persian history, and such a language. Musical. You see? So mixed, we are so mixed here in India. And so rich. The whole world is coming, looking for answers in India, but India is looking out at the world, shamed at their own country, wanting to be like America. Just like the magnificent peacock who thinks it's feet are ugly..."

Dadaji's chuckle was small; amused by the world, yet untouched by it, he found the reigning confusion of the planet to hold a simple solution; a solution few seemed interested to hear.

"You see, *pota*? This is why the world is not happy. Saadi

says what every wise man says, what every holy man says, that we are the same, we are of the same *saram,* essence. So while one part of the whole is suffering, how can we all not suffer? This is why the world is not rested..."

Raj said, "But where is it, Dadaji? Where is this essence, what is it? Why am I not at rest, if I live in this country that has so much of what you say everyone is seeking?"

"Oh, it is there, all of it, it is there, *pota*. No doubt. It is there. But you must become *saravit*, one who knows the essence, then become *rasagya,* one who tastes the essence. You see? You must want to find it with all your heart. Not that you become a holy man." Dadaji chuckled. "No. We have enough holy men," he again chuckled. "But your journey is your own. Nothing of what is on the outside can tell a person what is happening within. So you need to find this yourself."

Dadaji paused. "India is like Hollywood." Raj's mouth unwittingly gaped in surprise at his words. Dadaji, though, was laughing, his quiet, raspy laugh touching Raj's heart. "Yes, just like Hollywood, *haan*? This Hollywood, so this is not a place. There are big film studios in America, but are they Hollywood? No, they are buildings. There are movie stars, but are they Hollywood? No, they are just people. It is not a place, it is a tradition, a consciousness. So these movies and movie stars, big famous people with gold stars with their names on it, this is Hollywood, *haan*? But you touch that, on the street, this... what is it called..."

Raj smiled, "Hollywood Boulevard, the Walk of Fame."

Dadaji smiled, "Yes, yes, this street with stars. So you touch this star with Clark Gable written there, or Marilyn Monroe, did you find Hollywood? No. You will be disappointed. Because it is not something you can touch.

"So like this, India is something you cannot touch. Not anymore. It is here, but its *saram,* its essence, this is hidden. It is not on the surface. Like Hollywood." Dadaji and Raj laughed softly at his analogy. "So these people, they come to India, looking. But so much disappointment. 'India is a big mess,' they say. 'So much poverty, so much uncleanliness, so much corruption, everyone cheating. Where is this real India?' They come looking."

"Will they find it?" Raj asked softly.

"Yes, *pota.* It is there, all answers waiting to be found. But time serves the demands of no man, *haan*? Patience. Humility. These things must be there, then answers will come."

Raj said, "So you have the answers, Dadaji? Is that what you do every morning in your puja? Does it give you the answers?"

Dadaji smiled. "*Pota*, you have always been drawn to this side of your character, things of a spiritual nature, always reading, absorbed in literature and spiritual philosophy. These other things, they don't interest you. Why are you not out with your friends, why are you not having girlfriends like all your friends? Because you do not want to. It is that simple. You are more interested in the higher things in life, *haan*?"

Raj sighed. "Yes, Dadaji. But even if I am interested, still the answers don't come."

Dadaji leaned forward. "Then you are not asking properly, *na*?"

Raj stayed silent, ummoving, his eyes locked on Dadaji, who sat waiting. It was Raj's move. He felt a subtle shift, like the universe had moved a little. While he was certain that this journey, as Dadaji said, was his own – on his own time, on his schedule, at his pace – he felt that right now an opening had been made in the course of their talks, and would close if he delayed or spoke the wrong words.

He took a long breath, then said in a voice overflowing with hope, "Dadaji… please tell me the words to say."

Dadaji smiled. "Yes. This. This is the right question, *haan*?"

Raj sighed with relief. Dadaji looked at him for a long time, humming a tune to himself, a *bhajan* he would often sing to his deities in the morning. Raj waited.

"So, it is time. Time for *chhota pota,* little grandson, to become Rajendra, emperor of his own destiny, *na*?" Dadaji laughed. "But understand, *pota,*" Dadaji continued, "it is not some test, some examination you pass or fail and get a degree. It is a process. All your life you have been listening to words from scripture, songs of the temple, prayers by your mother, your father; you sit in here with me, so many years now you have been coming in the morning, listening and watching my *sadhana,* my practices, *haan*? I have told you, this is your nature. It is not some magic; you are ready. It is as simple as that, *na*?"

Raj understood and nodded silently. "So you go. Go, be the emperor of your fate. Look for it wherever you need to look. Don't be afraid." Dadaji stood and walked to the bookshelf that ran the length of his room. Raj waited: Dadaji had told him many years ago, and often since, "Silences are not empty spaces demanding to be filled; they are allowed to just be." And as Dadaji grew older, Raj understood that things took longer than they used to, and these silences were inevitable. He watched as Dadaji leaned on his walking stick, head tilted slightly as he searched the bookshelf for something in particular. He reached "F" and found it, gently pried it from the shelf, and walked back to Raj.

Sitting back down on the divan, Dadaji said, "Froude, he wrote this, *The Nemesis of Faith*, in the nineteenth century. So much controversy, much is in this book; you may take it with you, but this one part, I am thinking of this one part while you speak." He chuckled again, "Even it says, 'if you will hear an old man's opinion,' so it is appropriate now, *haan*?" Raj smiled as Dadaji turned to a bookmarked page and handed it to Raj, saying, "Out loud, *pota*. Let me hear you read this."

Raj held the well-worn book in his hands and began: "'*You must learn what life is now, not from me, but from life itself; but, if you will hear an old man's opinion, I will give it you. If you think you can temper yourself into manliness by sitting here over your books, supposing you will grow into it as a matter of course by a rule of necessity, in the same way as your body grows old, it is the very silliest fancy that ever tempted a young man into his ruin. You cannot dream yourself into a character; you must hammer and forge yourself one. Go out into life, you will find your chance there, and only there.*'" Raj looked up at Dadaji. "You could have written this yesterday for me, Dadaji."

Dadaji nodded. "So much has been written, so much is there, waiting to be found again and again, *na*? It is so, it is so. Every man must go and find himself. You ask why these people come here, this is a reason also, something inherent in all men and women. So you go and forge yourself a character, yes? That is what we all must do. And at times, sit and wait, like one who wishes to see the sunrise must wait through the long hours of the night. In the end it will come. Don't demand that it serves you. 'Seek and you shall find,' these are the Bible's words. 'Seek and you shall find.'"

Dadaji paused, his stare was intent and deep, but Raj did not waver. After some moments, Dadaji said, "And while you are seeking, you pray, see? You chant this mantra I will now give you. This is the Gopal mantra. These two things – seeking and praying – this is how we find ourselves. You see?"

"Yes, Dadaji."

Raj bowed his head and paid his respects as Dadaji leaned forward and chanted the mantra in his ear.

And the universe again settled into place.

2

The Taj Mahal and Devi

THE Kerala Express pulled into Agra Station, heralding its own arrival with the screech of steel on steel as it drew to a stop at the platform. The carriage doors opened and hundreds of people burst into life, all insisting on being the first on or the first off, a simultaneous impossibility to which Raj quietly surrendered. Carried with the wave of exiting energy, his feet found the platform and kept moving with the flow until he reached the main gate of the station.

He breathed a sigh of relief; travelling by trains was not something he would consider an "adventure," but it was certainly more than just buying a ticket and moving from one station to another.

It was mid-afternoon; the gates of the Taj Mahal would be open until darkness fell. Raj decided to visit the monument first and think about other things later. He avoided the hawkers and tour guides and found a taxi driver to take him to the parking lot as close to the main entrance as possible.

He still wasn't sure why he'd come to Agra; it wasn't the first place that came to mind when he thought of his motherland's mystic secrets. And wasn't that what Dadaji had encouraged him to seek? He was certain the millions of tourists from the world over didn't come to the Taj Mahal to learn the hidden mysteries of India's spiritual heartbeat.

But that they came here at all intrigued him; surely there was something more to this city than Shah Jahan's monument to love, the tomb of Mumtaz? Or was it the essence of that tomb they sought, the love that had been the source of its creation?

There had been a far more powerful kind of love pulsing in this city in its heyday; more famous than Shah Jahan, more influential, far-reaching, and advanced as an emperor, India's third, Akbar, who ruled from Agra, laid the foundations for a united empire reaching all across the nation, a uniquely Indo-Persian culture adorned with the jewels of artisans, poets, architectural geniuses, holy men of every flavour, scribes, calligraphers, bookmakers, scholars, translators: the kind of India the world still hoped to find when they landed.

Akbar, though a descendant of the Mughal Empire, was tired of the battle-won victories that made up the empire. Over time, he replaced the dominant and negative regime of the invading rulers who had made India their home and had instead created an empire that served all who lived within its boundaries, uniting and encouraging diverse and varied religious practices, and introducing and supporting culture and the arts. His own library held over 24,000 volumes in Sanskrit, Persian, Arabic, Latin, Kashmiri, Greek, and Hindustani that was the *lingua franca* of the period. And all this despite his being unable to read.

Raj felt that what Emperor Akbar had created, what he had hoped would be his legacy, was possibly far nearer to what everyone was hoping to find remnants of when they came here, yet he wondered if the tourists even knew the real history behind the city that was home to the famous landmark. He wondered vaguely, too, if Shah Jahan had perhaps sought to eclipse Akbar's tremendous reputation and legacy by building such a dominating monument. He certainly hadn't done much to maintain his grandfather's principles: he drained the economy, gave scant regard to the farmers, created famine across the land by redirecting all growth and grain to his capital. He slowly destroyed the nation while emptying its coffers, all in his vain desire to build a tomb for his dead wife: a woman whose contribution to the nation, the world, to anything, was questionable. Shah Jahan had murdered his brother to secure the throne, even. The families of the empire were always neck-deep in intrigue, especially amongst each other…

Driving through Agra, Raj tried not to take in the surroundings; he wanted a clear mind and unprejudiced arena for his thoughts. The journey was short, though, and they soon arrived. After paying the driver he found an electric shuttle car to drop him at the gates: no vehicles were allowed near the monument, its preservation a serious concern, the area marked as a pollution-free zone to protect the historical landmark.

Raj finally made his way inside, the entry queues of mid-afternoon shorter than the morning, as most visitors were lunching or resting; pre-dusk would see a swell of numbers before the gates closed in the early evening. He kept reminding himself why he was here: not to view the tourist site, but to try to understand what brought people here. Surely not just to see a building, despite how stunning it was? He was certain it was something more than simply a burial site of a rather ordinary woman. Mumtaz had been regal, certainly, but was hardly remembered for any lasting legacy, besides that of her tomb. He could think of no former emperors, kings, or queens anywhere in the world whose burial sites drew the world's attention.

Raj knew that even the most renowned historians, experts in knowledge of the Mughal era, were cynical of the reason for the Taj's creation: Shah Jahan's love for his wife. Yet in the emperor's biography, *Padshahnama*, Raj had read of how, on the death of Mumtaz, Shah Jahan's heart had indeed broken, his loss of the woman who was his equal in all respects too much to bear. Still, the emperor's own claim about the glories of the Taj Mahal – words carved into its pillars – were, Raj thought, excessively sentimental:

Should guilty seek asylum here,
Like one pardoned, he becomes free from sin.
Should a sinner make his way to this mansion,
All his past sins are to be washed away.

Was this the essence of this world-famous tourist site? Raj had found no religion, tradition, holy man, wise man, scholar – in fact, nothing or no one – that could support

Shah Jahan's words, that one was free from sin upon visiting the Taj Mahal. Mumtaz, while lauded for her noble lineage and for mothering fourteen children, was not renowned for her saintliness. That her burial site represented something more than fine architecture was doubtful.

But the monument itself was stunning. Raj stood near a pillar at the *darwaza*, the main gate, which bore the same calligraphy that graced the walls of the tomb. He gazed across the now British-style lawns and pathways that had once been exotic Persian gardens and was captivated by the beauty of the red sandstone mausoleums of Shah Jahan's other wives – and even one of Mumtaz's favoured servants – that lined the eastern and western boundaries of the grounds.

Raj walked across the lawns, and as he neared the monument he was entranced at what a phenomenally beautiful and enormous creation it was, one that was deservedly one of the wonders of the world. Despite its fame, though, the source of its beauty and the design itself was not Shah Jahan, but his father Jahangir's empress, Nur Jahan – known as Mehr-un-Nissa – who had designed and built a smaller version known as the Itmad-Ud-Daulah's tomb for her father, Ghias Beg, on the banks of the Yamuna River years before Mumtaz had died.

The Taj was a far bigger version of Mehr-un-Nissa's design and had taken twenty thousand workers and twelve years to build, with an additional ten years to complete the outlying buildings. The exquisitely detailed inlays on the white Markani marble were breathtaking: jade and crystal from China, turquoise from Tibet, sapphire from Sri Lanka and lapis lazuli from Arabia, diamonds from Madhya

Pradesh – altogether around thirty different precious and semi-precious stones in varied designs. The inlayers had been brought from South India, sculptors from Bukhara in Madhya Pradesh, calligraphers from Persia and Syria; even one specialist who carved only marble flowers. Raj knew these inlays weren't the originals; it was no secret, the shameful history of the British soldiers and officials defacing the stunning monument, hacking out all the precious stones from the walls and inner chambers. But the massive restoration that followed, launched by Lord Curzon, was completed in the early years of the twentieth century, its finishing touch a stunning lamp in the interior chamber, based on a design found in a Cairo mosque.

Still it was disappointing to Raj that something so detailed and beautiful could ultimately mean so little. He wondered what the other visitors and tourists were thinking: all this, just for the love of one woman? He was obviously still missing something.

Standing on the eastern platform of the mausoleum, Raj looked out at the Yamuna and across to the gardens on the opposite bank. Feeling suddenly overwhelmed at the futility of his visit, he wanted to be out of there and across the river, sitting on the quiet and peaceful banks and viewing all of this from a distance. He started to make his way towards the exit. It was just over an hour till dusk, and he knew where he wanted to be and what he wanted to be doing when it came...

* * * *

Outside the *darwaza,* Raj turned toward the eastern gate of the grounds and, passing through it, made his way down the track that ran alongside the boundary wall and towards the Yamuna. On reaching the banks, he saw a boatman resting on his haunches and smoking a *bidi.* With a slight upward jerk of his head and a raised eyebrow, the boatman wordlessly asked Raj where he wanted to go. Raj indicated the bank opposite. "*Bas?*" asked the boatman. "That's it? Nothing else?"

"*Bas,*" Raj replied. They agreed on a price, and Raj climbed in.

The Yamuna was wide and calm; Raj felt like he and the boatman were the only two people in the world. A flock of birds rose into the sky as the boatman's oar stirred the waters, and Raj turned to watch them soar westward over the dome of the Taj Mahal. It was a short ride across the water; when the boat bumped into the land, the boatman helped Raj clamber onto the bank, committing to wait until dusk to take him back to the other side.

The boat had stopped near a crumbling ruin, and Raj walked along a low adjoining wall, which led to a clearing above the bank of the river. The former beauty of the ruin was evident still; it was the only remaining one of the four domed octagonal towers that had been built on raised platforms to mark the corners of the gardens that had once lain within.

As Raj reached the clearing, he stopped. This, then, was the legendary Mehtab Bagh or Moonlight Gardens. Originally, one of Emperor Babur's eleven *charbaghs* – Persian-style gardens divided into four quadrants and lined with a network of paths, waterways, exotic trees, shrubs, and flowers – that had been built more than a century before the Taj Mahal, it was here on the bank of the river that Shah Jahan had stood and appreciated the view of the monument to his beloved Mumtaz on its completion, a view that inspired him to have this southeast corner of the original garden rebuilt, its width identical to that of the Taj Mahal, its view perfect.

Legend speaks of Shah Jahan's wish to build a twin black monument on this bank for his own burial site, but he was imprisoned by his son, Aurangzeb, before his plans could reach fruition. Even now, Raj knew, many spoke of the rumoured Black Taj. But is was just that: a rumour. Only a few years back, he remembered, archaeologists had reconstructed the original central feature of Shah Jahan's carefully designed garden: the pool. As the moon rose, they realised they had discovered the infamous "Black Taj"; the moonlight illuminated a dark reflection of the Taj Mahal in the pool's surface. It was a wondrous revelation of Mughal and Persian beauty and expertise, their obsession with symmetry, the positioning of the pool, and the layout of the gardens all combined with the artfulness and grace so typical of the culture and style of the day.

And the emperor had been right. Raj looked across the Yamuna and understood how perfect a viewpoint this was. The monument shone in the now-setting sun, the visitors small and ant-like, swarming around its base. Waterbirds waded at the shore, idly picking at the river's surface. It was a beautiful scene.

As the arrival of dusk coloured the sky, a mist began to rise from the Yamuna. Raj realised it was the time that he always chanted the mantra Dadaji had given him that day in his room, encouraging him to go and find those things that would satisfy his heart, mind, and soul with this mantra as his guide. It was indeed the reason he was here. Finding a large, flat tuft of grass, Raj sat facing the river, letting the chaos of the day drift from his mind, and allowing the peace of early evening to settle around him. As he prepared to chant the mantra, his thoughts turned, as they always did, to Dadaji.

* * * *

After Dadaji had given Raj the Gopal mantra, he had told him to come in the evening also. "Dusk," he had said. "Morning, midday, dusk: this is when you chant. If you are at home, then I am here, so come."

And so he had. It was a serious, mature practice to undertake, Raj thought. He felt very grownup about it, anyway. It made him feel responsible, older... like he was ready, going forth. Into what, he didn't know. Or how. But it was something. And because it was from Dadaji, it meant so much more to him. He would absorb his mind in the mantra, praying for direction, offering the words with a strong desire to know himself, his purpose, and his place in this world, in life, with God. Yes, he felt serious and directed.

Dadaji had spoken so many things to Raj that morning. "Clean, *pota*. The mind has to be clean. There are six senses, and the mind is the king of these senses. So when it is clean, then all the senses are clean, *na*? So you clean first the body; always be clean when you chant. Bathe. This is first. But this is external – how is the body clean inside also? You keep the body pure, already your whole life you have done this, what has gone into your body is pure, no pollution by unclean things: meat, alcohol, drugs, these things, *na*? Meat, it is not some lifestyle choice, *haan*? Compassion. How you can be compassionate, how one can know what is right and wrong when one is eating violence?" Dadaji shook his head, sadness in his eyes. "So many people looking for answers to life, but how to hear, when the mind is not clean. And the mind is not clean because the body is not clean. What to speak of the heart... this is not possible. Not possible."

Dadaji paused. "If you want to grow a beautiful flower, do you plant it in the snow, or cover it with cement? No. It requires fertile ground, then it will bloom, it will give a wondrous scent, it will attract with its beauty.

"So the senses, the body, all must be clean. Then the mind is also, and you can chant the mantra. And if you chant this way, then the heart is touched. The mantra reaches there. That is what you want: that the mantra reaches the heart. The heart is the seat of the soul. You want that your soul directs your journey in life? So, then, this is how."

From that time on, Raj's mornings with Dadaji changed. Their relationship deepened and the bond between them grew stronger. Dadaji had planted a seed in Raj, a seed he watered daily, nurtured; he felt joy when tiny buds started to grow, and waited for the leaves to unfurl, the flowers to blossom.

Raj had always visited the Chhatarpur temple near their home on festivals or special days. Now, since Dadaji gave him the mantra, he went as often as he could. He would find a quiet place near the altars and sit, sometimes deeply absorbed in his mantra, sometimes watching the comings and goings of the pilgrims, tourists, and locals.

The temple – one of the oldest and largest in Delhi – contained many altars laid out in a circular pattern across the acres of land it occupied. He had his favourite two places in the temple: the first in the small pavilion of the Shiva-Parvati altar, where pilgrims would file through, yet seldom come near the wall to the side where Raj sat, his gaze always on the beautiful silver and gold form of Parvati, in particular, whose own gaze was locked always on that of her son, Ganesh, in the altar at the opposite end of the pavilion.

The second place he sat was in front of Devi. Though the temple's principal deity was Katyayani, she was only on view once a year for some days at the end of the auspicious month of Kartika, in November; the rest of the time she presented herself in her form of Durga, a stunningly beautiful silver form whose soft, loving face was appealing, kind, and welcoming. This was, in short, his Devi: the form of Katyayani that was the object of his meditation while he chanted.

* * * *

And now, a few short months later, he was here, sitting on the banks of the Yamuna in Agra, the still-bright, pearly silhouette of the Taj Mahal across from him. Amber and pink streaked the sky as dusk began to bloom, and Raj watched tiny splashes rise from the Yamuna as the waters flickered in the last light of day. It was a surreal and spectacular sight, and he allowed his eyes to close as he began to chant, thinking of Dadaji, of his wisdom and affection.

The light changed. Deep inside his mind, Raj withdrew the natural impulse to open his eyes and look; *it was nothing, let it be.* The light was fading, if anything, not growing, he reminded himself. He maintained his absorption in the words, drifted with them as they reached a higher place, still here but somehow not, subtly higher than the ground upon which he sat.

"Rajendra..."

It was distant, at first. A woman speaking his name. Again he resisted the impulse to look; there was no one there, he told himself.

"Rajendra. You asked a question. Will you not hear the answer?"

He opened his eyes. The universe had definitely shifted.

Everything about her sparkled, thousands of tiny lights leaping around her exquisite form, from the intricate gold belt that adorned her waist to the tinkling bells dangling from her armlets and bangles, and the shimmering jewels on her fingers. Her throat was decorated, a gorgeously jewelled throne to her milk-soft, moon-like face, her cheeks reflecting the twinkling diamonds and shining gold of her long, swinging earrings. Endless strings of pearls draped her hips, their elegant movements making lustrous waves against the gossamer red silk that swathed her body, falling in liquid folds to the ground. Droplets of the Yamuna's waters splashed around her, sprinkling like weightless diamonds to the ground near her toes, which peeked from the golden hem of her sari and glistened like blushing rubies.

Blue-black curls framed her face, and above her dark, long, *kaajal*-rimmed eyes, her eyebrows swept delicately across her brow like the graceful wings of a songbird. Her eyes danced, her head tilted slightly, and the musical lilt of her voice mesmerised him.

A thousand words flooded his mind, yet none of them sufficient to address this… this… *goddess. Who was this?*

"For so long you have worshipped me, sat in my temple, offered prayers, asked for answers to your questions. Yet I stand before you, and you do not recognise me? Look with your heart, Rajendra: I am Devi, whom you worship as Katyayani, as Parvati, and as Durga." She held her arms open, smiling at Raj. "Now do you see?"

All Raj could think of was how impossible this was: gods and goddesses didn't *appear* in front of people. Did they? No one he knew, at least.

"Why would I not appear before you?" Devi asked, answering his question. "Is it imagination, these prayers you speak, this mantra you chant, these desires in your heart to understand the essence of life?"

Stunned first by her beauty and then her words, Raj realised he hadn't yet spoken; that this goddess whom his family had worshipped for centuries stood before him was unfathomable, but more real every moment she lingered. He half expected her to evaporate in the blink of an eye; Devi, however, was not moving, though the air around her vibrated with her energy.

"So?" she said.

Raj gathered his senses, stood quickly, and then offered her his *pranams*. "My deepest respects to you, Sri Devi," he said, and bowed down before her.

He felt her touch his head as she said, "Stand, Rajendra. I have already received your worship and respects. Your mantra has brought me here; I have heard your words, listened to your heart, and so I have come."

"But why to me, and why here? I don't understand... you can appear anywhere, but why here, in Agra?"

Devi smiled and turned slightly, her long, lotus-shaped eyes sliding slowly to the domed outline of the Taj in the early evening sky. "Many do not know what it is they seek; they know simply that they are curious of a different nation or culture, or they are unfulfilled and, like you, they are looking for life's meaning and purpose: *saram.*"

She turned back to Raj, and he thought he might lose consciousness: her beauty and energy were almost too much to bear. "But why am I here, you ask? Among other qualities, I represent royal power, universal sovereignty, knowledge, kingdom, fortune, and beauty. These things lived here when the empire was ruled by pious men. For centuries, beyond the reach of man's memory, historical records, or tradition, I have been witness to the bountiful results of a properly ruled empire, where culture and order were welcomed, where godly men were given shelter and respected by the people, by rulers who sought their counsel and direction.

"Dharma was honoured. People lived their lives not confined by religious dictation or fear of recrimination, but with joyful commitment to the ideals by which they were raised, and by which they lived." Devi paused, raising one eyebrow slightly, then continuing, "Certainly evil and suffering have always co-existed with success and righteousness: this is to be expected. But in a cultured empire, such things are dealt with swiftly, and to the satisfaction of most.

"Those qualities I represent, they lived here, too, and thus everyone lived in harmony. Is it any wonder that people long to know the secrets of the past, and come here to seek them?"

Raj understood and nodded. "Yet..."

Devi tilted her head slightly, smiling at the questions rising in Raj's mind. "Yet... what of this monument to love?"

Raj was somewhat embarrassed at his ignorance, but Devi's smile did not indicate any disappointment in his questioning mind. Again her eyes swept over the river to the Taj Mahal as she said, "Yes, this is a monument, but not to love. It is a folly of attachment. It serves no purpose."

While Raj had thought this for some time, still he was surprised to hear the words coming from Devi, the demigoddess of the material world, whom the entire Hindu population of India worshipped. He said, "I fear India's people would be disappointed to hear this from you, Devi," he said.

Devi laughed a small, melodious, sweet laugh that took Raj's breath away. He had to keep reminding himself this was not a dream, that he was standing on the banks of the Yamuna speaking with a demigoddess, *the* demigoddess, Devi, opposite the most famous monument in the land, in the world, but which she had called a folly of attachment. "Do not be so sure, Raj," she said.

Raj was surprised. "What do you mean, Devi?"

"Tell me, Rajendra... tell me of the great love stories in

India's past. Tell me of those whose names are spoken by people the world over, burned into the minds and hearts of all, even written into Bollywood scripts, their love for each other the cause of their fame? Who are they, Rajendra? Tell me..."

Raj looked away, across the river's still-shining surface, thinking of Devi's words, and those of his history professor at university, who had often spoken the same words as Devi. Raj recalled those words now, and said, "I can only think of... perhaps... Radha and Krishna... Sita and Rama..." his words trailed off as he wondered what Devi would think of his response.

Her smile didn't change. "Yes. We have no Romeo and Juliet; no Antony and Cleopatra, no Virgin Queens who ruled the hearts of the people while ruling their land. We have Krishna and his eternal consort, the most challenging, misunderstood, and beautiful story of true love. We have the most adored and esteemed ruler in history, Ramachandra and his Sita Devi. We have so much more than a foolish love story, you see? This land is home to thousands upon thousands of monuments to this love of Radha and Krishna, or Laksmi and Narayana, or Ramachandra and Sita Devi. These monuments are your temples – the repositories of your prayers – and the altars within are the homes of the personalities you venerate and long to serve."

Devi turned to face the Yamuna, and Raj, standing to her right, followed her gaze and looked eastward as Devi lifted her arm, its movement sweeping across the river as she spoke: "This river was once the playground of Krishna and his friends, its shores the place of their sweet pastimes. These banks were decorated with gardens leading all the way to Vrindavan and Mathura. Cultured people, educated rulers, godly empires: these elements combine to preserve those things that have meaning. It should be no surprise to you, then, that so many come to this place and feel some magic."

Again she laughed her melodious laugh. "But it is not the magic of this tomb they are feeling. No, this is but sentiment. Consider carefully, Rajendra: Akbar the Great was overthrown by his son with the assistance of his own harem of wives. Such betrayal! Alas, Jahangir, despite his successful reign, had the same fate visit him... as fate is wont to do. His sons, Khusrau and Khurram, both attempted to overthrow their father's rule but were defeated. Khurram murdered his brother, and eventually, on his father's death, ruled the empire: this was Shah Jahan."

Raj considered the lofty price paid by these men to fulfil their desire to rule, and the undercurrent of turmoil and intrigue that went on regardless of how successful their rule.

Devi sighed and turned to Raj. "Do not mistake my words for a lesson in history, Rajendra. One can read of these things anywhere. It is not for this purpose that I come. It is to show you the illusion of this monument, the godly yet misled men behind it, and the culture and history that people seek, all of it based on the oldest and most powerful of spiritual love, that of Radha and Krishna, Rama and Sita. It is no coincidence. Think, and decide for yourself what it is even the rulers of this land were seeking. It is the same thing you are seeking: the ultimate success of life, the essence of being.

"Rajendra, I came to show you that there is always something other than what you see on the surface. But you must find this yourself. By your own intelligence and good sense you know what is not. So now go and learn what *is*."

Raj was relieved in so many respects, yet more questions arose. "But how do I do that? Do I simply go to all these places that everyone is drawn to and wait?"

Devi laughed again. "Yes! That is precisely what you must do. What *you* must do. But remember, dear Rajendra, there is always something more than what you see. Even the person who encouraged you to come here, who has set your course and laid your foundations, he is more than you realise. You see him only as Dadaji, but know this, Raj; he is your spiritual guide and guru. Bear this in mind, and you shall find your way. But listen, Rajendra, and I will tell you a story. Then I will leave it in your hands.

"Many centuries ago, a great king encountered a wandering holy man. The king noticed that this holy man seemed exceptionally happy. He was curious, and asked the holy man about the cause of his happiness.

"The holy man replied, 'I have taken shelter of twenty four gurus: the earth, air, sky, water, fire, moon, sun, pigeon, and python; the sea, moth, honeybee, elephant, and honey thief; the deer, the fish, the prostitute, the *kurara* bird, the child, the young girl, the arrow maker, serpent, spider, and wasp. By studying their activities I have learned the science of the self.'"

Raj was fascinated: this seemed like the kind of thing Dadaji would say, sharing stories whose depth and meaning were hidden in the wondrous detail of his telling. Devi continued, "From the earth he had learned how to be sober, and from the mountain and the tree, he had learned, respectively, how to serve others and how to dedicate one's whole life to the benefit of others. From the wind he had learned how to remain uncontaminated by the objects of sensual indulgence."

Devi paused, looking up at the sky: like an artist's canvas it was splattered with rich colours and cloud formations in the deepening dusk, reflecting on the waters of the Yamuna. "From the sky he had learned how the soul is both indivisible and imperceptible, and from the water he had learned how to be naturally clear and purifying. From fire he had learned how to destroy all the inauspicious desires of those with whom he came into contact."

Devi indicated the setting sun with her left hand, the rising moon with her right, and said, "From the moon, he had learned how the body undergoes growth and dwindling, and from the sun, how to avoid entanglement – both the sun and the moon come and go, appearing and then disappearing, not affected by anything that goes on in their presence. You see, Rajendra?"

Raj was absorbed in Devi's words, and nodded without speaking. She continued, "From the pigeon he had learned how too much affection and excessive attachment are not good for one."

They both turned to look across the waters at the Taj Mahal; it was obvious that the lesson of the pigeon bore more than a passing resemblance to Shah Jahan's own folly.

Raj's attention was drawn back as Devi approached the end of her absorbing tail. "From the python he learned how to accept whatever comes of its own accord or which is easily obtained." This appealed to Raj, and he wondered how he would remember all the things Devi was saying. "From the ocean, the holy man had learned depth and gravity; he does not become elated when he achieves desirable things, nor does he become distressed in their absence.

"He learned that, like the moth who is enticed by the fire and gives up his life, the fool who cannot control his mind becomes enchanted by so many things: youth, beauty, and the body, along with its glittering ornaments and fine clothing."

Devi paused and smiled. "You see, Rajendra? Just as a bee goes from flower to flower to collect the nectar, so should an intelligent person collect the essential truths from all scriptures, be they great or insignificant. And just as the honeybee collects nectar daily, a mindful person does not hoard, as he knows his greed will destroy him. Like the elephant who avoids capture, a sober man is not lured by what the world offers him, and is not deterred from his spiritual path.

"He learned that just as the thief waits for someone's hard work to accumulate, so the false guru will take wealth and gifts given by the hard-earned money of his followers; that as the deer is lured by the sweet song of the hunter's flute and thus loses his life, so that music which does not raise the consciousness or purify the heart serves no purpose and wastes one's life." Again Devi looked down at the waters. "Just as a fish is caught on the baited hook and must die, so an unintelligent person who is under the control of the insatiable tongue will also end up losing his life.

"From the prostitute's clientele, the sage learned that the hope for sense gratification is the root cause of all suffering, and one who gives up such hankering attains transcendental peace. He learned that, like a bird, one who is unattached to his possessions is qualified to achieve unlimited happiness. From the child, the sage learned that freedom from anxiety allows one to experience supreme peace and bliss. Even from a young girl who was grinding rice and bothered by the clanging bangles on her arms, the holy man learned that where many people gather there is every chance of quarrel and gossip.

"Why, Rajendra, even a serpent educated the holy man, and this I think is important for you: he learned that if one sought the answers, which you are now seeking, that one should travel alone and not be concerned about his living arrangements, be always careful and grave, not reveal his movements, take assistance from no one, and to say little. And finally, from the wasp, the holy man learned that everyone, under the sway of affection, hatred, and fear, attains in the next life that upon which he fixes his intelligence in this life."

Devi stopped speaking, looked over at the Taj Mahal and again back at Raj, her head tilting slightly, a deep and thoughtful look on her face.

"You will see in time, Rajendra, that this is how one attains real benefit through his own intelligence. Thus, one sometimes acts as one's own spiritual guide. You have Dadaji, but in time you will see all the ways that your intelligence can guide you. As I said, there is always something other than which you perceive initially. Always. Remember this."

Raj was still silent; there was so much to absorb. Devi's melodious laugh interrupted his thoughts: "Do not be concerned, Rajendra. All these words will revisit you when they are called upon."

Bowing his head and closing his eyes, Raj thanked Devi and offered his respects. He was overwhelmed with love and affection for this goddess, who had appeared of her own volition and given him a lifetime of wisdom and guidance in but a few minutes. The expression of gratitude forming in his mind, he lowered his hands, raised his head, and opened his eyes, words of praise poised on his lips... and she was gone. He turned to look behind, but knew it was futile. As mysteriously as she had appeared, so she had left.

Raj looked downriver toward the crumbling tower at the shore of the Yamuna where the boatman sat waiting patiently, unaware of the extraordinary events that had just occurred, simply waiting on a young man who struck him as serious, self-content, but somewhat distracted, unsatisfied with the results his journey to Agra had engendered. Yet, as he watched Raj clamber down the bank towards him, the boatman was struck by the glow that suffused his face and features, and, reaching out to help him climb into the boat, was nearly felled by the scent that wafted from Raj as he brushed past.

The boatman watched Raj settle, baffled by the young man's change in countenance. He looked back toward the bank from where Raj had come, wondering what had caused the change. He saw nothing.

But he knew he wasn't imagining the perfumed air that Raj carried with him.

Scratching his head, he gave Raj a curious look, climbed into the boat, and with his oar, pushed them across the now-darkening waters of the Yamuna.

He would not forget this man for a while...

3

Black Acres of the Night

THE train strummed rhythmically along the tracks to Delhi as Raj stared out the window, lost in thoughts of Agra. Fields of blooming yellow mustard flowers reached far across the landscape, undulating to the music of the wind like freshly washed sheets on a clothesline, flapping in the crisp pre-spring breeze.

He had hardly slept the night before, eager to return home and speak with Dadaji, the memory of Devi filling his mind and thoughts. There were so many questions he wished he had asked, but felt certain Dadaji would know the answers; those she had answered would, he thought, take some time to unpack and restructure into something he could digest.

Raj arrived and made his way through the chaos of

New Delhi station, switching platforms and boarding a local train to Chhatarpur Station, minutes away from his home.

* * * *

Everyone was surprised when the heavy front gate of the property opened and Raj entered. Mr. Singh was the first to see him, and called out in excitement, alerting the family and bringing them to the garden in welcome: Mammi, Bapa, Ma and Meenu, Mr. Singh. Raj laughed; it had only been thirty hours, yet he had known there would be a drama on his return: it was an inherent part of the Indian psyche, he thought to himself.

As his mother fussed around him, petting him, stroking his head, and squeezing his arm, he laughed again and said, "Mammi, please; it's hardly *Devdas*..." and they all laughed at the reference to the classic Bollywood movie, whose opening scenes portrayed the homecoming of the son after a ten-year absence, celebrated with opulence and extravagance.

Entering the house amidst a hub of chatter, questions, and merriment, as he reached the central courtyard Raj's eyes were drawn to the first floor landing where Dadaji stood at the railing, drawn from his room by the excitement downstairs. Raj's face lit up, his heart felt soothed, and, promising the others that he would tell them everything at dinner – including, his mother was prodding, why he was back so soon – he ran up the stairs two at a time, and into Dadaji's warm embrace.

"Ahh, *mera pota*... the emperor Rajendra returns! Have

you conquered the world so soon? What is this, you came back so quickly?"

Raj was still smiling when Dadaji spoke, but as he thought of the things he wanted to tell Dadaji, his smile faded, and Dadaji read the depth in his eyes. "*Achha*... I see. Come, come, *pota*. Let us talk," he said, and led Raj into the familiar and secure sanctuary of his room.

* * * *

When Raj finished speaking, Dadaji was silent but for his lifelong trait of humming to himself as he thought. Raj knew to wait, as did everyone who knew Dadaji. There was a lot going on behind that distractedly hummed tune: a wealth of knowledge, experience, intuition, and spiritual depth, all gathering themselves into the right order to form their answer before leaving the confines of the heart, the mind, the intellect, and then, finally, the mouth.

The humming stopped, and Dadaji finally looked at Raj, shaking his head slightly, and said, "What fortune is yours, *pota*. It is incalculable. Devi herself. This..." he paused, still shaking his head, "...so rare, *so* rare." He smiled, reaching forward and patting Raj firmly on his knee, chuckling with joy, "Such fortune!"

Raj knew that this was just the beginning, Dadaji's appreciation for what was a remarkable and blessed event: Devi appearing to him personally. Yet he knew that the words that would follow would tell him what was really on Dadaji's mind. There was a moment's pause while Dadaji allowed that special moment to be relished. Then he spoke quietly, almost casually: "So, *pota*... Devi's question, it was very good."

Raj was momentarily thrown by Dadaji's words. He expected Dadaji to speak of Devi's answers, to explain in detail, to expand upon them, to guide him and lead him to deeper understanding. He said, "Her question, Dadaji? I don't understand..."

"Yes, yes, *pota,* her question. I can see you gave it little thought, but it is in fact the heart of the matter." He paused again, waiting for Raj to understand what direction the conversation was taking.

Seeing Raj's hesitation, Dadaji prompted him, "When Devi appeared before you, *pota,* what did she say?"

As Raj thought back to that moment, he suddenly realised what Dadaji was alluding to. Their eyes locked, and Dadaji nodded slowly, encouraging Raj to follow the train of thought he had boarded.

"For so long you have worshipped me, sat in my temple, offered prayers, asked for answers to your questions. Yet I stand before you, and you do not recognise me? Look with your heart, Rajendra: I am Devi, whom you worship as Katyayani, and as Durga." She held her arms open, smiling at Raj. "Now do you see? Is it imagination, these prayers you speak, this mantra you chant, these desires in your heart to understand the essence of life?"

Raj was silent for some time, then said quietly, "I had doubts. But even they did not make sense to me, Dadaji. Devi was standing before me: what was there to doubt?"

Dadaji's soft chuckle soothed Raj's mind. "*Arre, pota*! This is the duty of the mind! It has only one function, you know this: to accept or reject. Simple. One function, two options: accept or reject. Anything else is simply a space in time while the mind decides which of those two options it will take. One function, two options, *bas*!" Dadaji chucked.

Raj nodded, these words of Dadaji's no news to him: he had heard them many a time over the years. "But Dadaji, you have often said that to doubt is evidence of one's intelligence, that to question indicates an intellect behind one's choices, as opposed to a blind faith."

Dadaji nodded, "Yes, yes, very good. This is true. But you see, *pota,* that space of time before the mind accepts or rejects, that space wherein the questions you speak of are formed, for one who possesses a strength of conviction this space is non-existent, *haan*?" Dadaji paused, allowing his words to sink in. He leaned forward a little and said, "Why would you doubt the possibility of something you have known all your life?"

Raj looked troubled, his answers forming slowly. "So my moment of surprise or momentary disbelief, this was a sign of weakness?"

Dadaji made a tutting sound, shaking his head. "No, *pota*, not weakness. Perhaps a pause that you will never make again, certainly: this is learning by experience. But it is necessary to understand this point in order to answer the question you asked yourself on your journey home, do you remember?"

Although on the train Raj had been absorbed in the details of his experience with Devi, he had deliberately stemmed the flow of questions that inevitably begun, not wanting to speculate, imagine, or concoct meaning until he had discussed his thoughts with Dadaji and built a strong foundation on which to base his questions. When he was finally able to do so, he had told Dadaji how one point in particular had troubled him, how Devi had spoken of the "godly yet misled men" who had ruled this nation, and the regret he felt afterwards for not asking her to elaborate. Raj told Dadaji he had wondered on the train how they were "godly but misled," that he was intrigued at what kind of influence had entered and caused such decay in the kingdoms, had changed the nation's landscape between then and now, so much so that those empires no longer existed; they had degenerated and disintegrated, their heritage destroyed, now only a relic, a memory: simply a part of history, and nothing more. Now, the world was filled with chaos, unruliness, disorder. Governments were corrupt, power was abused, wealth misappropriated, and the people were always either cheated or cheating, or both. While Akbar had always been one of Raj's favourite historical figures, a worthy example and ideal emperor, the beginnings of the Mughal Empire were not auspicious. His ascendants – Timur, Genghis Khan, and Babur – and indeed, his descendants, especially Aurungzeb, had invaded with violence, demolishing the Delhi Sultanates and ruling with fear as their weapon. Although Akbar's grandfather, Babur, had wanted to rule a peaceful and successful kingdom, his establishment of the Mughal Empire in Delhi was by force, toppling the Lodi Dynasty and leaving in his wake a trail of devastation.

Raj wondered what ill wind had swept the Mughals into this land. Was it fate, providence? Was it simply geographical? Or was it, as many were fond of saying these days, just "meant to be." He wished he had asked Devi.

But Dadaji hadn't commented then, listening only to the overall experience in one telling, waiting until the end to address what he knew was the heart of it all.

And this, Raj realised, was it.

"You asked what had caused these men to be misled. And this, *pota,* this is what you must now seek, this is your next step, to understand what it is that enters into an otherwise successful endeavour or practice only to destroy it, to wreak havoc."

Raj frowned. "But Dadaji... you know the answer, *na*?"

Dadaji chuckled again. "Yes, *pota.* But you need to build your strength of conviction, your faith in the practices you undertake, the path you have chosen to walk on, those things that you accept because they are tradition or condition. This is not wrong, to accept like that, but even better is that they are *yours.* Your choice. Remember the words of Froude I had you read to me, about how one must journey forth to forge one's own character?" Dadaji paused. "It is said, *pota*, that a first-class intelligence simply accepts things by hearing, a second class intelligence has to experience things before accepting their validity. You have heard me say this, *na*? Perhaps not in so much detail, but you understand, *haan*?"

Raj nodded, remembering again the years of wisdom that had left Dadaji's mouth and soaked into the the walls of that room, and into Raj's being.

"And you do accept what you hear, this is obvious, I have no doubt. You are a first-class boy, Rajendra." Dadaji leaned forward and held Raj's hand, squeezing it with a strength that belied his years. "But you see, *pota*, our character, our faith, our intellect, all are developed and strengthened when we meet with challenges. They will grow or they will crumble: the latter will prove they had not taken root, the former will add to the wealth that already sits inside you. Do not fear. Have faith, chant with faith, pray with faith, forge your character, and live accordingly. You see?"

Raj nodded, accepting quietly the lessons that were piling up inside him; they needed space to breathe, they needed to be sorted, filed, and processed. He looked up at Dadaji. "Yes, Dadaji. I understand."

Dadaji patted Raj's hand, sitting back and nodding. "Good, good. See, *pota*, so many things, they are not 'instant,' *haan*? Be patient, and you shall be rewarded. Know what it is that can assail and distract you, and learn to deal with it. Know also what it is that aids and directs you, and learn to practice it. You see?"

Raj nodded more firmly. He understood there was more to learn, but that this was Dadaji's own test, based on what Devi had taught him. *I hope I'm up to it,* Raj thought to himself, *because at the rate things are going, I'm likely to bump into that test on the way down to dinner...*

* * * *

Dadaji wasn't the only one Raj had been longing to see on his return from Agra; he was just as eager to visit Devi at the temple near his home. He was excited about seeing her, as tired as he was. The night in Agra had been a long one. He hadn't slept at all, but had wandered the banks of the Yamuna until it was dark, wanting to burn into his heart forever the imprint of Devi's presence and words.

It was a most extraordinary experience, and she had not left his thoughts for a moment since. He had considered taking the next train home from Agra, but the four-hour journey would have meant arriving home too late at night, which would alarm his family and result in long explanations of what had happened, why he had come home the same day he had set out on his journey.

And so he had spent a sleepless night, sometimes lying wide awake and completely still on his bed in the guesthouse, going over and over again in his mind what he had seen and heard; at other times wandering the streets, lingering at the doors of temples and mosques, sometimes entering, sometimes, if they were closed, yearning to sit in the calmness within; at other times he sat on his bed, chanting his mantra, meditating on the words, repeating them again and again.

Finally, at 3 am, he could wait no longer. After showering and changing, he had packed his small bag, its contents mostly unused, unneeded, and had walked the short distance to the train station. An express to Delhi had arrived soon after, and he had reached home before midday, his longing increasing by the hour to see both his Dadaji and Devi.

After a few short hours with Dadaji, and after extricating himself from his family – who wanted to hear of his visit to Agra and the reasons for his swift return – he had finally managed to set out for Devi's temple. A few minutes by scooter and he was there.

He had been at Katyayani Mandir for some hours, sitting before Devi in contemplation of all the things his tired mind and body had experienced in the last thirty six hours, her words and presence even more fresh, despite his fatigue. He felt different now, having seen her in person and spoken to her. Dadaji's words, too, repeated themselves over and over in his mind: "*Know what it is that can assail and distract you, and learn to deal with it. Know also what it is that aids and directs you, and learn to practise it.*"

Raj sat beside a pillar to the left of Devi as people filtered through, his presence no obstruction to their passing. He gazed at the deity of Devi in her form as Durga. She only appeared as Katyayani once a year for a few days during November, at the end of the auspicious month of Kartika; for the rest of the year, she was hidden, out of sight in her rooms in the depth of the temple, yet showed herself daily as Durga. As Katyayani, her beauty was indescribable; as Durga, her features were refined and delicate, when normally – in her other manifestations across the country – she portrayed herself as heavy and threatening; especially in West Bengal, where she was the principle deity – dark, menacing, and feared. Here, though, she was gentle, refined, and beautiful.

But now the temple began to fill, the approaching close of day seeing an increase in devoted visitors as they, too, neared the end of their day, stopping in on their way home from work or leaving their nearby homes to offer their last prayers of the day.

The chatter grew louder, the space in front of Devi more and more crowded, and Raj decided to leave, knowing he could find elsewhere the solitude and space he longed for to chant and meditate, confident that he carried Devi with him, knowing now he could see her anywhere he turned. He realised that her personal presence had instilled in him the understanding that he already held in his heart: that the deity form was, in truth, non-different from her personal form; not, as some might conclude, a mere idol.

It was the kindness of Devi that she graced the altars of temples the world over, to deepen the personal relationship of those who worshipped her. This was another facet of his history professor's teachings that Raj had appreciated so much: his academic understandings and descriptions of one's relationship with a temple deity, which were, at the same time, shared and supported by the spiritual and philosophical teachings of that *siddhanta,* or branch of spiritual learning. It wasn't imagination or flights of fancy, but a very real process of developing one's love for Devi, or any deity. He thought of the words of the poetess, Mirabai, whose devotion to Krishna was famous within India and beyond:

If the worship of stone statues could bring us all the way,
I'd have adored a granite mountain years ago.

He smiled at the wry observation of the undeniably devoted yogini. Paying his respects to the deity of Devi, he made his way through the people and out into the street.

As he pulled his scooter into the road, Raj suddenly decided to detour first towards the quiet gardens nearby before going home. Qila Rai Pithora was the oldest of the seven ancient cities of Delhi, and his Sultanpur home was in the district of Mehrauli, the second oldest. The gardens lay in a quiet corner past the ancient stone walls of Qila Rai Pithora, and were a beautiful, quiet sanctuary where birdsong was prolific, shade and sunlight lived in equal measure, and visitors were few. He entered through the wrought-iron arched entrance, and heading past the neatly bordered lawns and lily pond, found a quiet corner near the tree-lined boundary of the park, a little away from the shade. It was still the ideal weather to soak in the last rays of the sun.

He removed his shoes and small backpack and sat on the grass. The sky surrounding the sun had started to turn the colour of an unearthly coral reef, writing the remnants of day in the sky with pink-orange streaks and signing off with promises of a beautiful tomorrow: *pink sky in the morning, fisherman's warning/pink sky at night, fisherman's delight,* Raj remembered his mother's words from when he was little.

As the last prayers of the day at the temple had seen a rise in the noise level, so, too, the park's resident birds were busy in the last light of day, their songs frantic as they rushed to finish their duties before night fell. Raj heard the song of the *bulbul*, the nightingale, and his mind flew instantly to the words of Zeb-un-Nissa, the imperial princess – the daughter of the Mughal Emperor Aurungzeb – and her beautiful poetry...

King of all the roses, be thou kind
unto the bulbul, whose unquiet mind
makes him a mad faqir in loving thee...

Her *ghazals* were Persian literary art, and Raj wondered if this emperor's daughter had been in the thoughts of Keats, too, as he penned his famous *Ode to a Nightingale:*

The voice I hear this passing night was heard
In ancient days by emperor and clown.

Raj shook off the thoughts of kings and poets and princesses past, and focused his mind. The time was perfect: only thirty minutes or so of light remained, after which darkness, both subtle and physical, would begin to settle.

He thought of Dadaji's words on the morning he had given him the Gopal mantra some months back, of how the modes of energy shifted according to the time of day: goodness dominated dawn, passion midday, and ignorance nightfall. Dadaji had spoken of how the Muslim *adhat*, or call to prayer, correlated with these times, and how their *salat,* the prayer itself, was offered at morning, noon, and night. Although they offered two extra prayers – one in the afternoon, one at night – still the three other times, like Dadaji's and Raj's tradition, followed the sun's course as it rose, peaked at noon, and finally set.

Raj relished the memory of Dadaji's words. Like a newborn leaf unfurling, its tender form expanding, gently growing and gaining strength, so the words of his dear Dadaji were, over time, gradually revealing the deeper import of the mantra.

As he closed his eyes, deeply absorbed in the thoughts of the mantra's effects, ready at last to chant, Raj realised the breeze had changed, a sudden coldness had descended, and the air had turned: it was sharp, silent... *different.* Slowly, unwilling to break the mood, he opened his eyes, and his heart almost stopped.

Striding towards him was a vision of unbridled darkness, the black tendrils of its presence snaking into the ether: a tall, powerful, Stygian figure, his black robes swirling in the ice-cold wind and his features fierce. The surrounding gardens dwindled into nothingness in his presence, everything fell away, vanished, the entrance of this awe-inspiring person dominating the atmosphere. Though there had been few people in the vicinity to begin with, it was clear to Raj that those who might have remained after this person's arrival were not privy to his presence.

Raj was stunned into immobility. The instinctive physiological response of fight or flight had abandoned him: his mind was uncomprehending, his intelligence vanished, his senses drawn unwillingly into absorption in the apparition before him.

Three vile, terrifying creatures growled and hissed and snapped at the man's heels, their burning red eyes paralysing Raj with fear. *Was he hallucinating? What was this?*

As the man began to speak, Raj's terror reached new heights and he wished that he had somehow managed to find his feet and run. The voice was ethereal, carrying its own sonic echo that drenched and silenced the immediate area, enhancing the depth and clarity of his voice, and creating a bone-deep dread in Raj.

The figure came to a halt a few feet before him, arms akimbo, hands dramatically posed on his hips, his booted feet stamping to a standstill, shaking the ground with his arrogance, his stance portraying his mood of ownership and domination.

"*RAJENDRA*!" his voice boomed. "*At last we meet!*"

The words, unsurprisingly, were sinister, and Raj had no response. *At last we meet? Who was this?*

Unexpectedly, the man threw his head back and laughed, his long, black hair flying in the wind, his teeth flashing, his attendants still growling, snapping, and hissing, no doubt eagerly awaiting the order to lunge at Raj.

Lowering his head and staring at Raj, a wicked smile wreathing his bearded face, the man cocked one eyebrow, his brow creasing and lifting with a satire that left Raj chilled. "What is that you ask? '*Who is this*?' Dear Rajendra, you do not *know*?" Again the wicked laugh rent the air, lowering the temperature further. "Why, I am Kali! So very pleased to meet you," he said in a mocking voice, bowing deeply in theatrical farce.

Raj would never have thought a moment ago that anything could now surprise him, yet this revelation didn't just raise the bar, it evaporated it: *the personification of the era in time, Kaliyuga, was standing before him.*

"Surprised, *Rrrrrajendra*?" Kali mocked, rolling the r's with a sneering humour. "Don't be. I am the lord of this *yuga,* this age, remember? I own it. *It bears my name!*" he roared, and again the raucous and spine-chilling laugh burst from him. "Surely you do not think that a demigoddess can appear before you in Agra, yet I cannot appear anywhere in this world of my own volition, *hmmm*?"

Raj was baffled. "You... you know about that?" he asked in a small voice.

"Dear Rajendra! I know everything that is happening in my realm. As Devi is the presiding deity of this world, so I am the presiding deity of the age, Kaliyuga. I am Kali, in person! I can appear as and when I like."

"But... but why would you? What do you want with me?" Raj asked, his eyes flicking from one creature to the other, fear rippling through his body.

"'Want' with you, Rajendra? Why nothing, my dear

boy. *I want for nothing!* But you asked a question, and I am compelled to answer."

Raj was bewildered. "A question?" he repeated, his mind trying desperately to understand when or what he had spoken that had been construed as a question, and one that would draw the attention, what to speak of the presence, of Kali.

"A question," repeated Kali. "All of your 'seeking life's essence' and wondering to where the culture and order of this land has fled," he continued, his lip curling in disdain, "where righteousness and piety have hidden themselves, leaving open the doors of a cheating and dark world, that all other base qualities might enter and cause people the world over to leave the shores of their motherland and seek answers in this great country!" He sneered again. "Devi can speak all she likes of 'godly yet misled men' who once ruled here, and speculate as to what it was they, like you, sought."

Raj froze again, the thoughts moving rapidly through his mind, grinding to a sudden halt. These words of Devi, "godly yet misled men," were the very heart of his talks with Dadaji this morning. *What was happening?*

Despite the seeming impossibility, Kali's face darkened, an edge creeping into his voice. "But know for certain, dear Rajendra, that those men of whom Devi speaks, the former rulers of this land – and many of the people who lived under their sovereignty – shared the same desires: the lust for and hoarding of gold, the unruly taking of sexual liberties, indulgence in wine, liquor, and opium, and a disregard for the life of other living entities in the bid to satisfy tongue and belly."

A thought snaked across Raj's mind. *He's right.* He felt it somehow wrong, though, to agree with such a nefarious being, and thus remained silent.

Kali interrupted, jumping to another tack. "You admire Emperor Akbar, do you not, Rajendra? And those of his *ilk,*" his tone dripping with disdain.

Raj nodded, afraid to speak, unsure of where his answer would lead.

"Hmmm. Yes, Akbar was truly a king amongst men, an emperor indeed. 'Akbar the Great.' He, unlike others, abstained from the demands of the lower urges of mind and body." Despite his words of praise, Kali snorted in disgust. "Moreover, he was a righteous and kind man, seeking to unite all the religions in his empire, even desiring to create but one single religion under whose shelter the whole land would prosper." Kali stroked his trim, dark beard, contemplating. "A great man, indeed; protector of all, including animals. A godly man, cultured, intelligent, educated... a lover of the arts, not countless harems of women."

Raj was afraid to speak or move; he knew Kali's eulogising wasn't genuine, but a derisive lead-in to more cutting attacks on the principles, dharma, godliness, and good qualities that Akbar embodied.

"*Ahhh*, but his *offspring,*" Kali said, smiling with gleeful indulgence, his face glowing at the thought of the insalubrious descendants of Akbar. "That gloriously wretched dog of a grandson, Aurangzeb! My, my... did he know how to spend! He squandered the wealth of the empire and its people on his narrow-minded visions of ruling, even imprisoning his own daughter, whose qualities were much like her great-grandfather Akbar's."

Kali had been gazing into the distance as he reminisced about Aurangzeb's pitiable nature. Now he suddenly laughed and, leaning forward slightly, peering into Raj's face, he said, "Why, dear Rajendra! You and Princess Zeb-un-Nissa have *so much* in common! So dear to your forefathers, lovers of poetry and literature, well-read people of languages." He laughed in obvious amusement at the idea of Raj and the great-granddaughter of Emperor Akbar being so similar, belitting the qualities that Raj, like the imperial princess, held so dear.

"You see, though, do you not Rajendra, that in the end these great kingdoms and empires are nothing but moments in the course of time, now relegated to mere history: that is truly the legacy these men have left, even your dear Akbar!" Kali emitted a short, surprised laugh and shook his head slightly at what he considered the futile respect Raj held for former rulers.

Then, drawing himself up to his considerable full height, he exclaimed with anger and pride, "I should be ruling this entire planet!" He paused to contemplate, no doubt for the ten-thousandth time since his appearance on earth, the legacy that he felt was rightfully his.

Without thinking, Raj said, "But then only greed, falsehood, robbery, incivility, treachery, misfortune, cheating, quarrel, vanity, and all their counterparts would roam the land, the touch of their footprints poisoning the earth." He stopped suddenly, wondering if Kali or his vicious attendants would strike him down. The atmosphere weighed heavily upon him, the moment open, undecided. Kali's glance was like cut glass slashing the air, his attendants' eyes glowing red, their growls lower, deeper, and meaner.

Kali pulled back, stared down at Raj, and, somewhat to Raj's surprise, said, "You're right. And it is the fault of another one of your *damned emperors*. Thousands of years ago I was cursed by the righteous Emperor Parikshit, a gracious man who out of kindness spared my life but confined my area of control over this world and the beings within to only those realms where the pursuit of gold, intoxication, sexual promiscuity, and the slaughter of defenseless animals were rampant."

Raj interrupted again, becoming angry at the twist that Kali added to the truth. Bravely he said, "But you trembled in fear in Parikshit Maharaja's presence. You surrendered to him, you bowed down at his feet and begged for mercy. A warrior does not surrender: you were a coward! You relied on the godly principles Parikshit lived by and with which he ruled his kingdom, you hypocrite! You relied on the principle that a surrendered soul must be given shelter. He thus spared your life, but still he restricted you. You were in fact cheated out of your reign. He should have killed you!"

The sharp chill in the air peaked, silence descended, and Kali's glare threatened to slice Raj in two. *What the hell*, thought Raj, with anger. If these beasts were to tear him to pieces on the command of their lord and master, let it be for a reason. He glared back at Kali, his fear evaporating, and said in a steady, grim voice, "Only to the less intelligent do you appear powerful, but those who are self-controlled have nothing to fear."

Kali seemed to increase in size, the sky darkened, and lightning bolts crackled through the ether, illuminating Kali's monstrous face and exhilirating the beasts at his feet. Lifting his head in arrogance, his shoulders back, Kali suddenly changed tack, waving his hand in a dismissive gesture, proudly demanding of Raj. "What of it? What did it matter, in the end, this so-called 'curse' of Parikshit's? Little did the great emperor know that, on his demise, the qualities and characteristics of this age – of me, Kali – would once again rise and take dominance!" Suddenly, Kali, throwing his head back again, laughed with malicious joy. "Dear, dear Parikshit! Of course," he mused, "when the emperor ruled, people were still pious and this kind of behaviour actually *was* confined to specific areas of society. They did not run free."

Raj had heard many times from Dadaji this ancient tale of Parikshit Maharaja's brief meeting with Kali thousands of years ago; he was stunned that this personality whose name graced the pages of Dadaji's *Puranas* now stood before him, mocking the sacred edicts that had held sway during Parikshit's rule, yet which had weakened over the course of time to the point where the qualities of Kaliyuga – the age of hypocrisy and quarrel – now ruled the earth: nothing was hidden, and no shame felt by the residents of this planet for their abominations against Mother Earth, other living beings, and even themselves.

True, Kali was not able to escape the confines of Parikshit's curse. Yet he could expand the areas to which he was confined, cause their boundaries to widen, increase their size, all with the help of societies that now *did* allow such things free run. He had spent centuries perfecting his art, and now every corner of the world bore signs of his footprints.

Kali reigned supreme.

He took a step closer, and Raj involuntarily shrank

from the threatening intensity of the dark figure hovering over him. "Yes, Rajendra, people come from the world over to this land, yearning for the days of old, seeking answers, longing for righteous leaders, godly cultures, peace, guidance, religion, spirituality, liberation – any or all of those things that existed without challenge before I descended. There are few places in the world where they can now be found. And this land prospered like no other when they did, it is true."

Raj was cautious, yet his fear of the situation lessened. He suddenly understood that Kali would not harm him. The thought calmed his mind and made him focused. The creatures still paced at Kali's heels, but were controlled. He looked up at Kali and said, "These things you speak of – the pursuit of gold, intoxication, sexual promiscuity, and animal slaughter – are the very elements that destroy the four principles of dharma: truthfulness, austerity, cleanliness, and compassion."

Kali smiled, his eyes widening, his mood excited. "Yes! Yes, Rajendra! You are a good student of your Dadaji, no?"

Raj was momentarily surprised to hear Kali speak of Dadaji, but remembered his reference to Devi and his claim of knowing all that he chose to know. He accepted that Kali's words held no threat.

"But why would you destroy dharma?" Raj's tone was demanding; devoid of any mood of submissive enquiry, he refused to show respect to this being.

Kali sighed, his body slumping slightly, again adding a theatrical flair to his speech. "I am merely doing my duty, Rajendra." Kali held his hands at his chest, his fingers touching his chest, a victim-like naivete in his mood. "It is not I who am weak, but the residents of this world, those who balk at the thought of austerity; whose self-absorption in the gratification of their own senses sullies them; who seek shelter in intoxicants; and who claim it is their 'right' to abuse and slaughter gentle beasts and feast upon the charred remnants of their bodies, poor defenseless wretches offered in the sacrificial fire of gluttony and envy."

Raj's mind again disloyally released the thought. *He is right.* The world *was* full of people like this, as much as it was full of those who yearned for knowledge and meaning, who sought to embody the qualities of compassion, kindness, truthfulness, cleanliness, humility, and other such principles. Raj sighed. He did not understand where this was going. His mind was still reeling, his fear and bewilderment not completely abated.

"But fear not, Rajendra," Kali said. "The curse of Parikshit Maharaja still stands; alas, I can only rule in those fault-ridden areas of the world. If one wants to find these things that Devi speaks of, these higher principles and qualities, then one should simply avoid those places I dominate where these activities are taking place, where they are available. Truly, they weigh one down with an incalculable burden of karma."

Again, Raj's anger rose at Kali's trickery, at his attempts to dupe Raj with his evil duplicity. Losing the final remnants of his fear, Raj scrambled to his feet and snapped one word at Kali: "*Lies!*"

The beasts rose up and growled, and Kali's head snapped back in a mixture of surprise and delight at the prospect of an oncoming battle. Raj didn't wait for a response but continued, "Your aim is to kill higher principle wherever it thrives. You enter the arena of good qualities and yield your weapons of conflict wherever you can, preying on the weakness of man and longing for, *counting on*, his downfall."

"Yes, that is precisely what I am doing, Rajendra," Kali said, not a morsel of guilt or regret present in his voice or being. "But please understand: I am not the devil incarnate." He burst into another bout of raucous laughter. "Oh dear boy, I know your fear reached stratospheric heights upon our arrival, but I am not here to *harm* you..."

Raj's anger continued to grow, and he looked with disgusted fascination at the creatures still growling and salivating at Kali's feet. Seeing his eyes wander over them, Kali laughed again, saying, "Do not be alarmed, dear Rajendra; they are hardly the veritable 'hounds of hell'! Actually they are harmless. They just like to be a little, let us say, *dramatic*, shall we?" His menacing laugh fading, he looked down at the creatures and issued a sharp command as one would to a savage dog: "*Hut!*"

Suddenly, the three creatures became still, fell silent and, like shape-shifters in a science-fiction movie, morphed with gel-like fluidity into human forms: two men and a woman.

Was this really happening? Raj staggered backwards, stunned, and wondered whether, if he shook his head or closed his eyes and opened them again, these apparitions might be gone, this illusion dissolved. His mind could not keep pace with what he was seeing: three creatures of indeterminable species metamorphosing into humans. And what astonishing human forms they were!

"Meet a few of my attendants, dear Rajendra," Kali said, his arm sweeping carelessly toward the three. "Kama,

Krodha, and Lobha."

Raj was stunned, the hair on the back of his neck bristling: *was this possible?* Kali's attendants were the living forms of lust, anger, and greed: Kama, Krodha, and Lobha.

Kali watched Raj's reaction with relish. "You see, Rajendra, we all have our duty," he said, again raising his hand and indicating his attendants. "We are simply here to serve the people, are we not, my dear friends?" All four laughed, sharing their inside joke with malicious delight.

Raj's eyes wandered back to the three attendants. The most prominent was the woman, Kama. Standing to Kali's left, as he spoke her name she had draped herself over him, hanging off his broad shoulders, her lascivious smile directed at Raj. Now she slowly unwound herself from Kali, and stepping forward a little, spoke in a voice that had drunk the liquid form of seduction, which now tainted her breath and the air around her. "Hello, *Raaaaj*," she drawled.

Raj swallowed.

She was stunningly beautiful in every dangerous way imaginable. Although unmoving, she seemed to writhe, her energy flitting around Raj like sharp electric currents zapping the air. He was fascinated, and drank in every detail of her. She was restless and reckless, her eyes darting here and there, never still: seductive, then distracted; wanting, then bored; demanding, then dismissive. Her movements were sensual, her form beyond shapely, her bluish-purple clothing – what there was of it – almost indescribable.

Her stance was predatory, sensual, and her features exquisite yet threatening. She wore a large pearl and diamond *aarsi*, a thumb mirror, something that seemed very dear to her heart (*did she have one*? wondered Raj), and with long, graceful fingers, flicked open the cover every few moments, gazing at her reflection with an almost salivating glee, gorging on her own beauty. Smokey smudged *kaajal* lined her long dark eyes, and her lips shined with both rouge and the tip of her wet tongue, which skimmed their surface repeatedly. She was enthralled with herself, only distracted by something that might give her pleasure or satisfy her, and even then only momentarily until the next appeared.

She delighted in every slight sensation that her being, her ornaments, and her revealing clothing produced: from the swinging jewels touching her cheeks at every step, to the sound of her anklets, each bell tinkling with the promise of a thousand pleasures.

Raj thought of the poet Bhartihari's words, that in her graceful movements and twinkling eyes every woman possessed both a beauty parlour and an armoury. Yet before him stood not just a parlour but an entire emporium of female weaponry. Her mission was to enjoy, and she did so by drawing to her the senses of her victim and seducing their minds, thus controlling them.

This, then, was Kama: lust personified.

A wild and mad desire assailed Raj. The elements of scent, movement, beauty – all bewitching and seductive – formed a troop, armed and poised, ready and willing to serve their mistress's mission: to conquer, take, enjoy, bewilder, and indulge in any sensual adventure she fancied.

And she fancied them all.

Raj looked away: he knew her purpose, and Kama was no doubt far more experienced in getting her way; he didn't want to cross her.

As he diverted his eyes they fell on the menacing form

of Krodha, who appeared to have been waiting patiently for Raj's gaze to drag itself away from Kama.

Krodha was dressed in dark red, his clothes similar to Kali's, but not as opulent or dramatic. Raj's eyes swept over him: everything was perfectly tailored, the cape he wore pushed elegantly to the back, his form clad in *churidhar* and a long *kurta*. Raj could see that Krodha had immense pride in his appearance, and as he noted the arrogant angle of his head – held high with more than a touch of disdain – Raj knew that he was looking at what Dadaji had spoken of over the years: anger born from the pride of harsh austerity and high knowledge that turns on itself and creates an ugly righteousness, which in turn unleashes itself as anger. Raj had seen it, too, in some of his father's friends, and one or two of the parents of his own friends.

Krodha's face, though, was menacing, like the sun setting over the ocean's storm-engulfed, raging waters. His eyes flashed like burning copper, his brow was heavy, his countenance dark. Raj knew it would take very little to turn his mood swiftly from dark to vicious.

Krodha sneered at Raj, no doubt ready to unleash a torrent of abuse for whatever reason took his fancy. His attention was diverted occasionally by Lobha, who was in cohoots with Kama, their playful grabbing at each other and shared jokes always a point of contention between the three. Krodha barked stern chastisements at Lobha, which only resulted in a moment's silence, then a burst of wicked laughter from both Kama and Lobha in an arrogant disregard for anything that might interfere with their pleasure.

Kama vacillated between lovingly soothing Krodha's mood and stroking his arms and back, to sneering with contempt at his inability to enjoy. His chastisements were useless; Kama had no concept of anything being unavailable to her, was not ruled by boundaries or orders. She thought with her senses, tasted everything or wanted to, smelled everything or tried to, devoured every sensually attractive person or thing around her.

Krodha's existence was, in fact, a secondary one to Kama's. Although born from the brow of the creator, Brahma, he was, in some ways, Kama's offspring: the first time she ever experienced the inability to enjoy what she craved, from her sprang Krodha, a frustrated and uncontrolled energy.

Raj wondered if Krodha ever experienced even a moment's happiness or joy, and quickly concluded he did not: it was not his role, his purpose, his dharma. Raj knew from years of hearing the *Bhagavad Gita* spoken by Dadaji that anger created delusion in a person's mind, and from delusion, one forgot the tenets of proper behaviour, of right from wrong, or the treatment of others. Thus, the intelligence was lost, and anger was all that remained.

This, then, was Krodha: anger personified.

Raj's attention was distracted by a loud slap as Lobha struck out at Kama, who was snatching at his gold earrings, wanting them for her own pleasure. They were bickering like children, slapping and grabbing and squabbling for possession.

As Kama waved her arms in deflection and mock-attack of Lobha, Raj was momentarily dazzled by the flashes of gold and precious stones that sparkled with her movements: golden snake-shaped *bajubands* wrapped themselves tantalisingly around her bare upper arms, almost alive. The snake heads leaned out, their tongues a bright red, their eyes tiny rubies, seemingly ready to strike and poison anyone nearby who might obstruct Kama's endless indulgences. Her breasts swelled from her jewel-encrusted bodice, the golden chains that hung from her neck sliding and sparkling over them like a sunlit river flowing down a hillside.

Raj again dragged his eyes away from the distracting vision of Kama and turned his attention to Lobha, marvelling at the frightening display of manifested ill-will and lowly qualities that were enacting their dramas before him as if on stage. The squabbling again turned to screeching laughter, as Kama and Lobha entertained each other's longings. They were, in fact, exceptionally close, though Raj doubted they were what one might term "friends." He wasn't sure how these three really functioned, but he didn't believe that the finer elements of friendship, love, and care for others entered their realm of thought, action, or deed.

Lobha was an interesting personality to observe; his appearance and mood were deceivingly playful and mischievous, but Raj did not doubt for a moment that this was but a thin veneer that hid an always unfulfilled need to accumulate and hoard more and more and more, an unceasing driving force that beat within his chest in place of a heart.

Again, Raj thought of some of his grandfather's and father's friends, excessively wealthy businessmen whose social and public faces were philanthropic, charitable, generous, lauded as examples in society, but who, in fact, only acted in whatever capacity was required to expand their empires, increase their storehouses of wealth or fame, and be seen as gods amongst men.

Dressed in deep brown, traditional garb similar to Krodha's, yet without the distracting dramatics of cape and colour, Lobha portrayed the image of a man eager to be taken seriously, a man of depth, the respected and admired lord of all who moved in his circles. In his playful mood, his existential quality of greed unleashed in the snatch-and-grab antics he was engaged in with Kama, apparently in humour, but driven nonetheless by his undeniable nature.

And this, the last of the trilogy, was Lobha: greed personified.

Kali stood quietly, watching Raj's response to his three unruly attendants, observing with interest how Raj's face reflected fascination, sympathy, curiosity, disgust, fear, and to Kali's surprise, sadness.

He finally said to Raj, "What ails you, Rajendraji? Are you feeling sadness for the world, for those lost on their way through life, for the unhappy women and children who are left forlorn by unscrupulous persons? Are you lamenting the bewilderment of so-called leaders who have fallen under the influence of these qualities you are observing?" He laughed again, unleashing a torrent of malicious derision into the air.

Raj was suddenly livid. He recognised the words Kali spoke and knew they were not his. They were the words of Kali's long-despised enemy, Parikshit Maharaja. The first time the emperor encountered Kali, all those thousands of years ago, he spoke those very words to dharma personified, who, in the form of a bull, was being beaten by Kali. Now Kali laughed, the edge creeping once more into his voice. Unstoppable, he continued mocking Raj's sympathies. "Are you grieving the passing of culture and social order in the world? These days the general populace does not follow the art and etiquette for eating, sleeping, drinking, mating – anything! They are inclined to indulge in these things anywhere and everywhere, however they please. *As is their wont.*"

The malice in the air rendered Raj silent; he was unsure whether his previous conclusion that Kali would not harm him was actually true. Kali possessed an evil that was, to Raj, incalculable in its appearance, depth, and manner. Despite his claims that he was not "the devil incarnate," Raj understood that this was the most accurate description of Kali.

"And so you see, Rajendra," he continued, "I am everywhere. No longer am I banished to the distant corners of a village, town, or city. But am I to blame? Indeed, I do not 'cast spells,' perform magic, bewilder the mind of any individual! It is not I who am responsible for their condition. It is they. Do you see, Rajendra? It is but the mind that is the root cause of these three who stand before you – Lust, Anger, and Greed – and their absentee companions, Illusion, Madness, and Envy, to name a few."

Raj thought of Dadaji's words the morning he gave him the mantra, of how the mind must be clean, the body unpolluted, the consciousness focused. His reply was filled with contempt. "No learned or pious man, or even one with basic common sense, would put his faith in the mind. It is akin to placing a welcome mat at the door of one's being and inviting you and your filth to enter."

The air sizzled, the attendants growled again – even in their humanlike forms – and Kali, stung by the savage intelligence of Raj, curled his lip in disdain and anger. With Kama, Krodha, and Lobha at his side, he glared down at Raj, who felt even more sharply the uncertainty of his future. Then Kali spoke:

"Know this, dear Rajendra: you are the master of your destiny. And in that regard, you are also the master of mine."

Raj, stunned at Kali's words, didn't know how to answer. Kali's smile was sinister. "I seek only to accommodate those who long to enter the marketplace where my wares are sought with fervour."

Kali and his attendants fell silent. The air began to change again, the chill departing, the darkness lifting slightly.

"Everyone chooses, dear Rajendra. You are indeed a fortunate soul, that the circumstances of your birth and upbringing have given you knowledge of the transcendent, the intelligence to choose those things that serve your desire for self realisation. But know this, Rajendra: you are not immune!"

Raj took a deep breath, his eyes closing momentarily as he absorbed what Kali was saying. As he began to answer, he opened his eyes and was again stunned. They were gone! The gardens and surrounds were as they had been: not a single trace remained of the presence of Kali and his attendants, Kama, Krodha, and Lobha.

He spun around and looked behind and all through the gardens: nothing. He looked down at the ground, thinking he would see the pawprints the "creatures" might have left from their initial forms, but again there was nothing. He looked across the grounds of the gardens and saw couples wandering together, one family in the distance packing the remnants of their picnic, an elderly couple out for their evening constitutional. Everything was as it had been.

Raj looked down at his hands, watching the slight tremor caused by his still-trembling body. He needed to get home, and quickly. He didn't know what he was going to say to Dadaji, but he knew he had to get out of here: the memory of their presence was too strong.

As he looked to the ground to find the small backpack he always carried, a glint caught his eye, and he noticed a shining object nearby. He took a step towards it and bent down to pick it up, holding it in his hand: it was one of the small, round, diamond-studded bells from Kama's anklets. He thought for a moment, then closed his hand around the trinket. Picking up his backpack, he slipped the bell into a side pocket, and began to make his way out of the gardens.

Dusk had settled. Raj quickened his pace, his long strides swiftly closing the distance between the green surroundings and his scooter. As he walked by the reed-lined pond at the centre of the gardens, the swans gliding over its surface uniformly pivoted, paddling smoothly away from his intrusion – Kabir's "*tell me, O swan, your ancient tale*" swimming in unison in his thoughts – and the frogs perched on rocks at the waters edge jumped at the sound of his feet, plopping into the pond with a splash like suicidal lovers leaping from bridges.

Raj knew how they felt.

4

The Gupta Empire and Saraswati Devi

IN the weeks and months that followed his still-indigestible audience with Devi and the unsettling encounter with Kali, Raj assimilated the enduring consequences of the meetings, consequences he knew would transpire only over the course of time. He approached the days that lay in wait with trepidation, sometimes fearful, sometimes excited at the prospect of what would be unveiled.

It was an arduous task: more than just a memory or experience, both personalities had impacted his past, present, and future in every sense. During his morning talks with Dadaji, Raj admitted he was sometimes afraid to plan his next move despite understanding that the world was open to him, that he now carried with him far more in the way of wisdom, intelligence, knowledge, and, perhaps most importantly, faith in what the future held.

While the indelible image of Devi embraced and comforted him, Raj was suspicious and vigilant when it came to that of Kali. He remembered the odious stain the reprobate's words had left: "*You see, though, do you not Rajendra, that in the end these great kingdoms and empires are nothing but moments in the course of time, now relegated to mere history... but those men who ruled – and many of the people who lived under their sovereignty – shared the same desires: the lust for and hoarding of gold, the unruly taking of sexual liberties, indulgence in wine, liquor, and opium, and a disregard for the life of other living entities in the bid to satisfy tongue and belly.*"

He knew that while anything Kali spoke was filled with untrustworthy intent, these rulers had, by Kali's influence, become weak, overwhelmed by their power and wealth, and had allowed human frailty to have its day, succumbed to the weakness of the mind and flesh, and ultimately contributed to the destruction of their own empires.

But still... he could not shake the sense that something, *something*, must prevail, find itself a new home in the generations that followed. It must; why did he feel so much attraction to it, if it were not something of substance? He was not alone, surely? He knew he wasn't: his thoughts were haunted with the question of why so many foreigners came to India to seek the substance they felt their lives lacked. *What were they looking for, and where was it?*

He had felt the pull in Agra, the sense of order and strength from a city that had once flourished under a qualified ruler. But was it enough? So much of the culture was gone, lost to the past. He constantly questioned whether it were merely his own desire that impelled him – which was ultimately a waste of energy, hankering for a world that no longer existed – or whether there was something to be discovered, applied, lived by, that lay silently in wait until someone found it and brought it to life. *Was that even possible?* Raj wondered.

And so, while the clues to what his future held were within his view, the answers lay further afield than he had so far been willing to travel. Not only physically but mentally, emotionally, and spiritually. He often felt overwhelmed, yet found comfort in Dadaji's presence: he knew Raj's fears and took great care to gently remove them, clearing his mental path and allowing an unobstructed passage into his future.

In the weeks that followed, Raj had again immersed himself in his beloved books, but it was not the same langurous stroll through literary escapes that had formerly been his succour: this time he was consciously seeking that which might reveal the source of his interest in those lost empires, those personalities whose lives had touched his in irrevocable ways. Kabir, Zeb-un-Nissa, the Alvars, Jayadeva, Surdas, Chandidas, Lalla, Wordsworth, Sa'di, Keats: the list was long, the poetry and beauty of his literary idols his only real interest.

In particular, he again absorbed himself in the work of Zeb-un-Nissa: her cultured upbringing and erudite scholarship – a remarkable and unusual feat for a woman in the sixteenth century, and even more so for a sheltered daughter of a Sunni Muslim – had formed a foundation to her life and promised a rich and fulfilling future, a future of which she had ultimately been robbed. Imprisoned by her father, Aurangzeb, she spent twenty years in solitude and confinement, the culmination of which was the exquisitely crafted, bittersweet poetry that, after her death, became the *Diwan-i-Makhfi,* so named because she had, in her years of freedom, written anonymously as Makhfi, The Hidden One, fearful that her expressions of love and longing for her Lord would anger her father, filled as he was with hatred for other religions. During confinement, Zeb-un-Nissa had no need for disguise, exposed as she was as an envoy of religious freedom; her writing, in her father's eyes, her sinful disqualification.

Raj's own upbringing had been similar; perhaps not one of the extremes of both regal opulence and imprisonment, but sheltered by a cultured and religious family, educated in the fine arts, and encouraged to explore his spiritual, literary, and poetic nature. He could not help but wonder how different Zeb-un-Nissa's life might have been had she been born a male heir to her father's empire, although with the upheaval inherent in the Mughal dynasties amongst male heirs, she most likely would have died a lot younger, either in battle or at the hands of a challenger to the seat of her father's kingdom.

Regardless, her expressions of spiritual hunger and her love of the arts, literature, poetry, and language had been Raj's own, and he felt a kinship with this imperial princess whose artistic and expressive freedom had been cruelly wrenched from her.

Zeb-un-Nissa's writing swam through his head constantly. The memory of one of her *ghazals* – sometimes just a line or even a word triggered by something or someone in the course of the day – was as much a part of his life as rising in the morning. Each word was heavy with the pain of confinement, her sorrow pouring like liquid from her quill…

And never did the blossoms of success
within my hope's enchanted garden bloom,
And my fair beacon-light of happiness
is sunk in gloom.

From words filled with sadness and despair, Zeb-un-Nissa would then lean towards a fierceness of pride that no doubt sustained her throughout her lonely days…

Down in the dust and sunken in disgrace
My honour lies for all the world to see,
But why should I bear shame upon my face?
What is the honour of the world to me?
Although the times on my unhappy head
Have heaped the burdens I can hardly bear,
I have not wept; I smile in pride instead;
Upon my brow are graved no lines of care.

The thoughts of Zeb-un-Nissa fresh in his mind, Raj crossed the landing now to Dadaji's room. It was midday, and the house was still, the marble cool beneath his feet while the sun warmed the outer walls. He would sit with Dadaji and chant their mantras together, perhaps talk a little, and then join the family for lunch.

He paused at Dadaji's door, savouring as always the scents and sounds coming from the room. He entered, again as always offering respects to Dadaji's deities, then to Dadaji. He then sat, listening to his grandfather's quiet voice muttering prayers in a sing-song melody, watching as always the incense smoke curl towards the ceiling. He felt comforted by their ritual continuing within Dadaji's own.

Raj cherished every moment he spent with Dadaji in his room. It was like entering a timeless vault where nothing outside mattered, had no meaning or impact… or at least little enough that it could not bide its time until he emerged.

"So Rajendra…" Dadaji smiled and paused; Raj waited, wondering what path the talks would take this morning. "You have been busy with your studies. This time your own empire is capturing your mind, *na*?"

Raj smiled at Dadaji's reference to their family name, Gupta: a lineage that traced its roots back to the empire that ruled India from the fifth to seventh centuries. "This is your intrigue, *pota*?" Dadaji chuckled softly and nodded, both making light of, and approving, the track Raj's thoughts had taken.

"I don't know, Dadaji…" Raj began. A frown creasing his forehead. "It seems too long ago to be of any significance. Gupta is a common name: how do we even know we are connected to the Gupta Empire?"

Dadaji moved his head slightly in his nod-shake fashion. "Yes, you are right: what 'proof' does one have of such an ancient connection. History is only as accurate as those who decide how it shall be written, *haan*?" He paused, and Raj knew the pause only too well as the precursor for something beyond conversation; a setting of the stage whereupon a drama would now unfold.

The silence in the room deepened; Dadaji continued,

"It is natural to question history. But the name is the same, and everything has its roots, *na*? Is there somewhere else you know of that this name existed? Is there a Gupta family line that is not related to the source? And what is the source, *pota*? Does it matter, you ask? Perhaps not. But how is it that some Guptas are still villagers and some, like our family, are city merchants, wealthy and educated? Is it just modern changes to village life that saw our family direction change?"

Dadaji frowned and shook his head. "See, you need to understand what is history. It is not one person's written word. Look at the history in this country. If 'historical records' were our only source of knowledge, then according to those who recorded it, we are all uneducated, idol-worshipping heathens who needed converting to Christianity, *na*?" Dadaji chuckled. "But the truth is something different, and it is known to be different by its continuity. Think of this, *pota*.

"History is also eternal. Four, five months ago there was winter, now there is a new season, and in another two or three months, summer again, monsoon. This calculation of one year is history, but the summer and winter seasons are also eternal. There is a saying, 'History repeats itself.' Why make a distinction between history and eternity? Things are happening eternally; this is history." Dadaji laughed, surprising Raj. He certainly had a unique, simple, yet deep and pure way of seeing things, of explaining them. Raj knew that had he asked, Dadaji would have quoted reams of scripture and philosophy to support his shared thoughts. "It is all there," he would often say; sometimes elaborating, sometimes not, knowing that Raj had heard it all the years of his life, had listened to him reading his books and speaking the wisdom they held.

Dadaji continued, "Devi gave you the same advice as I did, Rajendra. Things are not always as they seem. So do not be content to accept what others accept as truth, fact, history, *haan*? So many people today, they are not content to accept, and they are learning for themselves, finding the truth, discovering the real history. How? Because it is there. It is there."

He paused again, shaking his head: "This is my motherland, and I am an old-fashioned man. But still I will say, Indians put so much nonsense time and effort into their *gotras*, their line, their family, this-that caste, all this class-conscious living, so much wasting time."

Raj wasn't surprised; he knew his family had always been nonplussed by the caste and class preoccupation in India. In Raj's generation, it had lost some of its significance, but still it remained. He could never quite decide what was better: that it be done with completely or that it be retained and that the fully functioning class system's banishment was what ailed the country. "Dadaji, is there no purpose in knowing or living by one's caste or *gotra*?"

Dadaji shook his head. "Actually, there is no 'yes or no.' You see, nothing is of no value, that is always there. But what will a person do with his pride of birth? If he uses it for the benefit of others, then alright, it has value. But if the only value is pride in one's family, then it is useless. More than useless, it is a burden on society.

"You see, *pota,* so many men, they come from what is considered a low-class family line or background, *na*? But one's actions are more important than one's birth. Always remember this: your *gotra* is one thing and it is always there, you are born with it, it is fixed. But your future? You can become a king among men even if you are born on the street, *haan*?"

Raj's frown persisted. "So am I wasting my time wondering if there is any merit in my family lineage, Dadaji?"

"No, no, this is not a waste. But while you are going back in time, looking for the answers, always remember to leave the door open so you can bring what you find back with you and apply it in the future. Do you see, *pota*?"

Raj nodded, but waited. Dadaji was silent, but he knew there was more to come. "If you manage to find that you are of emperors' blood, Rajendra, then you must ask yourself what it is this information will contribute to your future, *na*?" Dadaji paused, choosing his words carefully. "But if you find nothing, then what is it you will do? This longing you have for the days of old, it is only a waste of time if you do not apply it, make it count in this life."

Raj frowned again. "Dadaji, I don't understand. I am just one person, I am nothing, no one. How can I apply my love for culture and the beauty of its literary and artistic jewels to something that might have meaning to a stranger, or a foreigner, to anyone? How do I become something or someone of value?"

Dadaji smiled and nodded. "This!" he laughed his raspy, muted laugh. "This is the question. Low-born man, high-born man, king, pauper, rickshaw-walah, prime minister: it doesn't matter, you become a king among men. Don't be so certain, *pota,* that these empires were idyllic and perfect. Look at your Zeb-un-Nissa: imprisoned by her own father.

So she lived in a cultured empire, but who was able to help her? No one. She was in prison."

Raj nodded, an understanding beginning to form. Dadaji watched the wheels of Raj's mind turning, and continued softly, "But see now what she is doing. Hundreds of years later, here you are, wanting to bring her into your own life and the lives of so many; wanting the environment she lived in; wanting so much of that time to once again exist."

Leaning forward, Dadaji patted Raj's hand and said, "So this is what you must seek now, my little emperor," Dadaji smiled. "How to give your love, your culture, your knowledge, your faith to others. Zeb-un-Nissa did, and she will continue to do so for centuries." Dadaji squeezed Raj's hand and said quietly, "Will you, *pota*? This is what you must keep in your mind and heart as your compass: will you bring what it is you love from the past into the future, not for your own indulgence, but to benefit others? Do you actually believe it is timeless, and not just 'history'? Do you know what value knowledge, culture, and godliness have in the river of eternal time?"

Raj stared at Dadaji, speechless. He leaned back against the wall for support and rested, thoughts swirling in his head, finding their place, organising themselves... and in their movement, turning on every light bulb in his brain.

Yes, he thought. *Yes... finally...*

This is what Raj had wanted to hear. This is what he had waited so long for, even the smallest clue to what he was meant for in this world, what his value was, what use his study, his love of literature and poetry, history and culture, his passion for empires lost and emperors fallen.

Dadaji watched in silence, knowing at last that his dear

grandson was ready to step into who he was and for what he was born: even if he could not yet know how enormous his impact on this world would one day be.

"Understand, *pota*, that at one point you must stop seeking. It is said that questioning is a sign of intelligence, and so one must utilise one's intelligence in the search for their purpose in life, as you are doing. This is good. This is good." Dadaji nodded and again patted Raj's hand. "But do not make a life of it, *haan*?"

"But when do I stop, Dadaji? How will I know when to stop?"

"I told you, *pota,* you must know what it is you are looking for. Oh, but the details, those you cannot know. Those you cannot know. They will flow like small inlets into the long river that is your life, whose waters are your path, its tides your principles. But are you being carried along in the currents or are you mastering the waves, avoiding the rocks and waterfalls?" Dadaji's raspy chuckle warmed Raj's heart. "You must learn to chart your course, Rajendra. Chart your course. Do not simply be carried along on the water's surface; master the currents."

Dadaji's analogies always struck Raj as practical and tangible, not clever riddles. And Raj knew Dadaji was right: he was, at present, being carried along on the tide of his life's moving waters, a passenger rather than the clichéd "captain of his own destiny." Dadaji had told him a few times, seemingly in joking reference to his name, Rajendra, to become the emperor of his own fate. But he now realised this had been Dadaji's message all along, his gentle and unchanging persistence that Raj step into what and who he was destined to do or be in this world, even if he did not yet know what it was. Because for sure, one principle ran strongly in their family, their customs, their tradition, their history: that everyone was born for a purpose in this world. Be it a purpose confined to their own small circle of life, or one that reached out across nations, still there was a purpose to everyone's life.

Some would argue or speak of randomness, but Raj believed that the randomness existed only in one's choices: one could choose to step into their destined path, or choose to float and be carried along in the waters of life.

He knew which option he preferred. He wasn't interested in being washed up on the proverbial shore of an unlived and unfulfilled life. At this point he didn't even care if he ever reached his goal, or if he even knew what it was, but he would never sit still or die wishing that he had tried harder to find it, to *be* it.

Dadaji had been silent but now interrupted Raj's thoughts. "Your Gupta dynasty, your Mughal dynasty, your own life that only now seems to be starting, with this step into adulthood... do you think these things are unconnected? I do not think so. But this is for you to know.

"So now again you go, my little *musafir*, go. You are not a seeker now, you are this, a *musafir*, a pilgrim. Do you understand?" Raj smiled at Dadaji's choice of words. "A pilgrim has a purpose, *na*? See the difference: a tourist, he will visit some place and his mind is open, he is full of wonder, maybe he knows something of the place he visits, something has piqued his curiosity, *haan*? 'Oh this place looks nice, let me go there,' this is a tourist. You see?

"But a pilgrim, this is different. A pilgrim has intent, *na*? So, *mera musafir*, you may not know the answers when you go somewhere, but you know the questions, you see the difference?"

Raj nodded, again filled with gratitude for his Dadaji's love, his seemingly story-like words weaving tales that captured the heart and mind and yet were truths drawn from a deep well of wisdom.

"So... you know where you will go now, *musafir*?" Dadaji laughed, and Raj too.

"I think so, Dadaji. I... no. You're right. I *know*. Yes. I know." He paused, thinking. "Like you say, I may not know the answers, but I know the questions now." He paused. "Is it right for me to feel that the questions were always there? Is that the same as saying I have always had this knowledge inside me? Is that pride?"

Dadaji firmly patted Raj's hand and sat back; there was a finality in his gesture that struck Raj. "That is the perfect question, Rajendra. You are a humble boy, and this 'humble,' it does not mean weak or dull." Dadaji frowned, shaking his head. "So many have the wrong idea of what humility is, *na*? It is a strength, not a weakness. And you have this strength. This is the perfect question, and it is born from the quality of humility that flows in your blood.

"You have begun your search for the perfection of life, and perfection is never attained until one is satisfied at heart. This satisfaction of heart has to be searched out beyond matter, beyond what we can see or perceive with just these senses, the eyes, the ears, like that, *na*? So to satisfy your heart, you will keep going until you find what it is you are meant to find, you understand *pota*?"

Dadaji paused, his eyes never leaving Raj's, then said, "The answer is yes. Yes, you always knew, all of us, we all know. We all have this in us, this knowledge. But how is it awakened, how is it drawn from us, what do we feed it, how do we nurture and nourish it? That is what you must take care with. Sometimes we see that it becomes a monster, fat with pride and self-interest. You know this saying, 'A little knowledge is a dangerous thing,' yes? Also it is true that too much knowledge is dangerous, but only if it is unaccompanied by humility, you see? Otherwise, humility and knowledge, together there is no limit to what they can achieve. Together, they will lead you to the perfection for which your heart longs.

"So let your ego be controlled by your mind; let your mind be controlled by your intelligence, and let your intelligence be guided by your soul. Don't reverse, don't let your spirit be drowned with ego and mental speculation. Always remember this recipe: the soul is in charge. You understand, Rajendra?"

Raj nodded, the enormity of Dadaji's words evaporating any response he might have spoken: there was no need. Dadaji's conversations were like that – when they were finished, it was obvious. There was nothing left to say, at least for now. Dadaji's talks always culminated in the highest and most complete perfection of reason and wisdom.

They were done.

Dadaji looked at Raj, a smile playing with the sparkle in his eyes and one eyebrow slightly raised. "So?" he said to Raj. "Then?"

Raj smiled. His head was lowered and he idly toyed with the hem of his shirt as he chose his words carefully, conscious of Dadaji's explanation of the difference between a tourist and a pilgrim, between a drifting seeker and one who sought answers to questions, of one whose humility and knowledge would lead them to find the perfection of life for which the heart and soul yearned.

Raj spoke quietly. "The Gupta Empire, they ruled in Patna and Gaya, in Bihar." He gave a soft laugh. "Funny... now they are both popular tourist destinations, so many millions of tourists are drawn to these cities." He looked up at Dadaji. "In the beginning, some months back, my question was why people came here, why they came seeking answers. Why India? Why leave their homes?"

Concentration formed a small frown between his eyes. A field of words lay before him: he had to take care not to crush any delicate sprouts of thought and possibility that had sprung from the soil of Dadaji's wisdom.

The room's silence enveloped them, and Raj said quietly but firmly, "My fascination with and love for these ancient empires – the Gupta Empire, the Mughal Empire, others – they are not coincidences; they are not meaningless." Dadaji nodded slowly, encouraging Raj but staying silent, noting with satisfaction that the questioning tone had left Raj's voice, replaced with a mood that reflected his conviction. "Even historians can tell you that Akbar was influenced and impressed by the Gupta Empire's tactics, reign, beliefs, and processes. The similarities both empires shared, they are not accidental."

He looked down again, thinking of Akbar now not as a ruler but as a man who, perhaps a little like himself, had looked to mightier empires than his own, had sought their wisdom, learned their ways, emulated their successes, longed for a world that reflected the ideals and principles upon which those empires had been founded and by which they were sustained. What an interesting realisation: Akbar the man, not Akbar the Great, Akbar the Emperor, or an historical figure, but a man with longings for lost times and principles.

Dadaji waited, his small smile encouraging Raj to continue, hoping that Raj's next step would not see him veer off course and into the banks of that river of his life, but that he would master this small current and surge forth.

Raj's next words sounded hesitant, but they were what Dadaji had been waiting for: "I also know it is no accident that I have such a love for all the things these two empires encouraged and developed and are famous for. I know that my attraction to Akbar's great-granddaughter, the Imperial Princess Zeb-un-Nissa, is no small thing. I know that there is nothing that flows more strongly through my mind and heart than the love for the fruits of a poetic and beautiful writer whose words were born from a heart filled with the same longing that my own is beginning to reveal: that a godly and powerful culture is not a matter of history or geography or birth or caste, but is the nature of the soul."

Raj fell silent, and the house seemed to shift and settle. Dadaji sighed deeply, a relief filling him. He smiled, his eyes filling with unshed tears. He nodded and said, "*Ji.* It is time. Your chanting, your prayers, your longings, they have awakened in you a purpose and understanding that in most remains covered by the smallness of life." He paused then said, "It is a rarely achieved milestone in a person's life when one understands that we are meant to transcend the very smallness of this body, mind, and senses, and realise the infinite nature of the soul and the possibilities of that state of being.

"Understand, Rajendra, this mantra is no small thing. Don't limit it. Don't serve the smallness of mind and body. These words, they unlock the subconscious, the eternal soul. It is always there, all things are there, but how to open the vault they hide in, this is what so many spend their lives trying to learn. You are doing that: this vibration of sound, this music of the soul, it opens the heart. It is mystical, yes, but it is not magic, it is not fairytale or love songs or wishful thinking. It is a science that is deeper than a thousand oceans. Do not stop. You have come a long way but you have far to go. Keep going, *mera pota-musaafir.*"

They both laughed softly at Dadaji's tweaking of the lifelong affectionate name he had called him, *pota,* "my dear grandson." Now he was the dear grandson-pilgrim. He prayed he would not disappoint his beloved grandfather.

* * * *

The March heat had yet to settle on Delhi when Raj boarded the train to Patna. It looked like it would be a late summer, and he was grateful. Travelling was best done in the cooler months, but this journey couldn't wait: he was eager to reach the state of Bihar, the seat of the Maurya and Gupta Empires so many centuries ago.

It was dusk as the train headed east out of Delhi away from the setting sun, and darkness had fallen as they passed through Mathura and Agra. Raj was excited; he had made speedy arrangements after Dadaji had encouraged him to go to Patna. The ancient city had long fascinated him on an historical and scholarly level, but as he had progressed through university and become more deeply absorbed in the history of arts and literature, it had appealed to him more and more, and his history professor had found in him a willing partner for long talks after class had ended.

One of the oldest, continuously inhabited places in the world, Patna had been the seat of learning and fine arts and the former capital under the rule of both the Maurya and Gupta Empires, until the Mughals moved the throne to Delhi. The peace and prosperity created under the leadership of the Guptas enabled the pursuit of literary and artistic endeavours. Science and political administration reached new heights, and it was known during their rule as the Golden Age of India. Dotted with shrines, temples, and monuments to Sufi, Jain, Hindu, Muslim, and Buddhist saints and gods, the city was host to millions of tourists annually, from both India and overseas.

Raj slept fitfully, the hum and roll of the train sometimes lulling him to sleep, sometimes bouncing him awake. The train arrived in Patna thirty minutes early, which was another remarkable event in India's history, Raj thought wryly. It was just after 3:30 am when they drew to a stop at the platform, and he was grateful for the quiet hour of morning and the extra time he had to reach the Ganges before sunrise.

Patna sat on the southern bank of the sacred river, its streets empty in the pre-dawn as the taxi made its way around Gandhi Maidan towards the water. Raj saw the statue of the Mahatma in the park, and wondered if it were uncharitable to prefer the original, more graceful name of the Maidan, Patna Lawns. The renaming of streets, parks, and buildings after famous Indians seemed to be a favourite pastime of the country that he and so many others he knew wished would stop.

The river was only a few kilometres from the train station, and the quiet streets saw them pass through the city easily. Raj thought of its history and the unique flavour that had for centuries attracted so many people annually. In Patna's long-lasting prime years, it drew a wealth of people whose purposes for visiting were varied. Sufi saints lived here and attracted others with their liberal approach to spirituality and humanistic values towards religion, and the tomb of the first woman Sufi saint, Hazrat Bibi Kamal, was here; nearby at Champaran was where Buddha met his first spiritual teacher and had lived for five years; Hindu, Buddhist, Jain, Muslim, and Sikh temples covered the city.

The Gupta Empire was responsible for the first university in the world, said to have contained nine million books, and it was a tangible sense of history Raj felt as the city rushed by outside the window of the taxi as it headed towards Patna College, which graced the banks of the Ganges. The academic history of the Bihar region was equalled by its religious and spiritual harmony, also the legacy of the Gupta Empire: the Jain Jal Mandir on the Lotus Lake, the Vishnupada Mandir and the Jama Masjid in nearby Gaya, the Catholic Padri ki Haveli in Patna, all of them remnants of the united spiritual flavour of the seat of the Gupta Empire. Raj thought of the creation of modern-day interfaith groups and decided that there was really nothing new under the sun. This region had been the birthplace of such endeavours. This, Raj knew, was where he was meant to be, the next stage of his journey. He smiled to himself, wondering when his journey had acquired stages, curious at what might manifest here that would lead to his next destination.

And with the unplanned thought of a "next destination," Raj suddenly realised his life had become a remarkable and unique adventure, and he was overwhelmed with a deep sense of gratitude to his well-wishers. The Lord he worshipped, his Dadaji, his family, and the unseen benefactors who graciously guided him whether he was conscious of it or not.

* * * *

Krishna Ghat covered the sloping banks of the Ganges in front of Patna College, a bathing *ghat* whose steps led down to the waters edge and served as viewing platforms and seating, covered throughout the course of the day by drying clothes worn by pilgrims and locals who came to bathe in the holy river. The view was expansive and clear to the faraway opposite bank. There were other more popular and central *ghats* in Patna, but Raj had chosen this one because it was frequented mostly by students, whose days started later than other visitors, assuring he would be alone for a while.

Perhaps not solitude but certainly peace and aloneness were unusual experiences for most inhabitants of India: be it city or village, the rarity of having no one nearby or no event or ceremony or celebration – even the sounds of a normal day – consuming all the space on the ground and in the air, such moments were cherished by some but alien to others. Solitude was different: it could be found within, yet Raj knew it was not something that most of his fellow countrymen hankered after; indeed, they perhaps avoided it, feared it, even. Such was the social nature of the dwellers of this land, regardless of tradition or religion.

Not he. Raj certainly loved the sounds of life in his country: sometimes chaotic and mostly always festive. But it was rarely quiet, and thus, the moments of silence were more precious than they might be to one for whom solitude and silence was a given, or at least easily accessible. Like the beauty of the rain after burning months of sun, or a sumptuous feast after too long a hunger, these silent moments were treasured.

Now he relished the absolute stillness of the air that held the faintest hint of a mist, one that would dissipate long before the sun rose. He drank in the quiet, uninterrupted moonlit view of the expanse of sacred water that lay before him, its surface unbroken by humans, boats, or the birds who, led by the exquisite notes of the Magpie Robin's song, were just beginning to waken. His view to the opposite bank unhindered, Raj placed his overnight bag down on the steps, found a *gamcha* from inside and removed his outer clothing. Tying the familiar, red-checked, cotton garment around his waist, he prepared to enter the still, welcoming, cooling waters of the river that coursed through the country like an arterial vein: life-giving, nourishing, crucial.

Bending down to offer his respects to Sri Ganga Devi, the goddess of the river, he sprinkled a few drops on his head, purifying himself before allowing his feet to touch the sacred waters – a process that millions across the country followed on the banks of rivers from dawn till dusk every day, without reminder or thought. Such was the depth of the sacred conditioned habits of those who dwelt within this land.

Lowering his body into the coolness of Sri Ganga's waters, Raj was again grateful for the early hour. In only thirty minutes from now, the devoted regulars would start to appear at the *ghat*, which reached long past the college grounds and on whose steps sat a small temple of Radha and Krishna. The *pujari* would soon arrive to lead the worship, followed by the regular attendants to morning prayers, all of them taking a cleansing dip in the holy river before entering the temple for the regular 4:30 am *arati*, daily prayers and song.

It was 3:45 am. Raj had wasted no time and taken just minutes by taxi to reach the banks; now it felt like the world belonged to him, if only for this small window of time. He felt the heavy, reassuring weight of the dark sky, as yet unbroken by the threat of morning, its stars no longer twinkling but still visible for some moments before colour would streak the sky, rendering them ineffective.

The dawn neared and soon he would chant the Gopal mantra, but for now he drank the remains of night like they were nectar. Soon, in the very first moments of dawn when the darkness of night is replaced physically and subtly by day, the elements of ignorance, sleep, and stillness would be replaced by renewed life, awakening, and light. He would wait, then.

The quiet cloaked him, and thoughts of the purpose of his visit sat in the back of his mind; he willed them to remain there and not crowd his morning. The city awaited, his desire to understand the depth of the culture the Gupta Empire created and the effect it had on its residents crept stealthily around his mind and thoughts; he would give that desire a free run soon enough.

A drop of the water he had sprinkled on his head slid from his hair, landed on his nose, and splashed into the water. Raj lowered himself further, sliding beneath the surface, his body and mind filling with gracious thoughts, remembered poetic words piercing the silence of the moment: *descend lower, descend only into the world of perpetual solitude...*

Beneath the water, a heavy sense of gratitude and fulfilment weighed him down, drawing him into the depths: embraced, pressed, comforted, held. He wished this moment would last... might *be* his last. Was there any more perfect a way to leave this world? Had he been older he may have allowed himself to be drawn deeper into the waters. But life had not yet claimed him, what to speak of death. It was far away, his time...

Raj broke the surface smoothly and softly, causing barely a ripple. He stood in the shoulder-high water, then lowered himself a little so his eyes were level with the surface. What a vision, a view, from this angle – a world of possibilities and breadth and scale! He loved the music of the lapping water, its lilting notes enhanced by the silence of the end of night.

Nearby, empty boats bobbed in a slow-motion rise and fall at the water's edge, tied to posts near the steps; they would fill with passengers dozens of times during the day and ferry them across to the other side, returning again filled with more passengers, and so the day would pass...

He heard a small splash, and wondered fleetingly if it were leaping fish, little river beings joining him in the solo odyssey into the otherwise crowded waters. He turned slowly, his eyes still at surface level, relishing with wondrous awe the enormous and silent world he was viewing.

The white-feathered wing didn't register in his mind at first. It was out of the realm of reality; what lay before him was nothing but water, miles of surface, tiny laps of waves made only by him. No one else was here... nothing and no one.

Again the splash, and again he turned, following the sound. This time, the white wing was larger, more focussed, joined to a body... a bird... then, again, gone. Raj rose to full height, turning in the water, following the shadow and movement.

Before he saw it, the scent overwhelmed him. A dizzying perfume of an unidentifiable flavour and source, causing his mind to reel and his senses to cloud. Momentarily distracted by the aroma's power, the bird appeared before him without warning; larger than he thought a bird might be in this part of the river, and whiter, whiter than a bird should be. His eyes were level with its chest, and he stepped back, raising his head to look up, knowing even before he did so that he no longer occupied the world he had just moments before, where the predictable movements of time, people, space, and life never changed.

The words from T.S. Eliot streamed into his mind like a soundtrack without an off switch, inappropriate but insistent:

Here is a place of disaffection
Time before and time after

In a dim light: neither daylight
Investing form with lucid stillness
Turning shadow into transient beauty
With slow rotation suggesting permanence
Nor darkness to purify the soul

The bird's form glided and bent and swayed, revealing a long and graceful neck. A swan, Raj realised, whose luminescent feathers lighted the dark waters around them and whose radiance revealed... *her.* Seated upon the swan and draped in silken white cloth more brilliant than the swan, she shone brighter than the moon in the velvet-black waters, her fragrance engulfing Raj, his mind and senses drowning as he stood staring in disbelief, the vision of unspeakable beauty and the scent of lotuses drowning him... *and the pool was filled with water out of sunlight, and the lotus rose, quietly, quietly...*

The poetry stopped, one thought defeating all others: *it's happening again.*

The goddess of sacred rivers, of speech and wisdom, of writing, music, and learning, of the arts and sciences; the patroness of fertility and wealth – Saraswati Devi. Raj had surrendered long ago the ability to maintain his thoughts at these moments, what to speak of explaining his reaction to the appearance of these sacred personalities. "Stunned" was merely the beginning.

There was so much to absorb, inhale, hear. Her very name swam in his thoughts along with Dadaji's words from last year – *was it that long ago?* Raj thought. It seemed like moments, and simultaneously like a lifetime ago. "*Sa'di says what every wise man says, what every holy man says, that we are the same, we are of the same saram, essence… you must become saravit, one who knows the essence, then become rasagya, one who tastes the essence. You see? You must want to find it with all your heart."*

Saras, the essence of *swa,* self. Here she was before him, Saraswati Devi.

Raj could not tell where the form of the white swan ended and Saraswati's white silken cloth began. She was seated on long, soft-pink lotus leaves atop the swan, their curved edges draping gracefully towards the water, their pointed tips tracing wispy lines on the river's surface, melting softly and swiftly in the water. She was draped in gossamer-like silk, its fineness edged with gold, her upper arms lined with gold, her delicate wrists wrapped in fine gold, and her fingers twinkling with gold. She simply shone, sparkled, and lit the waters and the world around him.

Her wavy hair was held at the crown of her forehead with a gold ornament and woven into a braid with gold thread that flowed like a river through her glistening locks. Gold gleamed at her ears, and at her throat sat rows of translucent pearls. Tiny white jasmines, *jui* strung into a garland, adorned her neck; smaller garlands graced her wrists; even finer ones laced through her hair.

Across her lap sat an elegant, richly decorated *vina*, its strings sparkling, its long and slender neck so finely and ornately carved, leading up from the chamber, *kaddu,* itself a perfectly formed and exquisite round orb from which emanated faint melodies, pitch-perfect notes fluidly entwined and dancing in the air around him.

The long, tapered, beautiful fingers of one hand moved expertly across the *vina's* strings, the other held *japa* beads, a rosary. Saraswati's dark eyes sparkled, her beauty enhanced by the smile toying with her mouth, humour in her glance. She was enjoying Raj's reaction to her arrival, but decided he had had long enough to absorb her presence.

The music that filled the air was defeated by the song that was her voice. Raj felt another wave of gratitude towards the water that made him buoyant, otherwise he may have fallen to the ground. Her beauty – all aspects of it – was overwhelming.

The lilting laugh was panacea to ears that longed for fulfilment in sound, for the notes of such a voice to caress them and make them receptacles of love and not simply holes in the sides of his head. Her voice was unspeakably beautiful, rich and deep, or light and soft, he could not decide. "Rajendra... at last the day has come..." The playful cadence of her voice skipped into his heart and mind, defeating both.

Raj was unable to respond. Saraswati spoke, surprising him, "Let us move forward, shall we, Rajendra? Time may be eternal, but it is still of the essence, *hmmm*?" She raised one eyebrow and smiled, and he was pleasantly surprised at her wit. *I'm standing in the middle of the sacred river Ganges, alone, in front of Saraswati Devi, the goddess of... well, so much, and she's making jokes?* He was brought out of his daze by more of Saraswati's words. "Oh come, now, Rajendra. Must you take everything so seriously?" She laughed a warm and soft laugh, and he smiled, appreciating her humour and the use of it to make him feel at ease.

He said, "Well... you must excuse me, Devi. I hardly expected to be exchanging words of banter with a goddess before the sun had risen." He paused and smiled slightly. "One would have thought these things could wait at least until after breakfast..."

Her eyes widened in surprise, and she laughed with joy at his riposte. "Why, Rajendra, you *have* recovered with haste."

They smiled at each other, then Raj remembered himself, raised his hands to his forehead in a prayerful gesture and bowed his head. He was, after all, in front of a goddess. Despite their light exchange, the honour was her due. She bowed her head slightly in acknowledgement and said to Raj, "Come... sit on the steps, Rajendra, and we shall speak. Time is short; people will soon fill the emptiness of the *ghat*."

The swan glided like air to the steps some feet away and Raj followed, climbing out the river and up the broad steps. "Sit, Rajendra. Let us speak," Saraswati said. Taking a dry cloth from his bag, Raj folded it and sat upon it quickly, crossed his legs, and waited.

"So..." she began. "Do you know why I am here, Rajendra?"

Raj hadn't expected to be questioned and admittedly, had little clue as to what would draw Saraswati to him; the purpose that had brought Devi and Kali to him was still unclear. "Let us address those questions, then, shall we?" she interrupted, again reading his thoughts, as the others also had done. This was moving fast, Raj thought; he hadn't had time to absorb her appearance, yet Saraswati seemed to be fast-forwarding to a conclusion that she was determined to hasten him towards.

The scent of the lotus petals upon which she sat, the

sparkling ornaments, the luminescent white wings of the swan, all combined to dazzle him as he sat before her. Her voice broke his reverie: "You are seeking answers, Rajendra. You first wanted to know what draws people to this land seeking answers to their own questions. Devi explained this to you, did she not, that these cultures to which you yourself are drawn were based on godly ideals and values, managed by men of substance and integrity. When the principles upon which the foundation of these empires eroded, they ultimately fell: man *and* empire."

She paused, her brow creasing. Raj was mesmerised, still not sure he would not awaken at any moment and realise he was in a guesthouse in Patna dreaming of a meeting with another demigoddess. Her words cut through his distracted thoughts and brought him back to the realisation that this was truly happening. "Kali's appearance was confirmation of the words of both Devi and Dadaji." A slight pause, but Raj didn't ponder how Saraswati knew of Dadaji and of his conversation with Devi. "Kali is the chief of all agents whose sole purpose is to cause destruction and distress in this world, Rajendra. No doubt you knew this."

Raj nodded. Saraswati looked across the *ghat* to the banks leading up to the city, where formerly great emperors had lived – from the mighty rule of the Maurya Dynasty to its successors, the Gupta Empire. Emperor Ashoka, the Maurya Empire's finest, had been distressed at the burden that battles and wars had placed on his lands, and had turned to the peaceful tenets of Buddhism: compassion, humility, kindness, and care. He dedicated his life to his dharma of protection as the ruler of the land and vowed never to enter battle again. He spent the remainder of his rule providing aid to the poor and battle-torn constituency – especially to animals – and sent his men to outlying areas to ensure food supplies were bountiful, wells were functioning, trees planted, and healthcare provided. Most notably, he cultivated a peaceful and inter-religious environment, encouraging all faiths and practices to live together harmoniously, a legacy that the Gupta Empire expanded upon when they came to rule. Near the gardens at Qila Rai Pathora, where Kali had appeared to him, the Delhi Sultanate had erected pillars upon which were words carved on Emperor Ashoka's order, requesting the people of his empire and of future empires to live a life based on the tenets of dharma (virtuosity), to end religious persecution, stop the killings of man and beast alike, and be compassionate to all.

The Mauryan Empire was perhaps the most powerful empire ever to rule in India. Yet their success was achieved through conquering territories and defeating intruders to their expansive realm; conversely, on that dynasty's demise, the Gupta Empire was defined by and flourished on its powerful foundation of arts, culture, music, scholarship, and especially literature, much of which was poetry and drama. They were famous for their mastery of mathematics, medicine, and astronomy. Religious and meditative writing was encouraged and supported, and the empire produced great men of history including, amongst others, the *bhakti* poet Kalidas and the astronomer and scientist, Aryabhatta.

Saraswati's gaze swept back to Raj. "The cause of devastation of these empires – indeed, of the entire world – is the presence of Kali's assistant, Adharma, Irreligion. The three other assistants you met – Kama, Krodha, and

Lobha – are the offspring of Adharma." She suddenly stopped speaking, her brow creasing further. "Let me be clear, Rajendra. I am not speaking of institutions of religion, of churches and men and man-made laws, edicts created and announced to fool the masses and cheat those longing to take shelter of spiritual principles. No."

For a moment, Raj felt uncomfortable, and more than a little surprised. He hadn't expected the fearsome mood that had suddenly descended upon this divine woman in these sacred waters. But just as quickly, it evaporated. Saraswati sighed slightly. "You understand the principles and purpose of dharma. This has been taught to you all your life by your grandfather and parents. And now, the world over, people are becoming familiar with this word. Yet, they are strangely ignorant to the converse anti-principle of *adharma*: quarrel, bluffing, cheating, cunning – all of these qualities thrive and flourish in the empire of Kali."

Soft notes continued to escape the *kudda* of Saraswati's *vina*, drifting into the air of the silent, still-dark morning. Her pauses in speaking were brief; there was a purpose to her visit, and she meant to impart it swiftly.

Saraswati was facing the *ghat* on the western bank of the river. She turned slightly, noting the first dim hues of dawn threatening to break over the horizon of the river's eastern banks. As she turned, exposing the right side of her body, Raj remembered all he had learned of this goddess of knowledge and wisdom, especially that this part of her, her right side, symbolised the activities of the mind and intellect; her left side, the qualities of the heart.

She turned back to him and spoke with a hint of urgency. "Rajendra, there are things you must know before you go further into your quest for understanding your purpose in life, your fascination with and love for these cultures and all the qualities they were founded on, the art they produced, the beauty and depth of some who lived within those cultures, and those who ruled." She paused, and Raj felt as if he stood on the edge of a precipice, its unseen depths threatening to swallow him with all that they might reveal in the coming moments.

Saraswati stared into his eyes, her gaze unsettling him with its intensity. "It is not for me to answer all that you wish to ask. But I can tell you that this sense of purpose with which you were born and which has only increased throughout your life is not a whim, it is not random. It is indeed your life's purpose. Hundreds of years ago, you took birth in the empire whose cultural triumphs occupy your thoughts. It is not a coincidence that the Persian beauty of *ghazals* and poetry course through your blood. Rajendra, know this: you were the imperial princess in the House of Timur, the daughter of Dilras Banu Begum and the Mughul Emperor, Abul Muzaffar Muhi-ud-Din Mohammad Alamgir Aurangzeb. You were Shazadi Zeb-un-Nissa, 'The Ornament of Women,' Imperial Princess of the Mughal Empire."

The world spun on its axis, and Raj's thoughts slowed, sputtering to a stop. Nothing. He had learned from Dadaji the processes of the mind: the rhythms of thinking, feeling, and willing that began in the mind, which never stopped, was never empty, and which could never actually be blank; still, perhaps, but never stopped. Yet at this moment, he was only aware of his mind's methods: every other thought was locked out, unable to interrupt the vault-like door of his intelligence, which might lend some clarity to the words spinning around his mind: *You were Shazadi Zeb-un-Nissa, 'The Ornament of Women,' Imperial Princess of the Mughal Empire.* His Makhfi...

Saraswati Devi had been watching Raj's reaction, allowing him at least a few moments of silence before she continued; yet she knew that it would take Raj more than just some moments, minutes, or hours to digest what he had just been told; more than days or weeks, even.

Her voice was soft as she continued, "Now understand the purport to this knowledge, Rajendra. Knowledge acquired must be accompanied by humility and directed by dharma, that it might be used for the prosperity of mankind. This is what you must learn." Saraswati leaned forward slightly, her left hand leaving the golden strings of her *vina* and gently caressing the head of her swan carrier. "Like the swan, whose beak can draw milk from water, you must now learn how to extract purpose and meaning from this knowledge and utilise it for the good of all whom you might influence." The swan's white feathers sparkled as they ruffled in sheer bliss at the touch of the goddess's flower-soft hand.

Saraswati Devi looked back at Raj. "Remember what Dadaji told you: knowledge is powerful only when accompanied by humility. Knowledge that is dominated by ego can destroy the world. Your purpose is quite the opposite, yet it is not for me to tell you how this will unfold."

Saraswati turned once again to the eastern banks, and Raj's eyes followed; the tiniest tip of the sun had broken over the horizon, its deep orange-pink form announcing its intention to chase away the remnants of night.

Raj was stunned, too many thoughts swimming in his mind. "But... how can you not tell me more? This is... I mean, the enormity..." he fumbled for words, a thousand of them spilling from his mind to his lips and stalling there, devoid of clarity or support.

Saraswati's voice was soothing. "Rajendra, calm yourself. You have had millions of births! So now you know the details of merely one of them. It is simultaneously of little significance, and of utmost importance; balance will come. You will in time learn what import this news carries. Allow time to let this revelation settle in your heart."

The swan began to sway ever so gently, and Raj understood that Saraswati Devi was about to leave him. He felt the panic rise in his chest; Saraswati no doubt saw the distress in his heart reflected in his face. "Rajendra, how fortunate you are, do you realise? Of course you do. How many have the eternal administrators of this earthly realm visiting and guiding them in life?" She laughed again with her sweet, melodious voice. "Know that it will not always be this way. Think deeply and act intelligently. You must build a powerful foundation on which your future can rest. Understand this: your Dadaji has given you immeasurable wealth, and now you must follow the course of the river that is your life. Do you understand me, Rajendra?"

Saraswati Devi's glance was filled with loving concern, and it calmed Raj. Despite the thousand questions he longed to ask, he knew that he was not ready to voice them, and that as dawn approached the first stirrings of visitors would appear: any moment now this exquisite demigoddess would disappear from his view, taking with her any words he longed to capture and keep, to study later, to pore over and find meaning in.

"You have some travels left to embark upon before you will find the final answers. Go and find those things you seek, whose paths lead to the essence for which you long. There are sacred places whose environs are ripe for imparting understanding. These places are meant for spiritual cultivation. And your heart, Rajendra, is ready for harvest."

Saraswati again looked towards the eastern bank as the sun broke the horizon with a razor-sharp streak of orange and threw the last signs of night into the water, leaving in their place the soft pastel colours of a morning about to arrive. She turned back to Raj, the swan again swaying and bobbing in the water, ready to move. "Our time has come to an end, Rajendra, but do not be anxious. It is a time that will live in your heart all the hours and days of your life." She smiled, the beauty of that smile eclipsing the sadness of the moment. The swan suddenly turned, its left wing opening wide like a fan, splashes of water like falling jewels dropped from its tips, its movements like a flash of lightning. The air seemed filled with a golden sparkling mist and scented with lotuses. It was a magical and astounding vision.

And just like that she was gone. This time, Raj wasn't surprised; it had been a most graceful and beautiful exit, one that had seared his heart and left its mark. He didn't want to move, it was too extraordinary a moment to end; he sat still, allowing time to have its way with him.

Gradually, the air settled, a sound nearby broke his reverie, and he turned; the devotees of the temple on the *ghat* were arriving. The day was about to begin with their worship of Radha and Krishna. The priest's bell began to ring, a small *ding ding ding* that ushered in the new morning with the auspicious vision of the Lord and his eternal consort, Sri Radha.

Raj rose, walked to the open doors of temple, and bowed down to the deities. His heart was filled with love, tears rolled down his face. "Thank you... thank you..." he repeated over and over to the deities, the same forms as those in Dadaji's room. Ghee lamps lit the altar and a little gold flute sparkled in Krishna's hands.

As Raj turned to leave, he could swear he heard the flute, accompanied by a *vina,* their notes combining in a dance that praised the fortune of the sun, whose face had seen the beauty of Radha.

But he could have been mistaken.

* * * *

It was perhaps four or five hours after the train had left Patna that Raj realised he had seen nothing of the town, in the same way that he had seen nothing either of Agra. His audience with Saraswati had eclipsed the need for questions or touring of any historical sites. Indeed, her presence had rendered him incapable of thought or action beyond returning to the station, buying a ticket, and boarding the train home. He was grateful for the air-conditioned sleeper carriage and an upper-berth bed that would afford him some privacy. He wanted to think, uninterrupted. The train was not quite full, but had a busyness about it that distracted the occupants yet was still some distance from chaos or disruption. Raj was grateful, and allowed himself to dissolve into the memory of his day. *That was just one day?* He smiled at the realisation that only hours had passed since his arrival, yet his swift and spontaneous departure from this city was not regretted for a moment.

There was much to think about, an experience he wanted to live over and over again in his heart and mind during the coming hours alone on the train, thoughts of what he would tell Dadaji, wondering if he could ever tell his parents. Perhaps, but not Archana. He sensed she was too preoccupied with her new life to be able to absorb the depth of the meaning these events bore. He would wait some time before he told Archana. He couldn't have known it at the time but it would be another twenty years before he would...

As he thought of how he would tell his family, the train lolled and rolled, its rhythm sending him swiftly and deeply into a fatigued but blissful sleep.

* * * *

Raj never expected the response he got from Dadaji, who rose to his feet and began to dance around his room, singing a *bhajan* that came, as always, so quickly to his tongue. Raj was at first alarmed and then burst out laughing at Dadaji's unexpected expression of happiness. He jumped off the divan and tried to grab at Dadaji, laughing, "Dadaji! Dadaji! Stop!" and trying to pull him back down to the divan. "You're ninety two years old, for goodness sake, stop!" Dadaji was laughing and skipping, singing in between his laughter, "*Hema-gauri-tanu rai, ankhi darashana cai, rodana koribe abhilase...*" As Raj tried to stop him, Dadaji gripped Raj's forearms tightly, pulling him into his spontaneous jig, and they laughed together at his delight.

Dadaji finally let Raj move him to the divan to sit, still singing, "*Jaladhara dhara dhara, anga ati manohara, rupe gune bhubana prakashe...*"

Raj tilted his head and watched Dadaji with love. "Dadaji, your Bengali is lovely," he said, and they both laughed again.

Dadaji was not breathless; instead, his words flowed smoothly and evenly. "Yes, *pota,* this is Bengali. Such a sweet song. Narottam sings of the desire to see the golden-complexioned Radha with his own eyes, and of Shyama's cloud-blue form. So sweet, so sweet... you were very fortunate. Saraswati Devi is a munificent being."

They quietened, their joy melting into the moment, and they sat holding hands.

"Rajendra, it is hard to express in words how great your fortune is. These personalities, coming to you! I pray you are aware that this is beyond the realms of what this world has ever shown to most of its inhabitants, *haan*?" Dadaji squeezed Raj's hand as he spoke.

But even more surprising than Dadaji's spontaneous jig were the words that he spoke next, throwing Raj off completely: "So you know now who is your enemy in this world, who is the enemy of the spiritually inclined, the one who brought whole empires to their knees, who broke the back of culture, who considers history a laughing matter. His shadow has already darkened your doorway: Kali."

The happiness of only moments before did not evaporate, but Raj was surprised at the turn their meeting had taken.

"I... yes... I mean... sorry, Dadaji, I'm just a little..." he stammered, unable to gather his thoughts quickly enough and herd them in the direction Dadaji was headed.

"Listen, Rajendra. I told you long ago, and Devi told you also, that things are not always what they seem. Kali was saying to you that these great empires, their rulers, and those who lived under their sovereignty, all shared the same weakness: that they invited failure, that they contributed themselves to the fall of the empire, the dissembling of the culture. That rascal! Absolute *rascal*!"

The last words burst from Dadaji in anger, and Raj jerked back at the vehemence of Dadaji's mood. "This Kali, he sows only evil and degradation wherever he goes. Listen, *pota,* you went to Patna to try to understand how these empires ruled, what was the foundation for their success. You will never understand in this day and age, Rajendra. Not from direct experience, not by looking for it." Dadaji sighed deeply. "The culture and tradition is there, but it is weak. You are wasting your time seeking that which cannot be found. For this, you must look within."

Raj was silent. Then he spoke quietly, "Perhaps. Yes, no doubt. But Dadaji... this interreligious culture, this is how the Gupta Empire ruled, *na?* This is what defined Kabir and his poetry. It is how Akbar formed his empire. Imagine, a Muslim emperor establishing the interreligious principles of the Gupta Empire! I just... I mean, surely, in Patna, something tangible is there still... I felt that it was the source of this interfaith mood that exists today. Surely it had its roots somewhere..."

Dadaji shook his head. "Listen, *pota,* the elements of spiritual ethics these rulers shared and which they brought into their empires, it does not mean this mixed-up, helter-skelter, 'spiritual' this-that, which people are so fond of speaking of these days. No. Each practice the empire supported – and indeed your Kabir – had roots in *dharmic* principles, in spiritual ethics and philosophy, and these, together, made up the culture of life, of prayer, of the personal paths of every man, woman, and child who lived under the protection of these emperors. But see, with Akbar's empire, how shortlived it was. Jahangir did not think his father's legacy worthy of being maintained; Shah Jahan... well, he was busy building this monument to his wife that would last hundreds of years." Dadaji gave a small, hopeless laugh and shook his head again. "*Arre,* then Aurangzeb, the little despot. Religious fanatic, outlawing Hinduism again, making so much misery for those who were not Muslim – these interlopers, immigrants to this country, telling us we cannot worship how we have for thousands of years. Ill-mannered! But what his grandfather Akbar did, what the Guptas did, it was not then and is not now a random mental concoction. It is eternal and based on knowledge. But this modern day version, it's all mixed, and often it is seen that people speak of many paths but follow none."

Raj was silent. Dadaji wasn't finished, and Raj was both glad yet reluctant: he didn't want to hear that he was misdirected... not now, surely? And how was it possible, when the result had been meeting with Saraswati.

"Keep listening, *pota.* Saraswati Devi told you the same

thing, *na?* She told you to go and find the place where these things are practiced, places ripe for spiritual life."

Raj nodded, relieved. He remembered Saraswati's words, "*Go and find those things you seek whose paths lead to the essence for which you long. There are sacred places whose environs are ripe for imparting understanding. These places are meant for spiritual cultivation.*"

It was true, he had gone looking for the history of a practice that could not be found in a place or time, but which could only be lived.

Dadaji interrupted his thoughts. "And your own words to me before you left. Do you remember? I do. You said 'a godly and powerful culture is not a matter of history or geography or birth or caste, but is the nature of the soul.' Those were very powerful words. This is what I mean, that it is to be found within. Not that Saraswati Devi is wrong to tell you to go looking. No. But what is your compass. This you must know."

The room fell silent. Finally, Raj shook his head. "Dadaji, I feel like a fool. Why did you not say…"

"No, no, no! No, *mera pota,* it is good. It is good. Don't be anxious." He laughed a little. "How would you have met Saraswati Devi otherwise? Do you know of some other means? She came to you because your heart is filled with a powerful desire to understand, to seek the source of what it is you want to bring to life, to give to others. So, your action was not perfect, but she saw the purity of your desire and she stepped forward. This is not small, Rajendra*ji,* not small in any universe. *Sheeeee…*" Dadaji shook his head and made the sound he always made when something surprised him, a soft, sibilant *sheeeee,* a sound that always touched the hearts of the family. "And, simply, she redirected you, that's all. That's all. 'Go and find the essence,' she said. We spoke of this. The essence, *saram*. It is her name, the essence, *saras*. This is what drew her to you: your search for the essence. This you must find. Geography, history, these are just signposts, they will help guide. But they are not the essence. Don't lose your way *pota*. Kali – rascal that he is – he also warned you: he said you are not immune, *na?* So this was not a wrong turn, *pota*, not like that. But take it as a sign. Follow Saraswati's advice to the letter. To the letter!"

Raj nodded, relief flooding his mind and heart. He needed to slow down, think more deeply, not take all these events so lightly. He didn't feel that he *was* taking them lightly, but he seemed to be making mistakes. Yet still Saraswati had appeared. It was confusing. *What would I do if it weren't for Dadaji,* he thought, a thought that did not bear thinking.

"Rajendra, you wanted to understand how an empire supported multi-religious communities, *na?* But it is happening in the world now. Why go looking to the past for this? Don't worry, this was meant to be, your journey to Patna. But also it was meant to show you that you need not waste your time in this direction, *na?* So two things were there." Raj nodded. "Remember, Zeb-un-Nissa also longed for this, did she not?" He paused, his voice quieting. "You, as Zeb-un-Nissa, longed for this." Raj nodded again. "But in the end it was her jailer. It was her jailer, this desire. It was your jailer." Raj nodded slowly, understanding beginning to settle around him like a cloak. "You are thinking that Zeb-un-Nissa had so much more than you have, so much more wealth, of so many things at her fingertips: she was royal, she lived in a cultured time, she had so much opportunity. But did she? Of what use was it in her lifetime? So now Saraswati tells you, you were Zeb-un-Nissa. Do you understand what this means, *pota?*"

The silence in the room deepened. Dadaji spoke quietly, and Raj listened intently. "She was able to do nothing, *pota*. Nothing but write, and those sweet words have reached you all these centuries later, *haan?* These words *you* wrote, they are coming to find you. So many years, since you were young, you have cherished her words, repeated them in your mind possibly every day. And you were thinking all this time you were growing to understand her, to feel her love and pain and longing. But it is memory, *haan?* It is memory. So you see, it is she who is reaching out to you, *pota*. You think you are chasing her, wanting what she had, but do you see it is the other way around? She has returned; she was not finished. She was looking for you, *pota*. For your birth, your body, your mind. You see? *She wants what you have.*"

Dadaji's words were like tiny bombs that erupted inside Raj. His mind froze; the sound of his heart pounding filled his ears. *All this time,* he thought. *All this time I've had it backwards. This woman from centuries ago was seeking* this *life, not the other way around. She needed* this *birth.* He was, once again, stunned.

Dadaji's words from months ago suddenly returned to Raj's mind: "*While you are going back in time, looking for the answers, always remember to leave the door open so you can bring what you find back with you and apply it in the future.*" Dadaji had tried to teach him this before, but as he himself had often said to Raj, "There is teaching and there is learning, and they are often a great distance apart." Raj could not have learned this any other way, so deep and life-altering was the lesson.

He looked over at the tiny forms of Radha and Krishna on Dadaji's altar; again the words of Zeb-un-Nissa's *ghazal* flowed into his mind:

I bow before the image of my Love
No Muslim I
But an idolater
I bow before the image of my Love
And worship her
No Brahman I
My sacred thread
I cast away, for round my neck I wear
Her plaited hair instead

Still looking at the altar, his voice was small as he said to his grandfather, "You're right. I wanted this, Dadaji. As her, this is what my soul longed for. This birth. This time." He looked back at Dadaji. "And you. She wanted you as her guide. She came back because of you." Saraswati's words swam into his thoughts: "*Like the swan, whose beak can draw milk from water, you must now learn how to extract purpose and meaning from this knowledge and utilise it for the good of all whom you might influence.*"

He realised, though, that his words perhaps did not make sense to Dadaji. He repeated the *ghazal* to Dadaji, the words tumbling from him in an effort to bridge the gaps that random thoughts were making in his speech.

"She wrote this *ghazal* to Radha, Dadaji. At least, that is one understanding and it has merit, but it is something I understand to be true: she was dispensing with the boundaries of religion, writing not as a Muslim, not as a Brahmin with a sacred thread, but a lover who wore a plait of Radha's hair in a locket around her neck. Who could write such a thing but one enamoured with the pastimes of Krishna and Radha, who understood that it was she, Radha, who was the object of worship for Krishna, and who held this as her spiritual goal, what her soul longed for."

He knew that there was much he was leaving out, but perhaps for Dadaji, who lived by the tenets of *bhakti* and all it encompassed, it was more than enough. He knew far more than Raj ever would about this topic: it was the rhythm of his heart and soul, his very life.

This is what her soul longed for. His head was spinning. *This is what* I *longed for.*

Dadaji was nodding. *At last,* he thought. *At last. He is ready.* "So, *pota,* the door was left open as you went into the past, and you have returned with a wealth of knowledge and understanding. Now what will you do with it?"

Raj's mind was spinning in excitement, but Dadaji's words instantly sobered him. In reality, he had much to process and to prepare himself for, and it would take some time. "I am not sure, to be honest. But I will be practical, and I will think carefully before I act." He took Dadaji's hand. "But I know one thing I must do now, and that is speak to Mammi and Bapa. I don't think I can go any further until I do. Will you come with me, Dadaji?"

Dadaji smiled and nodded. "Yes, *pota,* now is the time."

Both rose from the divan, and as he looked around at the things that belonged to Dadaji, that *were* Dadaji, Raj wondered how many more times it were possible that he would leave this room a different person than he had been when he had entered.

5

Rishikesh

THERE was no way of knowing the profound future that was carved out for him of which Saraswati Devi had spoken; Raj knew only that it dwelt not here in the place and time that was his life in Delhi. He knew also he could not sit and wait for it to find him. It would come and claim him of its own sweet will, but he would prepare himself for its arrival as a gardener prepares the earth for the promise of spring's blossoms; his thoughts would be the scent that drew it nearer, his prayers the song that would turn its head, his heart the beauty that would steal its gaze. Captured, he would then fulfil the desires of that future, the only desires that mattered; all others were insignificant, redundant as soon as they left the mind and entered the ether. Raj wanted so much more, and it had been given.

Now he had to prepare himself for its arrival.

As the train climbed north from the plains of Delhi to the foothills of the Himalayas, Raj began to sense the life going on outside the window as an adventure, not ordinary at all but delightful, colourful, vibrant, nonstop, like a movie with different characters and plots and stories. It was other-worldly, a tangible taste of the culture he felt was elusive in modern cities. But there it was, rushing by before his eyes. He felt it also in the other people who shared the carriage with him, their hearts and minds filled with the excitement of their travels, some of them heading into the unknown. He felt their joy, and his own started to build. This *was* an adventure, this life!

The train wound its way through villages and towns, and Raj absorbed the changing landscapes of places and people with a satisfying curiosity. The countryside was beautiful, the people animated: colourful and busy, and all of them seemingly happy. He loved the variety and the uniqueness of India. The world was changing, but something about India never did. Raj had spoken to a visitor to their guesthouse last year, a man from Europe, he couldn't remember where he was from or if the man had even told him. His name was Peter; he was older, and shared with Raj his life story. When Peter had finished university some years ago, he, too, had travelled India and other countries seeking a little more of something he couldn't name before he surrendered to that inevitable pattern of life that awaited him. Peter had told him that in the past, landing in a foreign country was intriguing, adventurous, exciting, but that now all countries somehow looked the same, from the large, cattle-like electronically controlled arrival halls, to the freeways and fast cars and air-conditioned anonymity that graced each formerly unique landscape, and airports lined with expensive, glitzy stores that looked the same in every country, selling the same useless generic products: perfume, expensive trinkets, electronics. The world had morphed into one form, the huge, green freeway signs sometimes the only clue to one's location. Everything else was sterilised, uniform: "global villaged to death," Peter had said, which fascinated Raj.

But the blandness of modern advancement met head-on with a history and culture that India refused to shake: it was another world, and it seemed firmly determined to remain so.

The carriage suddenly became a bustle of movement, and Raj realised the train was pulling into Haridwar, the closest station to Rishikesh. He took a deep breath: solitude in the foothills awaited, but he first had to get through this city to reach the next. He began to feel the stirrings of yet another adventure…

* * * *

Raj walked over Lakshman Jula – the bridge that crossed the sparkling blue-green Ganges at Rishikesh – to the eastern bank, where no vehicles were permitted, only foot traffic. He loved Rishikesh – literally the place of rishis, saints – and everything about it, and had come several times over the years with his parents for the combined family holiday and pilgrimage. It was, at times, peaceful: further up the riverbank it was quiet, the waters empty, and the crowds absent. It was where he planned to stay.

But he wouldn't be booking into a guesthouse. For Raj had come to find a cave in the peaceful, slightly higher foothills that lined the city, home to many yogis and holy men who lived a simple life of solitude, meditating and aiming for nirvana, or liberation. Although that was not his goal, he did want the solitude and peace, and the mood in these foothills encouraged it, offered it freely, and sheltered those who came in search of it.

This was to be his alone time: a time of introspection and prayer, a time to meditate on his future, to pray for answers, to assimilate all that had gone before. And what a mighty load it was that had gone before: Devi, Kali, and then Saraswati. He thought of them daily, by the hour, by the minute almost, wondering what he was meant to do next, how their combined presence in his life would impact his future. *How not to fail.*

But to figure it out he needed time to become his own man. All his life he had lived under the wing of Dadaji, and for that he was immensely grateful. He wasn't lazy or foolish that he allowed Dadaji to rule him; nor was Dadaji overly protective or controlling. Still the natural time for separation and independence had come. More than that, Raj was painfully aware that Dadaji's days were short. He was ninety three now, the family had celebrated his birthday just a month ago, mid-June, and he would often say to them that it wasn't every day that was borrowed, or indeed every hour; every minute now was stolen time, he would say. It was time for Raj, then, to leave that safe harbour, to be independent: not the grandson, but the man.

He had gone to Dadaji's room on the morning of his departure, but this time to take leave of him and, at the same time, take his blessings, his wisdom, his love. As Raj had sat on the *pida* chair against the wall, listening to the ever-familiar sounds of Dadaji's mantras and prayers, his eyes had roved across the book shelves that went from floor to ceiling and lined the entire length of the wall, right down to the window at the end of the room. There were perhaps a thousand or more books there, Raj thought, and he could take anything he wanted with Dadaji's approval.

But he didn't want Dadaji's books. While he always wanted access to this library, he wanted to wait until he arrived in Rishikesh, feel the rhythm of the mountain and listen to where his heart led him. He would find what he needed there, and know that this treasure house of knowledge and wisdom would still be here on his return.

Now as he reached the end of Lakshman Jula and stepped onto the river's eastern bank, he turned right towards the laneway that was lined with stores. He knew what he was looking for. He walked quickly, knowing there was only a few hundred metres to cover. He was keen to extract himself from the busy walkways and head in the opposite direction he was walking: to go north, further up the river, into the quiet.

His eyes glanced over the stores as he passed, nothing holding his attention for long: gem stores, souvenirs, internet cafes, restaurants, trinkets. It was all the same, all tourist-oriented and bustling with business. He kept walking.

After a few minutes, he reached his destination. He remembered the little book store that sat at the top of the stairs leading down to the *ghat* at the water's edge: an ancient, tiny shop with bright blue window frames, crammed inside with books, all of them philosophical or scriptural. He walked slightly past the store, smiling as he approached the back of the statue he remembered on the corner: the goddess of learning, Saraswati Devi. Raj offered his respects to Saraswati, remembering her recent words that filled his mind as he turned back and opened the door of the shop.

The overpowering scent of incense rushed by Raj in the breeze created by his entrance. A bell jangled above his head, and as he closed the door he was enveloped in silence, the sounds of the laneway outside muted, distant. He loved this store, had been in here many times over the years: first as a little boy, then as an avid book lover, and now. And for the first time, he didn't know what he wanted. He was hoping it would find him.

A tall man came out from a curtained doorway at the back of the small shop, nodded quietly, and said, "Welcome. Let me know if there's anything I can get you." Raj nodded and smiled, his eyes wandering the shelves.

The store was much like the town in which it sat: truth lined the shelves disguised in many different forms, just as it lined the streets in Rishikesh. Present but elusive, hidden in the laneways, lost in the hazy clouds of incense smoke, drowned in the clash of *bhajans,* song, and chants all vying for supremacy, when the supreme lay not in noise or action but in the rarely seen soft eyes of one whose heart was its home. Thousands sat on the banks of the Ganges every day and night, staring out into the waters, all seeing the same thing with their eyes. Yet their hearts were often closed, or misled, or doubting, shut to the hugeness of life and consciousness that existed in the genuine spiritual realm. Instead they were content with the shedding of tears, believing it was their entrance into transcendence or enlightenment, as the local holy peddlars wanted them to believe. Yet it was nothing but sentiment pretending to be from the depths of the heart but in truth merely drops bursting from the choppy sea of emotions that flowed through the corridors of the mind, a wet, mental burden that soothed only fools and pretenders. He was neither.

The scent of the bookstore reminded him of Dadaji: the often-aged books were a comforting presence. His eyes roamed over the titles on the spines, some of them new-age, lightweight. He looked up to the category indicators, little signs hanging out from the shelves in old fashioned brass holders. "Over there," the voice said, and Raj turned towards the counter. The bookstore owner was pointing to an area behind Raj. He smiled at Raj. "I remember Mr. Gupta, your grandfather. He always went straight to that section."

Raj looked in the direction he was pointing and saw the category: Sacred Texts. "Ah, of course," he said, laughing a little along with the man.

"He is quite the philosopher, our dear Mr. Gupta. So many wonderful conversations and discussions I have had with him over the years. I pray he is well?"

Raj was quick to assure the gentleman that his aged grandfather was indeed alive and well, "Oh yes, he's doing fine. 'Fit with full faculty,' he often jokes."

The owner smiled, satisfied. "Please give him my regards. I know travel is difficult at his age, but I do hope we have his company again one day."

"I will certainly pass that onto him, thank you, sir,"

Raj replied and turned to the shelf now before him. He was in the right place: so many titles yet very few authors, the elite members of a small group of people throughout history who had managed to translate or write purports to sacred texts without changing the meaning and purpose. It was one of Dadaji's favourite topics of discussion, and Raj felt sure this was one thing Dadaji and the shopkeeper had in common and had discussed at great length.

He smiled to himself as he saw so many of the titles that graced Dadaji's shelves, and he took his time in selecting only a couple that he would focus on during his time here – the length of which was uncertain – and which would guide him on this leg of his inward journey.

His eyes were drawn to the end of the row, to a bright, orange-red cover dominating the others. Sliding it from the shelf, Raj smiled: *Sundara Kanda,* an excerpt from the *Ramayana,* specifically about Hanuman, whose mother called him "Sundara," beautiful, when he was little. Raj knew the book occupied space on the shelves of Dadaji's own library, and he had listened to its recitation many times when he himself was little: it was one of Dadaji's favourites, and had become his and Archana's too. Dadaji had often said that if one did not have time to read the entire *Ramayana,* then the *Sundara Kanda* would suffice, that it generated hope in the reader through its graceful and poetic telling of how Hanuman overcame so many obstacles to accomplish his task.

Raj hadn't expected to be holding this book in his hand; indeed, he had entered the store with the intent of finding the deepest and most appropriate book in the selection of sacred texts that would embody all the elements of purpose for which he had taken this journey. Yet, he had also wanted those books to find their way to him; he had intentionally remained open to whatever came to him, had not set his mind towards any particular book, and had prayed that the proper words would find him.

And now they have, he thought. What more fitting a tale to indulge his mind and heart in than Hanuman's own?

Still in the "S" section, Raj saw so many books on Shiva and tilted his head slightly, taking in the titles and wondering whether he should buy one. He was, after all, in Shivaji's realm: the Ganga flowed from its source, over Shiva's locks, and landed here at ground level first at Rishikesh: this was Shivaji's place. Everywhere one turned, the likeness of Shiva was present: *murtis,* or worshipable forms, cards, posters, even lookalike humans wandering the laneways of the town, dreadlocks in place, a loincloth, and smothered in ashes.

And perhaps... Raj nipped the bud of thought that sprouted in his mind, yet he had to admit its appearance was not the first: several times on his way to Rishikesh he had thought that maybe, *just maybe*, he was destined to meet with Shiva. He kept dismissing the thought, yet it wasn't born from pride or false hope or misguided thoughts. It was, if anything, a natural path for his thoughts to take, after his experiences in recent months.

But he refused to let the thought take root. It would be demanding and expectant if allowed to grow, and he refused to allow such thoughts to escape into the ether. *Let it be,* he willed himself. *Let it be.*

He wandered further along the shelves, seeing and dismissing so many titles and subjects. He stopped as he found *Bhagavad Gita,* and again smiled. *And I wanted independence,* he thought, remembering this book's eternal residence on Dadaji's bedside cupboard, its pages thin, soft, and worn. "Every man's *Bible,*" Dadaji called it. "*The manual for the human body. You buy a car, it has a manual. You buy a computer, it has a manual. You think something so complicated as the human being does not have a manual?*" Dadaji's hoarse chuckle echoed in his mind. Again Raj thought that something new, fresh, enlightening, and unread would find its way into his hands, but again he had to admit that Dadaji's influence pervaded his heart, mind, and thoughts, and he was grateful. His hand closed over the small, black vinyl-covered *Gita,* and he knew he was done here.

He paid for his choices, exchanged a few more words with the owner and took his leave, winding through the people all seeking food, drink, entertainment. Oh, and spirituality, that's right, he laughed to himself at the tourists and felt a little unkind in doing so. Still, while he could appreciate someone wanting to understand these things, he didn't think for a moment that white-water rafting on his country's sacred waters was going to lead anyone to enlightenment, and he was offended at the casual disregard these foreigners showed towards the river, even more offended at the rascal locals whose businesses catered to the demands of these sporting ignoramuses. He didn't want to think about it: it sickened him, and he wished there were something he could do to stop it.

Rishikesh was, in most respects, protected from the influx of outside influence and demand. Meat and alcohol were forbidden in the town. In this way it honoured the environment, which was a sacred place in a pristine location. It was the same as entering a temple or mosque, certain things were practiced and observed. So it was in a sacred town, and he wished all sacred towns presented and preserved themselves in the same way. Why Rishikesh and its keepers didn't extend that honour to its similarly sacred waters was beyond him.

On his way out of the busy lane, Raj stopped and bought some meagre supplies, just some fruit and nuts, enough to last him and yet very little in the grand scheme of things. He would drink from the middle of the sacred Ganges, bathe at the water's edge, eat in temples or, when necessary, buy some fruits. But he would do everything simply, no frills, no opulence, no rich food, no timewasting. He was here for a purpose.

Raj walked past the Lakshman Jula and continued for some distance, past the few houses, the guesthouses, and beaches on the river. After about thirty minutes, he found a sheltered piece of land some distance up the incline: an overhanging rock, a few small but shady trees, a good sized clearing, and a view of the river. *This is prime real estate,* he thought, wondering why no one was here. It seemed the perfect spot, and he knew the yogis and local residents had their stakes in the best places to live. Why was this one available?

As he was questioning whether he should stay or go, knowing with some certainty that it was someone else's space, he was surprised by the appearance of a yogi, wearing only a small piece of cloth around his waist, his locks of hair caught in a strip of cloth and tied on top of his head, keeping his skin clear and cool. The yogi offered his *pranam* to Raj, and he responded in kind. The yogi very easily took in Raj's appearance and belongings, and nodded in approval. "You will stay?"

"If I may..." Raj began.

The yogi raised his hand, sweeping away Raj's words casually, "Naturally you may, but this is the abode of one of our elder brothers. He is high in the mountains for some weeks, but will return. Until then you are welcome here. After, we will talk."

Raj looked around the area: apart from a narrow, one-man walking track, there was no other evidence that someone lived here. "There is no sign that anyone stays here; he is very discreet, then," Raj said.

The yogi inclined his head a little in agreement. "He is a supremely simple man who respects Ganga-ma and Bhumi-ma, the river and the earth. He would never leave a mark of himself on either."

Raj nodded. "I shall follow in his footsteps, then," he said, and the yogi again inclined his head in assent. "I am Subuddhi Raya." He pointed up the mountain a little. "I can be found above, should you need someone. I will tell others you are here."

Raj introduced himself, thanked Subuddhi Raya, and watched him walk towards his own corner of the mountain. He realised then that the yogi had asked nothing of Raj, like his name, where he was from, his purpose. Nor had he visually sought out the details of Raj's possessions. He was indeed a simple man, and Raj was grateful. He didn't want that kind of exchange here. He hoped he'd see Subuddhi Raya again, though.

* * * *

And so it was that he began his residency in Rishikesh on the banks of the Ganges. Rising early, always before dawn, he would first pay his respects to the earth, the sacred ground upon which he slept and walked, and to his spiritual guides: Dadaji, Devi, Saraswati. He would make his way quickly to the river, chewing on a teeth- and mouth-cleansing neem twig as he walked carefully in the dark, keeping his mind fixed on what he had read before sleeping. Reaching the river, he would quickly bathe, rinse his mouth, swim towards the middle of the river with his empty water bottles tied on strings around his neck, fill them, and swim back. It wasn't easy: the tides were strong and he didn't go far from the shore; just enough to find the clean rushing water from high in the Himalayas, and not the still waters at the banks.

He would then change into a fresh *dhoti* – the simplest form of dressing he could imagine – washing and wringing out the one he had worn to the river that morning. He would then take his water and laundry, and return to his cave, often seeing one or two yogis on the way, awake or asleep, walking to the river or from. He would then sit as dawn approached and chant the Gopal mantra Dadaji had given him, absorbing himself deeply in the words, losing himself in the sacred soundwaves, filling his heart and mind with the words over and over.

During the day he would often walk down to the river and swim, its waters cool and refreshing despite the heat. Monsoon rains cooled the land daily, rainwashed breezes freshened the air, and the nights were comfortable. It was a beautiful time of year to be in Rishikesh. Very few tourists braved summer and monsoon in India, and the land was, once again, theirs – at least for a while.

And so his days passed. Twice he had walked into town to phone Dadaji and the family to let them know he was well and happy. He had deliberately left his mobile phone at home. But they knew he was well; this was their land, he was no tourist, and there was nothing in Raj's plans or his behaviour that troubled his parents or caused them to worry. They were happy for him, supported him, and always prayed daily at their nearby temple for his protection. He was, in every way, surrounded by love, and protected by his Lord.

He recalled the conversation with his parents and Dadaji, telling them of his meetings with first Devi, then Kali, and finally Saraswati. His mother paled, a numb silence consuming her. His father responded more like Dadaji had: excited and happy for Raj, encouraging him to never forget, always be grateful, and maintain his consciousness and mood. All three – Dadaji, Bapa, and Raj – had, in the end, laughed at his mother's silence, breaking her shocked awe and drawing her into the joy. They had all agreed Archana should be kept from such discussions, at least for now. But for his elders, with their own knowledge of Raj's experiences, their support for his path and the choices he made had increased; they had voiced their encouragement repeatedly and had assured him that whatever he needed they would provide. Raj had been moved to tears by their loving support and generosity, and the embrace they had shared at the end of their talks had sealed their intimate pact.

Now, he read over and over the two books he had bought upon his arrival, each day bringing knew understanding, new insight, as though he had never before read the words. Sometimes he was frustrated, sometimes moved, but always challenged. Although he knew it would sound clichéd if he said it out loud, he was determined to find himself: not the boy he had been, but the man he was becoming, would become. This was his rite of passage, his quest.

He had a small glass lantern powered by a cotton wick soaking up the ghee that filled the base, never becoming solid at this time of year. Although he could read when he wanted, he would often sleep soon after night fell, and wake long before dawn. It was a pattern that Dadaji had practiced all his life, and while Raj and the rest of the family had not always followed suit, still it was the standard in the house, and it flowed through his being as easily as the blood flowed in his veins. It was even easier to live this way here in the quiet solace of these beautiful mountains, with the sounds of the sacred waters of Ganga Devi lulling him to sleep. There was so much to be grateful for, so much that Dadaji had given him, and he was reminded often throughout the day of the priceless gift his Dadaji was in his life. He couldn't wait to see him again.

* * * *

...and as the waves of Ganga Devi crashed in the distance and the cool monsoon breeze ushered in the deepest hour of night, Dadaji appeared to Raj; a dream, yes, but with so much clarity, like a private audience, a vision – not just a dream. But what was he saying? Raj tried harder to hear, the words finally audible. "Mera pota, *the truth is no longer elusive, haan? It is tangible, alive, not something distant to*

be sought. You have found it. You have found it. Now it is time to move on." In the dream, Raj was bewildered. "Am I to 'move on'? Am I doing the wrong thing? Should I leave?" The waves continued to crash and the breeze blew softly, carrying the scent of his life high into the pristine coldness of the mountains...

* * * *

It was dark and silent when Raj opened his eyes, waking to the cool morning, tar-black with a light fog dimming the sparkle of the star-studded, endless stretch of sky.

He lay still. There was no reason to move, no schedule, nowhere to be or to go, no one to see, nothing to hear. It was a wondrous sensation, the weightless beauty of this moment.

The shuffling sound – small, quick – intruded on his thoughts, alerting him and tuning his senses higher to a fine, sharp level: his sight, hearing, even his sense of smell, all sharpened. He breathed quietly, slowly, inhaling deeply, suddenly conscious of the scent. Listening keenly for sounds of movement, Raj again inhaled, wanting to be certain of what he had smelled.

The scent was sultry and warm, like the night air; a hint of saffron, perhaps, he wasn't sure. Aromatic, rich, and beautiful, he knew he had smelled it before, yet equally certain that this was a new experience.

He willed his breathing to remain slow, his body to stay still, his fear to recede. A minute passed, his initial panic abating with the practical thoughts that he forced into his mind. *There were no dangerous animals here, nothing that was a threat. A wild beast would have come to him, followed his scent, acted on instinct, and attacked. And it wouldn't have smelled like this...*

No. There was no threat. His heart slowing, his senses still primed, Raj quietly and cautiously sat up, then paused. Again, he heard the scraping sound: it was movement, but not footsteps. It was gentle and firm, not angry and menacing. He waited; again his heart slowed, his breathing evened.

Still sitting, he moved towards the edge of the opening in which he slept, sliding forward until the clearing in front of him was visible. And then froze.

The figure was huge. It – *he?* – sat hunched over, its head down, forehead leaning on its forearm, which rested on drawn-up haunches. Raj stared, his breath caught in his chest, the aroma stronger than ever: this was the source of the scent.

He watched and waited, the breath slowly leaving his body, his ribs feeling the strain. The figure was enormous, yet somehow unthreatening. *What is this?* The sky was too dark to help him identify the hulking shadow that sat just feet away from him. Behind the figure the half-moon shone dimly, blocked by the massive shoulders, head, and torso of the... *beast?*

Although now familiar, still the shuffling sound startled Raj as he saw its movement: a snake-like shape slithering across the ground between him and the form. It flicked and jerked, swatting at the air. It was the tail of an animal, Raj realised, yet the body it was attached to didn't really seem like an animal.

Raj had not yet moved, but he suddenly realised that

this being was fully aware that he had woken and risen and was watching, awaiting the creature's first move. He slowly slid forward to the very edge of the overhanging rock, sat upright, crossed his legs, and willed his body to relax, his hands resting, palms upward, on his knees: a non-combative, non-offensive pose, Raj thought.

The bowed head lifted, the nose rising in the air, sniffing. *A snub nose,* Raj thought. *What...*

The being turned towards him, and Raj's body and senses buzzed and tingled. His own repeated assurances that this beast was non-threatening clashed at full volume with the self-preserving primal scream that reverberated through his being. Still, he didn't move.

And then the beast spoke. "I am Hanuman. Do not fear me, Rajendra."

It had been nine months since Devi had appeared to Raj on the banks of the sacred Yamuna in Agra, then Kali in the gardens near his home, and almost four months since his audience with Saraswati Devi. Raj now marvelled at his ability to adapt to being able to hear the voices of these personalities, to see them, to converse. He swallowed. *What does one say to Hanuman?* he wondered.

Without hesitation, Raj bowed his head and held his palms together in front of his heart, offering respects to yet another divine apparition that had chosen to appear before him, the words leaving his mouth unchecked, "*Ramapriya namastubhyam, hanuman-raksha-sarvada.* I bow down with devotion to you, Hanuman, the beloved of Lord Rama and his greatest protector."

He lifted his head, silent. The sky was preparing for the arrival of dawn, but still, this King of the Monkeys was but a dark shadow, his features hidden by the night, his enormous outline barely illumined by the cloud-covered moon.

Hanuman turned, looking over his shoulder and up at the moon, then slowly turned back to face Raj. The heavy, still-like quality of his movements was deceptive: Raj knew everything about this legendary figure, of his speed, agility, and power. His tail alone could lash out and bind Raj. *Bind a herd of elephants,* Raj thought.

Hanuman leaned forward, starting to move across the fifteen or twenty feet that separated them. "Come," he said to Raj. "Sit where I sit, and I shall sit there; the moon will then light my face, and you need not stare into shadow."

The voice was as deep as a canyon, rolling like thick velvet from the form whose nearness was now beginning to excite Raj: *he was sitting opposite Hanuman, the famous servant of Lord Rama, King of the Monkeys... a legend.* He wondered if he should feel any hesitation, if this were a trick... *what if this were Kali?* The possibilities of Kali's reach were, he knew, unlimited.

Raj watched the enormous person move, his huge arms pulling his body across what was to him a small space, his legs making a quick yet heavy leap. Raj was simultaneously stunned and prompted to movement, scrambling in the opposite direction to make room for the massive form, a mixture of respect and fear motivating him. Hanuman settled into the space Raj vacated and said, "I am not Kali. I told you to not fear me, Rajendra." Raj wondered if he would ever stop being surprised at the presence of these personalities and their responses to his unspoken thoughts and questions. He hoped not: it would surely mean he considered these situations normal, which was as far from the truth as he could imagine.

The scent was strong now, its name bursting now into Raj's mind: *parijata*. He remembered that Hanuman slept under a *parijata* tree: a powerful, rare fragrance whose flowers bloomed at night, and now, as they sat together in the approaching morning, the air was tainted with the scent of the night-blooming tree. The bright orange stem of the tiny flower stained, leaving a long-lasting mark and aroma on the hands. This is the scent that had greeted him upon waking: an ethereal, tangy narcotic.

The dawn, impatient for its moment of glory, jostled with monsoon clouds that loomed like a legion of black-hooded Benedictine monks. Whatever light the sun gave this day would be feeble, and Raj was somewhat relieved; he wasn't sure if seeing Hanuman for the first time in the bright light of morning would be possible. The moonlight, however, was determined, and revealed enough of Hanuman's features to bury Raj in stunned silence. It was like watching a movie whose plot he did not know: nothing could have prepared him for an audience with Hanuman.

He was enormous, more than twelve feet tall and seemingly half that in width, his arms muscled, his chest bulging and broad, his waist tapered, his thighs massive and strong, his body perfectly formed and proportioned. Raj's eyes rolled over the unearthly body, and Hanuman allowed the inspection, quietly watching Raj's awe, giving him time to digest an otherwise unbelievable event.

His eyes roved over the massive body, taking in every detail. *He is beautiful.* Raj's own thoughts surprised him. They were not the words that one expected to appear first in the mind when resting one's eyes upon this personality. He was definitely not a monkey; that was far, far too insufficient a word to capture the form of Hanuman.

Yes, beautiful. Sundara. His eyes were a deep black, large and bright, their glance unspeakably soft; they reached towards his ears, long and curved like smooth mangoes. His mouth and nose were like that of a monkey, but again Raj found it difficult to settle for that word.

He was a dark reddish colour, his body powerful yet graceful, his nature imbuing every cell and muscle. Hanuman belonged to a race specifically created to serve Lord Rama, the Vanaras. They were a semi-divine creation: not human and not monkey, but with qualities of each. Twin lines of *tilak,* the sandal-paste mark of a devotee of Rama, lined his forehead, and gold rings sparkled at his ears.

After sufficient time had passed, Hanuman again spoke. "So, Rajendra, finally you have reached the foot of the king of mountains."

Raj answered, "...and I am greeted by the King of the Vanaras. Please forgive me, I have not greeted you properly." Raj looked around, and then back at Hanuman. "There seems to be nothing available that would be a suitable offering to you..."

Hanuman raised his hand and shooked it side to side, waving aside Raj's lament. "Please. It is not necessary. It is not why I have come."

Raj said, "Why *have* you come. And... why to *me*?"

"I am curious, Rajendra. It seems to me you are in the wrong place. Most who live here are absorbed in the impersonal concept of spirituality. Now all who visit here speak of 'yoga' and celebrate the exercise; they come here and think that standing on their heads makes them holy. And the false holy men here only encourage these practices, as it lines their pockets and swells their egos.

"You, however, are not without substance. Your upbringing has given you a foundation of a personalised philosophy of spirituality. So why are you seeking solace in meditation in these hills, which are the home of impersonal realisation?"

Raj had to admit that apart from the beauty of the environment, Rishikesh had never held any appeal for him spiritually. He could appreciate that those with no spiritual foundation might find something of what they sought here, but Hanuman was right. People didn't even know what they sought, and were easily fooled by those whose goal was to simply build their own fame and wealth. Certainly there were some genuine yogis and spiritualists in Rishikesh, but they weren't peddling their wares in the marketplace. He understood the source of Hanuman's question, and thought carefully before answering quietly, "I did not leave that foundation at home, my lord," Raj said, using the highest term of respect.

Hanuman shook his head. "I am no one's lord, Rajendraji. I am but a servant of my Lord Rama." He looked at Raj for a long time without speaking; rather than feeling discomfort under such scrutiny, Raj drank in the vision of this mighty warrior who lived eternally in the foothills of this sacred place. He savoured Hanuman's glance, grateful beyond measure for his personal audience. "Saraswati Devi told you to go to that place where you can delve deeply into the principles you already know, that you might realise them and apply not just mental activity to your thought process, but spiritual fuel. Yet you came here. Why?"

Raj was careful in his response, not able to distinguish the difference between Hanuman living here, and him visiting here – obviously there was something he was missing. "But you reside here, this is where you chose to remain. How is there some fault in my choice? I don't understand." He paused, thinking of Dadaji... and realising suddenly that Dadaji had stayed silent when Raj had spoken of Rishikesh. He now looked up at Hanuman and noticed the small smile.

"No, it was not Dadaji's suggestion," Hanuman said.

Raj felt that he had perhaps, by default, skipped over or missed the enormous depth and meaning of the presence of these great personalities in his life, of the rarity of their appearance, of his unspeakable fortune of having their priceless association, guidance, conversation. He paused. *Conversation. With Hanuman.* Again his head reeled...

But in truth, it lay deep within him and filled his every cell and pore and thought and action. Words were insufficient, like a speck of dust speaking of the glories of the sun, nothing he put into words could do justice to this, any of it. *To his life,* he thought.

That Hanuman had mentioned Dadaji – as had Devi and Saraswati, and even Kali – was not a surprise, in some ways, yet still life-altering. He had understood from his youth that his Dadaji was not an ordinary person. But that his name fell so easily from the lips of such exalted souls was nothing short of astounding to Raj. And he knew with certainty that they were not merely speaking of Dadaji as some bit-player in Raj's life, but that they each had a deep relationship with Dadaji, and he with them. *They knew him*, he realised, the thought making the hair on the back of his neck tingle and rise. *They know Dadaji.*

Before he could absorb his latest discovery, Hanuman continued speaking, "He had his reasons, Dadaji, but letting you think that you might find your answers here was not one of them. In time, you shall know the full extent of Dadaji's wisdom, but for now, I will tell you this. Are you listening, Rajendra?"

If before Raj had felt the world had stopped, he now could be sure it had switched course and was turning in the other direction. Everything seemed to shift and change, and he was beginning to tire of his own clichéd head-spinning.

Hanuman's voice resonated through him as he spoke: "I am a servant of my Lord, Ramachandra. This is the only wisdom I can share with you. That you came here seeking solace and a quiet meditation through which to reveal the secrets that lay in wait for you, I can only tell you, Rajendra, that you have come to the wrong place."

A blue whistling thrush, its human-like chirp loud and clear, sang a brief solo in a nearby tree, heralding a new dawn. But one glance from Hanuman and the bird swiftly changed religion, became instantly silent, and took flight, no doubt regretting its foolish notion that the arrival of dawn was more significant. Raj followed Hanuman's glance at the departing bird and said quietly, "Faith is the bird that feels the light and sings when the dawn is still dark."

Hanuman laughed and said, "Ah, Tagore. Yes, that can be true and false. This bird, then, is like most humans who visit here. He simply comes to this sacred place and assumes his presence alone gives him qualification, and thus, he can sing loud his tiny knowledge..."

Raj thought of the many people who had come through this holy city whose blindness caused them to act with ignorance: smoking *ganja* to find God, white-water rafting in the sacred waters of Ganga Devi, and gathering before saints and holy men whose agendas were merely to draw crowds who would worship them as mini-gods. *Fools and pretenders,* Raj thought again.

He was humbled at the thought of so many being so misled, while he had an audience with so eminent a soul as Hanuman. "I thought the solitude and meditation might at least give me the space to understand what it was I am destined to discover in myself, if anything..."

Hanuman nodded slowly. "I understand." Hanuman looked out over the edge of rockface and onto the waters of the Ganges below; it was dark and silent here, far from the mecca of the city centre to which thousands flocked each day. "If you wish to understand your purpose, it is not here. You might certainly learn something, but it will not fulfil your spiritual destiny and answer all your questions." He paused. "Your Dadaji wanted that you meet me." Raj was stunned. Again. Hanuman kept speaking, "He knows my life is one of service and devotion. This is not a proud claim, but rather it is all that I am made of. I have nothing else, and while the song of my Lord is sung here I shall remain and absorb myself in the devotion of His worshippers."

Hanuman paused, and when he continued his voice was barely audible: "My life has no meaning without service to my Lord. If one must speak my name, it is only when Lord

Ramachandra is mentioned. This is my only glory."

"But... do you not wish to be with your Lord?"

Hanuman was silent. Raj thought he had perhaps said the wrong thing, and thus, Hanuman would not respond. But after some time he spoke, "There is no question of never being without my Lord Ramachandra. He is not *in* my heart, Rajendra. He *is* my heart. But why am I here? Because my Lord asked me to stay, to help people like you, those who were seeking."

Raj was touched by the softness in Hanuman's eyes that permeated his words. "And your own path, Rajendra, it is so strongly impelled by your desire to fulfil your *dharma,* for this land to once more fulfil its dharma, for those who visit to see it in action, to sense it, to taste it, to take it into their hearts. This is why I stay, as this was my Lord's desire."

Hanuman looked away, across the river below to the city that still slept. "All these people..." he said, shaking his head. "And it is the same everywhere. Every holy site or city in India, their streets are now lined with merchants, trinket sellers, cheaters, profiteers, thieves, beggars, and charlatans. All these places, all covered over by time and deception and fraud, playgrounds not for the Lord and His pastimes, but for the unscrupulous, pseudo holy men and women who will rob anyone of their spiritual desires and trade them for fame, profit, adoration."

Raj listened to Hanuman's voice as the words fell like deep thunder from his mouth, leaving a subtle imprint on the morning mist. Hanuman continued, "Tell me Rajendra, how is it that the whole world knows of Rishikesh? You and I and many others know of its glories, but how does the world know? Because agencies the world over, whose mission is to make money, are promoting all these sites as places of pilgrimage, where, by performing yoga stunts, one can attain liberation and be suddenly 'spiritual.' That is why."

Raj was surprised as laughter burst from Hanuman. "Can you imagine, Rajendra? A world of people who think that yoga is the way to spiritual perfection and knowledge of... *a meeting with...* God? But... I am wrong, am I not? For these visitors have no desire to know God, do they? That is the burden the world carries, Rajendra: not that they wish to *know* God, but that they wish to *be* God. This is the highest pleasure in life, no?"

Hanuman laughed quietly and shook his head, falling silent. His voice was barely audible when he spoke again: "And so they come to Rishikesh longing for that highest of highs, that 'spiritual experience.' And along the banks of this sacred river live so-called gurus as dishonest as the street merchants, all of them awaiting their prey, dressed not in the cloth of a merchant behind a counter, but in saffron robes behind their *mala* – all of them, Indians and foreigners alike, donning saffron and pretending to be spiritual leaders. What folly binds the intelligence of the world that they cannot see through this..."

Hanuman was silent. When he again raised his head, Raj knew the conversation had changed: no more talk of the cheaters of Rishikesh. The energy had shifted and Hanuman's eyes were locked onto him. Raj felt his insides quiver at the long gaze that reached deep into his soul.

"One searching for diamonds is not fooled by broken glass."

Raj nodded. "Dadaji says that if one wants to purchase

gold, one must at least know what gold is, otherwise one will be cheated."

Hanuman smiled. "Your Dadaji is a wise man. Yes, Rajendra: one must know what it is he seeks before he can be sure he has not been cheated." He paused. "But gold or diamonds, they do not lie on the road and wait to be found. Tell me, Rajendra, is Dadaji not your life's treasure?"

Raj nodded. "He is, actually."

"And what is the substance of this treasure?" Hanuman asked.

Raj paused. "Well… I mean, I don…"

Hanuman interrupted. "It is not difficult, Rajendra. Think: what is the *substance* of what you call your life's treasure?"

Raj did not hesitate this time. "I love Dadaji, and he loves me, it is that simple. Or perhaps it is not simple at all. But that is what it is: love. We have a relationship and w…"

Again Hanuman interrupted, "Yes!" he said loudly, a smile widening across his face. He leaned forward slightly towards Raj and said, "Relationship. *This* is the essence of love. It is not a random object, but a relationship. Good answer, Rajendra. And a relationship means an exchange, no? So what is it you do for Dadaji?"

Raj paused. In the intimacy of their loving relationship, spanning the course of his life, he had taken for granted that Dadaji was there, simply there, a given, a trusted presence that was only shadowed by the long span of years that Dadaji had lived and which threatened to soon end. Yet when he thought of how that relationship survived, on what it was based, it *was* an exchange, a loving exchange, as Hanuman had said, and Raj looked back at Hanuman and said firmly, "I honour and respect him, I am his student in life, and I serve him."

Hanuman threw his head back and laughed with joy, his arms raised to the heavens, and shouted so loudly that Raj felt he would cause an earthquake, "*Jai Shri Raaaaaaaam!*" and continued to laugh with what Raj could only conclude was sheer bliss. It was contagious, and Raj was filled with joy, his smile spread wide across his own face, and he joined Hanuman in laughter, the shared moment thrilling them both.

As the laughter faded, a subtle energy seemed to gently bind them together; Raj felt connected to Hanuman through that one simple understanding, more connected than he had felt to anyone besides Dadaji or his family. He felt... he felt *love.* Before he could contemplate the meaning of his sudden realisation, Hanuman spoke, "This, Rajendra, is the essence of love's essence: service. It is not a secret, but it is a rarely achieved understanding. You are a fortunate soul whose life has been guided by the sage who is your grandfather. Thus you are equipped with the foundations that will carry you into your future."

Hanuman smiled and nodded. "This is what one's wealth is based on, Rajendra: spiritual service. Not 'liberation' or similar temporary goals. Most are simply looking for an end to suffering: that is the meaning these days of happiness. It is not really happiness at all but a cessation of distress or misery. But if one is looking for one's purpose, it is not found in liberation. Liberation is nothing: there is no better word to describe it than that, simply 'nothing.' As you have so rightly said, the essence of love is in relationship, and a relationship is an exchange. Between man and God, that exchange has many forms, the most intimate of which is achieved through service.

"So many millions may come to Rishikesh, seeking answers. But how many are told to find their relationship with God through service? I would wager few, if any."

Raj recognised Dadaji's own words in Hanuman's and knew this was what Dadaji had practiced all his life: *bhakti*, loving service to the Lord. He remained silent. Things were coming together in his mind, words were finding their place in this mystery that his life had become, a riddle to solve with the guiding presence of illustrious personalities, performed on the stage of his homeland's sacred sites. He spoke quietly. "You said that Dadaji wanted me to meet you."

Hanuman nodded once, and Raj continued. "And the reason was that your life is one that imbibes all the tenets of service and devotion."

Hanuman nodded again. "Your Dadaji sent you to me for this purpose. In *bhakti,* there are nine processes, and I am the representative of the process of *dasya*, service. Again, this is not my glory, but rather my only purpose."

Raj nodded. "And so this is the purpose of our meeting." Hanuman nodded again. "At Dadaji's request," Raj said. And again Hanuman nodded.

Raj spoke carefully and quietly. "Saraswati Devi told me of my past life, some hundreds of years ago when I was the Imperial Princess Zeb-un-Nissa, the daughter of the Mughal Empire's ruler, Aurangzeb." He waited. "You know this, then?"

Hanuman again nodded, yet remained silent.

"Then..." Raj began, and stalled. He shook some thoughts from his head and began again. "What is it, then, that Devi, Dadaji, and Saraswati want you to tell me of my future? You mentioned my future, and it is clear they all wanted me to meet you for this purpose. So now you have spoken of service. But what of my future?"

Hanuman took a deep breath, exhaling slowly. "Well... Rajendra..." he shook his head, a doubtful look coming to his face. "I can tell you so much. But it may be a burden to you."

Raj shook his head. He was adamant. "No! For years I have tried to understand what my life was meant for. So many go through life not thinking this, or only occasionally wondering, or sometimes always thinking of it but *doing* nothing. Even those who try, perhaps they fail and so they quit. Rare are the ones who achieve their life's goals and carry it as their compass in life. I want that. I *am* that!"

Hanuman watched Raj speaking, his look deep and grave. When Raj finished, Hanuman was silent for a long time. Then, to Raj's surprise, again Hanuman laughed: a deep, long, hearty laugh of one who was obviously amused – no, entertained! – by Raj's words. He didn't know whether to join in the laughter or to be insulted. And so he waited; as he did so, the small burst of ego left him, and he understood Hanuman's amusement was born from joy, not mockery.

Finally Hanuman spoke. "Good! I did not doubt you Rajendra." He paused. "But you have never had cause to speak the words you just proclaimed, have you? Therefore I wondered if you doubted yourself."

Raj opened his mouth to answer, and then closed it. It

was true: he was only twenty three years old. To whom or where or when had the need to pronounce his life's purpose availed itself? Hanuman watched Raj, considering that his daily mental and intellectual capacities were perhaps near breaking point, if not already gliding down the slippery smooth slopes of the Himalayas. "Listen, Rajendra, and I will tell you.

"You understand what it means that you were Zeb-un-Nissa in your past life. In so many ways it means nothing, as Saraswati Devi said. It is past, it is so long ago: another lifetime, yes, but also another world. How does one even benefit from knowing who or what they were in a past life? These are the questions you have been asking yourself."

Raj nodded slowly. Even knowing what he knew, he longed to hear it from an exalted person like Hanuman, and so he remained silent, and waited.

"Life after life, the conditioned soul takes birth as so many different people and species. It is no secret or mystery. That one may have no memory of this means nothing: most cannot even remember *this* life and its detail. The subject matter is a deep science, but we will speak of only one element of that science: what one brings with them into the next life. We will speak of what part of Zeb-un-Nissa you have brought with you to this life.

"You know all about her, of course, but in short, the princess was extremely intelligent, a cultured and refined woman, fluent in many languages, proficient in mathematics and astronomy, a poet, a writer, a musician. She was an aid to her father in her early years and held court with him, even advising him. She would have made a natural heir to the throne had she been born a man, perhaps, but it was not her time. In fact, the empire into which she had been born was at the end of its reign: it had come to its peak with Akbar and his heir, Shah Jahan, but it could not continue. Aurangzeb was a religious bigot who inspired hatred amongst Hindus and Muslims, when generations before Akbar had removed the binds of that bigotry. The empire was doomed, and Zeb-un-Nissa had little power to influence the future; worse, she even fell prey to her father's bigotry.

"Now, she wields that influence: or she can. *You* can. All that you learned and acquired and achieved in that life, those things are with you still. More than that, you have a strong desire to utilise them, to bring to this day, to this time, the culture and artistry that was your life back then, centuries ago. Am I right?"

Raj nodded. The dreams and thoughts that had lived only inside his head and heart, that had never had form, been spoken, seen the air or light of day, were now, through Hanuman's words, manifesting before him. Now, Hanuman was building them into more than just a form, but a future.

"Understand, Rajendra: you cannot *be* Zeb-un-Nissa again. That much is history. It is gone, out of reach, a dream. Nothing else. That woman is dead and she shall never live again. Do you understand?"

Raj nodded again, still too unsure of his words to allow them to be heard. Hanuman continued, "But her essence, her spirit, her soul: it is one and the same, yours and hers. Only the body that carried that soul is different, and a great many years separates both bodies. The soul moves from body to body, birth to birth. This is not news to you. The body changes: like one discards their clothing at the end of the day, so the soul changes bodies at the time of death.

"But the mind and intelligence of Zeb-un-Nissa, those you still carry; those things live on if our desire is strong enough." Hanuman laughed, to Raj's surprise. "Of course," he said, "most people do this, every day, every life they live."

Raj was confused. "They do?"

"Yes, but it has another name: attachment." And he laughed again. "So many lifetimes, bringing with them the same wants and needs and demands; never fulfilled, always wanting wanting wanting, so attached to their plans and their minds and their... well, to little else."

He stopped, now serious again, and looked deeply at Raj. "You should know, Rajendra, that this desire of yours is no such feeble attachment that results only in repeated frustration. It is noble, and it is a strong force that will have an enormous impact on the world. Your life will be one of great achievement. Surely you did not doubt this, with the personal guidance of demigoddesses, the great sage who is your grandfather..." he paused, smiling, and said, "...and even of my humble self."

Again Raj thought of how these things had been hidden within, of how he had been afraid that it was pride impelling him to think that his life was a rare one, that great things were meant to be if he were blessed with the guidance of such heavenly beings.

He nodded slowly. "I understand... though in truth it was never something I felt I could say to anyone."

Hanuman nodded and smiled at Raj's understanding. "Yes," he said. "To whom could you speak these things, but your grandfather? And even then, when? So far you have not been able to put these events into words, to appreciate or understand their meaning. Now, you can."

Raj was silent, and Hanuman allowed him space for his thoughts. After a few moments Raj said, "So what does it mean, then? What am I meant for, what is my purpose? If you were awaiting my visit to impart this knowledge to me, then please, tell me my life's purpose. Knowing now what I have brought with me, tell me where I shall take this knowledge."

Hanuman smiled and nodded. "You are an intelligent boy, Rajendraji. There is no doubt. As you have already been told, knowledge is only useful when partnered with humility and abandoned by pride. Otherwise it is destructive. As Zeb-un-Nissa you saw this repeatedly, a powerful view from your female perspective, and a regal one at that. This is one of the values of that birth. Now you have the chance to use all you were and all you acquired and all you learned as Zeb-un-Nissa, and apply it, now, here, in this life."

Raj was silent, a small frown between his eyes. "With due respect, my lord, I have asked this of Dadaji in the past, of how I, just one person, can change anything, do anything, have any influence; of how these cultures and empires that course through my lifeblood can be of any benefit to anyone." Raj struggled to find the words; he wanted to be brief, succinct. "Though my journey to your mountain has been one of understanding and learning and revelation, at this point I feel like I am back at the beginning, none the wiser, wondering how I am meant to do anything of value. Even knowing who I was, it is as you say of little value in some ways. It means nothing, and in fact since Saraswati Devi told me of my past life I have often felt moments of anguish and regret, that I was once an imperial princess in the Mughal Empire with so many resources at my fingertips, so much culture and learning and wealth and royalty and... so much. But now, here I am, a young man in twenty-first century Delhi, the son of a former cloth merchant, perhaps wealthy but still a normal family, my education limited by the age in which I live..." Raj shook his head. "This life is confusing..." he trailed off.

Hanuman smiled to himself. He understood Raj's dilemma; it was his purpose to alleviate these doubts and set Raj on his way with firm resolution.

"Fear not, Rajendraji. Nothing is wasted, neither your past, your present, nor your future. You *will* succeed as you have long desired as both Zeb-un-Nissa and as Rajendra Gupta. This I assure you." He paused. "Remember what Dadaji just taught you: it was not you who was seeking her, but her seeking you. Do you still understand this?"

As Raj stared into Hanuman's deep black eyes, he felt the weight of many lifetimes lift from him. He had a faith in Hanuman's words that was more than he could explain: a lifetime of honouring him alongside the other personalities in the temples he visited and at which he worshipped. This, as Devi had said, was no small thing, his prayers were not fiction, the answers not imagination. Deep within his heart he understood Hanuman's words and felt once again the subtle shift of the world as it accommodated this change inside him.

"So what should I do, then, to realise these longstanding desires I have held, to better the world, to instil culture and art and meaning, to live in a godly society, and to contribute in a real way to the lives of others?"

Hanuman could read the change in Raj and was satisfied. "Rajendra, you have read of my service to Lord Rama, why I fought Ravana and those who aided that wretch: they were agents of Kali, born for the purpose of raping the land, stealing its resources, creating terror, poverty, distress, war, and other disasters. And so they had to be destroyed. This was necessary. And you, Rajendra, while your future is yours to construct, it will be done by building on the foundation you already have. You are proficient in and naturally inclined towards the classic languages, literature, the arts, history, and culture. Your philosophical and spiritual grounding has been instilled in you since birth."

Hanuman paused, the depth and intensity of his mood suddenly vibrating through Raj. "You will be a leader in these fields. You will work in the international arena, bringing India's past into its present, resurrecting and maintaining culture, making this land's history known to the world, reestablishing the spiritual and cultural traditions it has lost, and introducing the world to the beauty this country has to offer in every respect. You will find your place in the higher echelons of these elements of the life you so rightly hold so dear. You will become a person of national importance and fame, and your reach will extend beyond this country, across the seas to other lands whose pasts echo this nation's."

He paused again, and when he spoke, it was beyond anything Raj could have expected. "Rajendra, you have met the purpose of your existence, and his name is Kali."

Raj was dumbfounded; he had asked, sure, but he could never have expected such an answer. And it seemed Hanuman was not yet finished.

"His agents have again taken birth in this land, this time in the form not of demons and other-worldly beings whose powers are, in modern times, confined to mythical adventures. Quite the contrary. They exist in the form of philanthropic billionaires and corporations, multi-national bodies of power whose sole purpose is to dominate and rid this country of its culture, to rob the earth of her resources and minimise those who would support religion, culture, and history. Kali will try to destroy anyone who is an obstacle and he will, for the most part, succeed. But there is one obstacle he cannot defeat so easily."

Raj hadn't forgotten Kali. How could he? But the purpose of his appearance had not been clear until now. And Hanuman still wasn't finished: "You, Rajendra, will be that obstacle. You will be the mastermind behind the resurrection of the multi-racial, multi-religious, and multi-cultured history that is India, the same culture that reigned thousands of years ago and which brought great men and women here from other lands, across borders and seas alike. All your work will be driven by the desire to see and experience once again the fruits of a cultured empire, not, as these past empires often were – like the Mughal Empires – founded on violence and warfare, but on the tenets of a godly society."

Hanuman stopped speaking and, signalling the end of their conversation, raised his hand. Raj saw the mark of a flag and lightning bolt on his open palm, and felt the hair on the back of his neck raise, tingling down his spine.

He was ashamed that he had even momentarily thought that this might be Kali donning the disguise of Hanuman. Overwhelmed by the words Hanuman had spoken, he was still and quiet.

Their discussion had finished, and Hanuman concluded with a few final words of advice: "But you shall find that essence within that will drive you to accomplish all that you must in the manner that reflects your long-held desire, not how things were done in the past. All these men, who were great emperors and who left their mark, they started as you are now – with hope and energy and perhaps not all but some of the right reasons."

Hanuman lowered his voice and said, "Do not be like them, Rajendra. Do not *become* them. Remember the words of Devi, and even those of Kali. Acquire that inner strength and resolution of purpose that these men did not have: learn what that means and how to achieve it, and be strong spiritually. Learn, Rajendra: give yourself, do not lose yourself."

A loud whistling scream from the returned blue thrush distracted them both. Hanuman stirred. "This time," he said, "our brave friend truly does hark the arrival of the new day. And thus an end to our meeting."

Raj decided that this time he would not be left wondering where, in the blink of an eye, his great benefactor had gone, as had been the case with Devi and Saraswati – and even the egocentric drama overkill of Kali. "So you will leave me now?" he said, smiling shyly.

Hanuman also smiled. "I shall. But I am always near. Yes?"

Raj didn't trust himself to speak and so he nodded,

his heart filling with a pain and sadness at the pending departure of this great warrior, this lover of God, this wonderful, peaceful soul. Tears, large hot tears, dropped from his eyes without warning. "I'm sorry..." he began, wiping at his cheeks. "Please know I will never be able to express how much this means to me, or repay you for your wisdom and kindness and... and love."

"Likewise, Rajendra. Go forth and conquer."

It was a moment or two before Raj realised Hanuman was being humourous. *Who knew?* he thought; *first Saraswati, now Hanuman.* His smile was large and genuine, and he was grateful that their meeting was ending this way.

"But you will repay me, Rajendra. Of that I am certain. Time will reveal everything." Hanuman rose, and Raj was stunned, again. First, by how swift and agile his movements, and then, by his size. He had guessed at twelve feet, but now saw it was closer to twenty. He looked up at Hanuman and said, "Is this... I mean... do you..."

Hanuman laughed and said, "Rajendra, I possess all *siddhis,* mystic potencies that enable me to do any number of things, including *anima* and *mahima siddhis:* the ability to become smallest of the small, and largest of the large. But you know this already, yes?" Raj nodded. "And did you think it myth or legend?" He laughed deeply again. "No, Rajendra, it is not the stuff of fairytales. I can be larger than you can perhaps imagine." Hanuman's hand indicated his body, "This is my usual size. Would you like to see the larger?"

Raj went to shake his head and refuse the display of mystical powers that would no doubt leave his hair standing on end. But just as suddenly he nodded, thinking, *how many times in my life will Hanuman, the King of the Vanaras, servant of Lord Ramachandra, ask me if I want to see his mystic siddhis?*

Hanuman stepped back into the clearing behind where Raj had been seated, and his form began to expand, upwards and outwards, unfathomably huge. Until now, Raj had thought the sky was without limits, but as Hanuman's body grew, Raj thought he would surely tear the sky in two, ripping a hole in the universe with his might and size.

He was filled with both awe and delight, the majesty of Hanuman's size and form and display of potencies equalled only by his unmatched humility. He was not showing off, but inviting Raj into an intimate moment that only they shared. Raj knew for certain that no one, near or far, could see this form that filled the mountainside, expanded through the sky, and covered the earth. He was, again, stunned.

After a moment Hanuman assumed his normal size, and as everything suddenly returned to "normal," Hanuman looked down at Raj. "So?"

Raj shook his head, breathless. "*Wow*!"

Hanuman, with a glint in his eyed, said, "Not quite Shiva, but still..."

Raj was surprised and embarrassed simultaneously, and stumbled over his words, "I... uh, no really, I didn't mean..." Hanuman laughed, enjoying Rajendra's reaction. Raj knew Hanuman was teasing him for the thoughts he had had prior to coming to Rishikesh, that he might be coming to meet Shiva, and he shook his head, gave up, and laughed with Hanuman, the bond between them sealed. Then, remembering himself, Raj bent to the ground, offering his obeisance to Hanuman. The great warrior-monkey shocked him by responding to the gesture in kind, bowing down before Raj. As Hanuman raised his head, he saw the stunned look on Raj's face, and smiled. "You have given me the honour of serving you, and your Dadaji. I am indebted."

Raj realised he had not yet asked about Hanuman's repeated references to Dadaji. As he went to speak, Hanuman again raised his palm, the bolt of lightning and flag again catching Raj's eye. "And now I must leave. Do not be anxious, Rajendra. We shall meet again. Rest assured. *Jai Rama!*"

Hanuman turned and walked away. Raj was prepared to stand and watch him until he could no longer see the form of the great Hanuman, but just as the thought crossed his mind, Hanuman was gone. *Just like that.*

* * * *

And so it was that he would for the rest of his life think of this as the day he came down from the mountain. He had arrived in Rishikesh only a month before, a young man of twenty three whose life had become, in a matter of months, one that resembled a fantasy, something he still could not understand, that did not merit description, and that only his grandfather and parents knew of. *Sure, if you discount the goddesses, Hanuman, and Kali,* he thought wryly.

After Hanuman's departure, Raj had sat quietly, losing track of time, allowing the experience to soak into his skin, his bones, his mind and heart. And in those hours, he decided he would leave Rishikesh, that his time here was well and truly complete and fulfilled. He walked down to the banks of the Ganges and took his final bath in the sacred waters, his mind and body tingling with the memory of the morning.

Returning to his temporary abode, it took him just minutes to gather his things and leave, taking with him only his *mala* – the sacred beads upon which he chanted – and the two books he had bought in the little store in Rishikesh in what seemed like another life. He had already given away the clothes he had worn when he had arrived, dispensed with his old shoes, and kept only one *dhoti* to wear and one *gamcha* for bathing. The lantern he used at night he left on the rock, knowing that one of the yogis nearby would be watching him leave, and that he would not return. They had a sense of these things, and they would take the lantern or leave it, use it or ignore it, it was hard to say. *They're a fairly detached bunch,* Raj thought. They had kept to themselves, and Raj felt the peace and quiet emanating from them whenever he was with them. Few words, if any, were ever exchanged. He thought to call out to Subuddhi Raya, but knew if the yogi had wanted, he would be here now. *Let it be.*

He picked up his cloth bag and slung it over his shoulder. Carrying his water bottles, he left without turning back, walking quietly and thoughtfully down towards Lakshman Jula, stopping only once very briefly. Then, dropping the water bottles in a bin, he crossed the bridge, climbed on a bus to Haridwar, got down at the train station some thirty minutes later, and soon boarded the train home to Delhi and Dadaji.

As he sat down in the train, holding his bag to him so

it wouldn't slide off his shoulder, his hand settled on the hard, small container he had bought at his one brief stop in the marketplace: a tiny, round, stainless steel container with a secure clip to seal it shut. Less than two inches in diameter and costing only a few rupees in the market, it now held one of the most precious items in the world.

For as Hanuman had left Raj, so too had he left a footprint in the dark, rich earth of the mountain upon which they had sat. Raj had enclosed the precious soil in his hand, and transferred it to what had been a worthless container but was now a sacred chalice.

* * * *

There is so much to be grateful for, where does one begin. Raj's thoughts filled with words that could not take form. Too fat with meaning to find their way into the ether, they rolled around inside his head like puppies in the sand, kicking, playful, filled with joy. They overflowed into his heart, where the happiness knew no bounds, expanding further until he was fit to burst. He had felt this way since Hanuman had left the mountain; he was not sure if he would ever again experience such a deep sense of happiness and fulfilment, and intended to relish the moment.

The words of his mother broke through his thoughts: "*When life is at its most beautiful, that is the time to be afraid.*" His mother was an unusual woman, that much Raj had realised through his relationships with the mothers of his friends and his aunts. She was peaceful, content, realistic, refreshing in her outlook on life, and never negative. But over the years he had heard these words from her so many times, and she was always right. He had found a *ghazal* many years ago by Zeb-un-Nissa that echoed the same mood:

But grasp thy joy; who knows,
Makhfi, what may to thee befall?
The firm foundations of the earth may shake,
The breeze that blows
may, if this empty life be all,
the bubble of our vain existence break.

He would not remember these thoughts a few days later; it would be some weeks before the words of both his mother and the *ghazal* would return to haunt him. Before then, the earth would definitely shake, and the breeze that blew would be an ill wind that threatened to never move on...

6

Vrindavan

THREE days: that's how long it took for Raj to tell Dadaji about his meeting with Hanuman. Despite the impact that Devi, then Kali, and finally Saraswati had had on his life, Raj knew without doubt that his meeting with Hanuman would have the most enduring consequences. The future of which Hanuman had spoken was overwhelming. For a long time, Dadaji did not respond. He sat staring out the window, sometimes coming back to his altar, sometimes taking books from the shelves in his room, seeking a particular reference, all the while silent, his brow furrowed in concentration and meditation. Dadaji hadn't spoken then for another two days, and when he did, it had been uncharacteristically brief.

And now, on the sixth morning, Raj felt that things had

returned to some semblance of normal. The morning was the same as every other: silence reigned, dawn hovered at the windows, and the distant and subdued sounds of Meenu making tea crept up the stairs. Raj crossed the landing to Dadaji's room, listening for the sound of the bell. He pushed the door. "Namaste, Dadaji," he said quietly as he entered.

But it was not the same as every other morning, and it never would be again.

Dadaji lay on his divan, but before he even entered the room, Raj knew that he was gone. There was a stillness, an emptiness that was beyond the means of the night or the hour of dawn to create, but which had entered as Dadaji had departed. Raj fell to his knees, scrambling to feel Dadaji's pulse, touching his neck, finding his wrist, one word sprinting in manic circles through his head, "*No no no no no no no no...*"

And suddenly, as though Dadaji had shaken him, he stopped, the truth blasting the panic from his movements and thoughts, emptying the room and leaving it laced with ice. Raj crumpled against the divan, laid his head on Dadaji's shoulder, his heart shattering and pouring in liquid form through his eyes as tears soaked his face and chest and agonised sobs shook his body.

Gone...

It was light when Meenu entered and found him in the same position, still crying in silence, his body trembling now in weakness and pain. The tray bearing the tea crashed to the ground, and Meenu backed out of the room, stumbling her way upstairs to reach Raj's parents – *and Archi, oh dear God, Archi, who was staying in her old room upstairs while her husband was overseas, who loved her grandfather dearly* – before they could wonder what had caused the commotion, to quell their alarm with... what? *Something worse...*

Raj's parents found him in the same place Meenu had, and from then on it was a haze for Raj: Archana falling to the floor in shock as she arrived in Dadaji's doorway, people crying, someone lifting him, and Archi, his little Archi, sitting together, holding each other on the *pida* in the corner of Dadaji's room, seeing everything yet absorbing little; so much movement, so many people, in and out, back and forth, Archana's tears the only thing that broke through Raj's daze.

And then they took Dadaji away. The tears became a river, and words poured with equal pain and swiftness into his mind: he could stop neither.

...what though the radiance which was once so bright
be now forever taken from my sight...

The day was a blur; family and friends coming and going, the cremation ceremonies, the rituals, fire sacrifices, the fasting, the visitors, and the constant, overwhelming pain of loss that tore through Raj's body with every breath. *His Dadaji.*

The next morning was worse. Had Raj known what pain would welcome him upon waking, he would have never again laid down to sleep. For as his mind rose from its unconscious state into that moment that was still just another day, a fresh day, everything new, a harbour, a shelter in its anonymity – *nothingness* – it then shattered as the memories flooded in and pain filled him, threatening to squeeze his soul from his body but failing.

Gone.

For days, he barely left Dadaji's room. He saw him in everything, heard him everywhere. It was sometimes too much and he would leave, only to find it was worse outside, away from Dadaji's things, away from Dadaji. And so he would quickly return and stay for more hours. Meenu brought tea and food, but both remained untouched. As the monsoon rains fell outside the window, she kept the ghee lamps burning and lit incense, but came and went silently, her own pain muffled by the constant movement she could not give up. Not yet.

All his life Raj had come and gone from this room according to the hours Dadaji kept, but now it was no one's domain. Though not empty, the life had retreated when Dadaji left, sinking in silence into the thick walls of the house, lying in wait to retell itself to the future. Raj watched the incense leave a trail of grey, smoky footprints as it climbed to the ceiling, filling the room with ritual and scent and history and love, all the things that were Dadaji. He stood and walked the length of the room to the back window that overlooked the market lane, opening the pane wide and letting in the monsoon air, rain-slicked from the night's showers. It was dark still; he looked out at the silent world, the view only so slightly different from his own window just twenty feet along, and pondered how different the view was from his mind, his eyes, his heart, than it had been from Dadaji's. A rooster coughed a half-hearted crow from across the lane, and Thomas Gray spilled through his mind...

The breezy call of incense-breathing morn,
The swallow twittering from the straw-built shed,
The cock's shrill clarion, or the echoing horn,
No more shall rouse them from their lowly bed.

Raj lent heavily against the wall, pain flooding his body and leaving him weak. *What will rouse me from my lowly bed now,* he thought. The dark stillness of the morning heightened the loss and sadness...

...and leaves the world to darkness and to me.

And so as the days began and ended, Raj took shelter of the Gopal mantra and the countless words Dadaji had spoken that now entered his mind unbidden, in no sequence, random but welcome. The mantra had meaning of its own accord, but that it was now such a strong connection to Dadaji made it all the more precious. He would sit in Dadaji's room morning, noon, and night, remembering when Dadaji had told him about the words to the mantra, urging him to go out and "be the emperor" of his own fate. He thought of the last nine months, of the extraordinary adventure his life had become. *Nine months,* he thought. *The time it takes for a new life to form, to take birth.* This was his new life, then: the one that would continue without Dadaji.

He remembered the dream he had in Rishikesh on what he had not yet known was his last night, of Dadaji telling him that this was now over, that the meaning of his life lay now in the future, not in memory or in the past, "*...the truth is not elusive anymore, pota...*"

He was reluctant to leave Dadaji's room, or the house; despite the months of travel and fearless adventure, he was incapable of walking out that room, so crippling the thought of going anywhere and leaving behind forever the *chhota pota,* the "little grandson," that he was to Dadaji. Now there was no one left to call him *pota.* He longed to hear Dadaji's voice once more. *Just one time please,* he would pray in futility, hearing only the poetry of Wordsworth that was like a blade slicing open his veins, allowing his life to pour out, flow away.

Stay near me, do not take thy flight!
A little longer stay in sight!
Much converse do I find in thee
Historian of my infancy...

Raj felt the deep, aching loss.

Historian of my infancy
Float near me; do not yet depart!

But it was hopeless. He could change nothing, nor would time adjust to accommodate his ravaged heart. He would never again be that little grandson clinging to the hem of his beloved grandfather's wisdom, love, strength, and support. He was *chhota pota* no more.

He was, now, only Rajendra.

And we, who seem
to live and move and love,
no more now than shadows on a wall...

* * * *

As the temple bell struck twelve times at midnight, the family slept, and Raj slipped from the apartment and down into the gardens, out the gates and into the laneways of the sacred town, longing to lose himself in the dark of night and filter his thoughts. He had crept into the dark of night, knowing that the family's sleep was light and any movement from him would waken them... he wanted to be alone. As he had left the guesthouse grounds, he heard the *chowkidars* talking quietly in the stillness of the night, their voices never above a whisper. They rose as he approached the gate, nodding silently as he left the grounds. They were used to it; so many did not sleep in this town, it was nothing new.

He thought of yesterday, their first day here; of how the movement of the heavy brass slide-lock on the door had stirred Raj; he had woken slowly, as he had every morning since Dadaji's death, allowing the pain to once again wash over him as the memory of life settled in his mind once more.

Gone.

His mind had filtered the sensations of awakening, realising slowly that this was not his room, remembering even more slowly where he was. He had forgotten for a little longer yesterday morning, and for that he had been grateful. The pain had washed over him eventually, though, its weight finding its place on him once again.

Vrindavan.

He had opened his eyes; the sound of the lock sliding back on the door had been Mammi returning from the temple across the laneway. Raj had reached up and lifted the blind at the window; it was still dark, but dawn would soon arrive. His eyes had swept over the wide verandah, across the pathway to the lawns bordered by heavily scented frangipani and night-blooming jasmine.

Vrindavan. Dadaji's place.

That had been yesterday. Now Raj wandered the back laneways, not sure of his destination but heading towards the Yamuna, his fingers rolling gently over the *japa* beads in his hand. The deep bellow of a cow rumbled through the still night, a peacock shrieked in the distance: the sounds of Vrindavan that Dadaji had so often spoken of. He saw ahead what seemed to be an ancient tree with two trunks woven into each other, dark and light, its branches reaching out into the thick, cool air, offering shelter. He sat on the ground, leaned back, and let the last two days empty from his mind, felt the weight transferring from his shoulders to this wise old soul whose strength seemed to lift the burdens from him willingly, a strength far greater than his would ever be.

They had arrived two days before, all of them, including Meenu and her Ma, who was more of a grandmother to him and Archana than their own had been; they had been so little when she died, and had never really known her. Yet Ma had lived with them, had been their father's *ayah* since his birth, as Meenu had been theirs.

The rooms of the guesthouse they'd checked into were small, and none of them wanted separate rooms, reluctant as they were to split, joined invisibly by the missing element of Dadaji. The reception clerk had instead offered them a rooftop apartment: privately owned, fully furnished, yet empty. It was quiet and spacious enough for the six of them, and they gratefully accepted. Yet despite the large separate bedrooms the apartment boasted, all six of them had somehow decided, without discussion, to sleep together in the lounge. They had already suffered too much separation and could take no more, longing instead to be supported by and give support to each other.

Dadaji's ashes had been brought here, to the place he said was his "ultimate goal of life" – the eternal playground of Krishna and his cowherd boyfriends and girlfriends. He had often sung to Raj the *sataka* written by the Vaishnava saint, Prabhodananda, in his glorification of Vrindavan:

Sri Vrindavan is my greatest attainment, my greatest deity, friend, teacher, religious duty, and wealth; it is my greatest glory, austerity, knowledge, and is eternally everything to me, everything I have searched for in this world.

So it was that they had come to perform all the ceremonies and rituals, ending at the Yamuna where the last of Dadaji would be sprinkled along with their tears.

It had been a long painful day, and Raj was glad they were here and not in Delhi where the air was thick with the absence of Dadaji. There was love here, and they needed it. It surrounded them in so many forms: love for the Lord in the temple, love amongst the large groups of pilgrims who had trekked long distances together to pay respects in the temples, love between the residents of this sacred town and the animals that were also considered "locals," the dogs and monkeys and cows. The whole family was in great need of this tangible reassurance and love; all of them were relieved to be here, in the place that Dadaji held so dear.

Raj swung his legs to the floor and stood, stretching; there were four divans in the main room, with Meenu and her Ma sharing one and Mammi and Archi another, leaving Raj and Bapa a divan each. As he watched his father sleeping, it suddenly occurred to him – conscious though he was of how strange it sounded – that his father had lost *his* father. They had all called him Dadaji, even Raj's parents had. What had started as a third-person address to their little children for their grandfather had turned into simply the name the family knew him by: Dadaji. He wasn't *papa* or *pita* or *bapa* or *bapi*. He was simply Dadaji.

Gone.

Raj shook off the sadness again, much the same as he did dozens of times a day, consciously moving it aside, not allowing it to settle. *Not yet.* Today would be a long day, emotionally draining, and the moment for which none of them were ready: the end of a chapter.

He heard Mammi in the kitchen and went to help her make tea, but Meenu had, as always, risen before anyone, bathed, dressed, and already made tea. As she turned to Raj, holding the tray with tea and cups, their eyes locked, Meenu faltered, their usual morning ritual now a painful memory. Raj stepped forward quickly, his hands under the tray, taking the weight from Meenu. "*Betho,* Meenu, *betho*... sit, don't worry, let me take this, *haan*?" She nodded silently, and Mammi took her hand and led her back to the main room, Raj following. The others had risen, Archi and Bapa were bathing, and Ma began making up the divans. As Mammi poured the herbal mix, they came together and sat in a circle around the table to speak of that one thing they wished would remain unspeakable: Dadaji's funeral.

In the end, it was simple. There had been no ceremony in Delhi – Dadaji's body was taken to the local burning grounds on the same day he had died, as was the tradition: his body had to be cremated before sunset. His ashes were placed in a brass urn and returned to the family. Where his body was to be burned had been of no significance to Dadaji. He simply desired that his ashes be sprinkled on the sacred ground of Vrindavan and in its holy waters, the Yamuna.

The river was but a few minutes walk from where they were staying, and they had left together just after dawn, walking down the back track that ran along the guesthouse entrance, turning at the end to wind through more back lanes until they reached the riverbank. The guesthouse had arranged for a *sadhu* from the temple across the path to oversee the depositing of Dadaji's ashes in the river, and after a ten-minute walk, the family met the *sadhu* at Keshi Ghat.

The ancient building that leaned over the river at the *ghat* was calm, strong, and quiet, the banks below scattered with people and boats, but otherwise still. Carved pillars graced the waters edge, and platforms reached into the Yamuna, graceful relics of centuries past. This was the place Dadaji had wanted his remains to be scattered.

The family climbed down the broad, steep steps and bowed to the sacred waters before entering, wading in behind the *sadhu* until they were waist-deep. The *sadhu's* assistant passed to him from time to time different items from an assortment of small copper and brass pots: a coconut, mango leaves, bright red *sindoor* powder, all exchanged while the *sadhu* chanted Sanskrit mantras that began with the sacred syllable *om* and continued throughout the brief ceremony.

The morning was still and cool; monsoon rains had fallen yesterday, and the sky was overcast, the slight breeze refreshing. *Dadaji would have loved this weather,* Raj thought, as he numbly watched the ceremony, holding Archana's hand under the water, squeezing it from time to time as he heard her sniffing back the tears. Although Archana had been firm about leaving her little Marcus in Delhi with the *ayah,* Raj could sense she missed him and longed to hold his tiny body in comfort.

The occasional splash and sprinkle from the Yamuna reminded Raj of Devi's appearance on the banks of this same river some months ago, as he had sat gazing at the Taj Mahal and wishing for the wisdom to understand his path. He thought, too, of Saraswati's pure white swan carrier and the drops of the Ganges that splashed his face as its wing gently broke the surface of the water. *I will think of these things later,* he thought, his mind overflowing.

After some minutes, there was silence. Bapa handed the *sadhu* the urn, and the mantras began again as the vessel that contained all that remained of Dadaji was held high and tipped into the breeze, its contents falling silently and softly in the Yamuna, dissolving in the current.

And it was over. The final offering of incense and a *ghee* lamp was all that was left. The young boy passed the huge flaming lamp to the *sadhu.* It was an offering both to the river and to the soul whose ashes now graced her waters, and Raj smiled a small, weak smile, knowing Dadaji would be pleased with the words of Kabir that drifted through his mind as he watched the flames dance across the sky:

...waving its row of lamps,
the universe sings in worship...

So it was that Dadaji was laid to rest in the eternal waters of Vrindavan. Raj's heart overflowed with the pain of loss and love for his Dadaji, pain that poured from his eyes and merged with the waters of the river.

Gone.

There would be only this day and the next in Vrindavan, days that were open to grief. Yet on their departure it would be left here; Dadaji had gently but firmly taught them over the years that there was a time and place for everything, but carrying it beyond that time and place was excessive. "To every thing, a season," he was fond of saying. So it was that Raj understood that come tomorrow, as they left Vrindavan to return to their home in Delhi, the pain and grief would stay here, and he would carry with him only the loving legacy of Dadaji.

Gone, but never far...

* * * *

The thoughts of the final ceremonies for Dadaji lingered around Raj's mind. As he leaned his back against the broad trunk of the ancient tree, Raj felt one weight lift, yet another settle upon him. The family was leaving tomorrow – *no, today,* he thought; *later today* – and beyond that moment, life was a mystery. He did not know what it held, and was afraid of the feeling that had started to linger around him: that he didn't care. *Does life, at one point, become meangingless?* He could only hope and pray that everything he had learned, everything he knew, all that Dadaji had taught him, would save him from the despair whose approach he felt lay in wait.

No temple bells yet sounded. It was still too early, even by the standards of this town – only two hours or so had passed since he left the guesthouse. For some of Vrindavan's residents, the first prayers at 4:30 am in any one of the town's thousands of temples was the end of a night of chanting, meditation, and song; for others, it was the beginning of their day. The whispers and quiet movements of its locals filled the air as they chanted and prayed, while silence reigned and the quietness invited the heart to open. Raj, too, chanted and prayed, processing the last few days since Dadaji's death.

He thought back over the past year, of the adventure his life had become, all of it due to Dadaji's wisdom and guidance: Dadaji encouraging to find his purpose in life; the trip to Agra and Devi's appearance on the banks of the Yamuna; his meeting with Kali and his associates in the park near home and the powerful effect it had had on him; the journey to Patna and the breathtaking appearance of Saraswati Devi in the Ganges; and recently, his retreat to the Himalayan foothills and his audience with Hanuman. *This is an extraordinary life,* Raj thought. *An unnatural life...*

He was blessed, he had no doubt. Yet there remained the question of what he was meant to do, to what the past year had been leading. He had felt certain that he was coming close to the answer, then Dadaji had died. *How can I feel cheated when I have been given so much?* The words of the mantra spilled from him into the air, joining other chants and mantras, all of them filling the space of the night with a sacred vibration that soothed his ache. The words of Hanuman tumbled around his mind, clarifying the question that remained unanswered in his mind: *"This, Rajendra, is the essence of love: service. It is not a secret, but it is a rarely achieved understanding. You are a fortunate soul whose life has been guided by the sage who is your grandfather. Thus you are equipped with the foundations that will carry you into your future."*

But how would that future now unfold? Why could I not have discovered it with Dadaji? Helplessness overwhelming him, Raj lowered his head, lent his forehead on his drawn-up knees, and cried.

The branch brushed over his head, its leaves gently caressing him. From the back of his mind came the thought: *but there is no breeze.* Again the caress, more firm. He thought it was his imagination, yet suddenly knew deep down it was not, knew that this was, once more, something beyond the realm of the ordinary. He raised his head.

He didn't recognise the person standing before him, wasn't even sure it *was* a person. Though it was pitch dark, she and everything around her shone like the sun, her lustrous glow illuminating the surrounding area. Raj was still and silent. While the appearance of other worldly personalities would never be anything but unusual to him, this one was even more so due to the one detail that set this remarkable event apart from the others: he had no idea who this person was.

He stared in awe at the being before him, her beauty filling him with a secure, strong warmth, a deep sense of relief, and he dived into its depths willingly. Her complexion was like molten gold, her blue garments decorated with pearls and flowers. She was wise, reassuring, and Raj understood that there was nothing she did not know. *But who was she?*

She smiled, lifting her right hand to stroke the bird that Raj now noticed perched on her left hand. Then she spoke, the words entering his ears like drops of ambrosia falling upon the lips of a man dying of thirst: "Ahhh, Rajendra... still your tears, dear son, still your tears..."

Her words were more than soothing; they mystically carried instruction and wisdom. No sooner had she spoken than his tears stopped, the pain lifted from his heart, and his eyes drank in her calming, gentle mood. "Forgive me," he said, "I mean no offense, but... who are you?" He felt the lacking in his words, that this goddess should have been addressed in a far more formal tone and gracious manner, received and spoken to with honour. But he was frozen still.

She smiled again. There was what seemed like a pause in the universe, as if the words she was about to speak were heralded by a chorus of angels announcing their arrival: "I am Vrinda Devi, the presiding goddess of these twelve forests known collectively as Vrindavan."

I'm not here. The words crashed into Raj's mind unbidden. *I'm not here. Not on this earth anymore. This is not where I sat down. I am somewhere else.* There was no logic or form to his thoughts; reason and order had abandoned him. While his mind slowed in an attempt to process what he was hearing and seeing, Raj felt his body moving as he rose to his knees, then bowed his head to the ground before Vrinda Devi. As his forehead touched the cool, sacred ground at her feet, he felt the memory of Dadaji's words pour into the forefront of his mind, flooding his thoughts...

* * * *

Raj was only three when he had gone to his mother one day as she sat in the downstairs office; he waited quietly in the doorway until she stopped writing and noticed him. She looked up and cocked her head slightly in question, seeing on his face the determination of a mission he had come to accomplish, curious about its source. "Raji? What is it, *beta*?" Raj walked to his mother's chair, her arm outstretched in a summons of welcome, now pulling him to her. He leaned on her lap, comfortable in her loving embrace, at home in the feel of her, the scent of her, all the wonderful things that created his formative mind and heart. She was pregnant with the child who they would come to know as Archana, who was due to arrive any day. Raj's head lay in her lap, his hand tracing light patterns on her large belly, his face a picture of concentration.

His mother smiled at her darling son's serious countenance. What could possibly trouble the mind of one so young, whose existence turned on the goings-on within the household, who knew nothing of the world beyond the gate? But her Raji had always had an air of calm graveness about him; always his smile was ready, his humour quick, but still the calm, serious exterior prevailed.

"Mammi, I love Meenu," he said, surprising his mother with the words. She was not in the least surprised at the sentiment: she knew he loved Meenu. They all did; she was family, as was Meenu's mother, whom they all called Ma and had done since she herself was young and living with Dadaji's parents. But it was a curious introduction to the conversation with Raj, and she was intrigued as to where it would lead. Raj continued, "But I think she should not sleep in my room."

His mother raised her eyebrows slightly in surprise; this was certainly not what she expected from her three-year-old son. Meenu was his *ayah* and had looked after Raj since he was born; it meant she slept in his room, too little was he to sleep alone. While she would have loved to have Raj sleep in her room, she had to consider her hard-working husband, who would not take well the demands of a baby in the night. Raj added, "Ma would like Meenu to come back to their room now, *na* Mammi?"

Gathering her thoughts, Raj's mother answered, careful to honour her son's serious intentions: "Why, Raji *beta*, this is very kind of you, to think of Ma like this. You are indeed my little gentleman, *na*?" She repositioned herself and scooped him up onto the now tiny space that was her lap, holding him to her. He did not resist, and she thanked the Lord for what she knew were now just remnants of babyhood, grateful that he was too young yet to reject the affection of his mother as boys so often did as they grew. She drank it in, smelling his head like he was a baby, yet finding only the scent of freshly washed hair and the lingering lavender soap Raji insisted upon – such an old little being her baby was. What three-year-old demanded lavender soap as he had! Pulling away slightly, she looked into his upturned face. "So, you wish to be alone in your rooms, then, *beta*?" Raj nodded. "Yes, Mammi. Meenu will have to look after the new baby soon, *na*? She should be with Ma until then." He frowned slightly then as a new thought occurred to him. Looking again into his mother's loving face, he said, "Do you think Meenu will be sad? I don't want her to be sad."

Raj's mother stifled the laughter that rose in her as it met with tears of happiness and pride and so many other feelings overflowing from her bottomless stream of loving maternal emotions. She chose her words carefully. "Well... I think Meenu will be a little sad at leaving you. But you're right, *beta*. Ma will be happy, and that's important, isn't it?"

The next morning, when Raj woke alone in his rooms, he heard in the still-dark morning – long before dawn would come – the tiny tinkle of the bell from Dadaji's room across the landing. He sat up in bed, listening, and then rose, left his rooms, walked around the railing, and stood at his Dadaji's door for the first time in what would become a ritual they would share for a lifetime, a lifetime of wisdom, love, and knowledge, all of which Dadaji was determined to instil in his only grandson.

After that first day, Raj would spend his morning hours staring at Dadaji's altar, at the deities of Radha-Krishna, his eyes almost level with the forms lit by ghee lamps in those early hours, just tall enough he was to stand in front of the altar and peer up at them as Dadaji spoke of the pastimes of Radha and Krishna, of the magical forests of Vrindavan, of Vrinda Devi, the goddess of the forest, of the *vana-devis*, the forest fairies who were her aides, and of the mystical pastimes in the secret land where Dadaji longed to live forever. Only with the blessings of Vrinda Devi, Dadaji would often repeat, was it possible to join Radha and Krishna in their forests, eternally. It was the stuff of fairytales for a child, yet it was alive and real and right in front of him every morning, not trapped in the pages of children's books or adults' minds. Little Raj would listen with rapt delight to every word Dadaji spoke...

* * * *

And so it was he had first heard Dadaji speak of Vrinda Devi, at whose feet his head now lay...

"Devi, forgive me. I am ill-equipped to understand what might be obvious to some. I cannot express my gratitude enough for the wonder of my life, but I fear I am a poor student."

Vrinda Devi's smile was gentle and kind. "Rajendra, your future is mapped, you know what it is that awaits you, yes?" Raj nodded. Despite how unclear he was about how it would all unfold, Hanuman's words were as though etched in stone. "Hanumanji explained to you what path to take and how to achieve the desires you have held so dear in your heart for many births. You are truly blessed by your association, there is no doubt." She paused and leaned in closer to Raj, her intensity increasing, the air surrounding her seeming to crackle with it. "But Rajendra, do not simply build an empire..."

With those words, past and present clashed in Raj's mind, visions and memories of empires lost, battles fought, war and famine and wealth and opulence and palaces all spun before him in a blur, swirling through the ether on the banks of the Yamuna where he now sat, ancient scenes and tableaus crashing into his mind and thoughts. His mind reeled, the words of Devi, Saraswati, Hanuman, and Dadaji, all combining to create a force that threatened to rob him of his life airs, so powerful was the turbulence, so heavy the import of the words they had all spoken. *This is what it has been leading to*, he thought, the understanding engulfing him like a tidal wave. And like every other moment in his life when he was drowning, it was Dadaji who came to his rescue.

* * * *

At the end of the fifth day of Raj's return from the Himalayas and his audience with Hanuman, finally Dadaji had spoken. Despite the amount of time he had taken to digest Raj's story, his words were fewer than Raj could ever have expected.

"*Pota*... yes, I can still call you *pota, na*? For now, yes, but your days as the young grandson are coming to their natural end, you understand, Rajendra? I do not know that there is much to say. Who am I to give a purport to the words of Hanumanji?" Dadaji paused, and Raj felt a curious moment of fear. There was something in Dadaji's words that was final, and he suspected it was the talk of his days as a grandson coming to an end. "Yes, little more to say, *pota*, but for this: don't become the same as the sons of these great men whose lives have inspired you, these sons who failed their duty, who disseminated cultures, failed their people, and who were responsible for the fall of the empires. Become instead someone for whom the world holds respect."

Raj was silent for some time, but as he went to speak, Dadaji held up his hand and shook his head. "No, *mera pota*, it is enough for now. No more words. You have much to think about, a life to plan. There has been enough said. Now... let us go downstairs. Meenu has already called, it is time for lunch. Yes?"

Although Raj was satisfied with Dadaji's words, still he knew there were some things that required discussion. But Dadaji was right; enough had been said. Now he needed to think, to let things take their course. Tomorrow so much could be discussed, but it would be different from all the talks they had had in the past. Tomorrow they could speak of details, of the future, of how to put Hanuman's blessings into action.

* * * *

But that time had never arrived, Raj now thought. The next morning Dadaji was gone, and now here he was in Vrindavan, Dadaji's final ceremonies over, sitting beneath a tree in the middle of the night, speaking with Vrinda Devi...

...and everything that had gone before was assembling itself into one neat, tangible, clear understanding that Vrinda Devi was handing him: "*Do not simply build an empire.*"

He looked up at Vrinda Devi and she smiled as if witnessing the journey his mind had just taken back to Dadaji's room, back to their last days together, the words

Dadaji had spoken that were, Raj now realised, filled with knowledge of his impending departure from this world. She nodded and said quietly, "Yes, Dadaji knew. But he also knew there was one element missing. And I am that element, Rajendra. Hanuman gave you everything; there is nothing more to say, Dadaji was correct. Nothing, but for this one element, Rajendra.

"You have not taken birth again to replicate the empire in which you lived as Zeb-un-Nissa. Your path is far more important than that. Listen now, and I will tell you what Hanuman told you, which is of the utmost importance:

"Service, Rajendra. Your life will be one of service, of that there is no doubt: to your country, to mankind, to your Dadaji, to Devi, Hanuman... and yes, to the Lord. Your entire life has been in preparation for this. Hanuman told you what you will do, how you will achieve your goals, how you will bring India's heritage and culture to the forefront, that you will be instrumental in making it once more the great nation it was. They have all spoken to you of 'godly cultures.' But think carefully: what does that mean? How does one build a 'godly culture?'"

Raj hesitated. *Do not simply build an empire.* There had already been so many empires, yet Kali had managed to destroy them all with his insidious presence and influence. Raj spoke quietly, choosing his words with care. "Hanumanji told me my life's purpose had been met in Kali. I do not know how this person is to be defeated, but I imagine that it can be achieved only from the powerful base of a godly culture. That much I know. The rest, I do not. I am sorry..."

"You are right. A godly culture is the fort from which

you will wage your war on Kali. Because rest assured, there will be another meeting between you, and this time you shall be the dominator. Empires have existed before: powerful empires, massive empires, empires with unlimited wealth. Yet all of them were defeated by Kali. They did not simply fade away with time; they were destroyed. Understand this, Rajendra: Kali's goal is to destroy anything of principle. These rulers, they may very well have been the representative of God, as an emperor of a land is. But even so, Kali sought out where within the kingdoms greed and envy and malice reigned, and he entered through the cracks those low qualities caused in the empire.

"You see, Rajendra, you cannot just create a culture and call it godly. To instil the principles of spirituality into the people of a nation, you yourself must be the representative of those principles. Do you understand? If you simply name the machinations of a nation's governing 'godly' and not actually invite God to rule, then you are doomed to fail. You cannot invite the Lord as a guest in a nation that claims to serve him." Vrinda Devi again paused, the intensity of her words increasing. "Because Rajendra, you have been taught the principles of how to treat a guest all your life, no? It is a part of the culture of this land. Why, even now this nation's international appeal to the world to visit its golden shores is based on the premise of *atithi devo bhava*... to 'treat the guest as God,' no?"

Raj smiled as he thought of the familiar song that the whole country knew, as did millions outside its borders. India's tourism industry had embarked on a marketing venture that was exceptionally beautiful in sight, sound, and impact, and which, most importantly for the Indian people, was proudly representative of the culture of how to treat the guest as God. The advertisements worldwide had been a huge success, winning awards for their beauty and artistry and musical score.

Vrinda Devi smiled and said, "Yes, it is a wonderful thing that India relies on its culture to present its best face to the world, no? But do you see the problem, Rajendra? This key word, *atithi:* guest. What is a guest, what does a guest do?"

Raj replied, "Visits, then lea..." He stopped, the sudden realisation of Vrinda Devi's words hitting him midsentence.

Vrinda Devi nodded. "That's right, Rajendra. The guest leaves. So you want to invite God to come to this nation as a visitor? No... of course not. *Do not simply build another empire.* Now do you understand this?"

Raj nodded. "Hanumanji said he is the representative of *seva,* of service to the Lord..."

Vrinda Devi nodded again. "Yes, Rajendra. And that is what you must hear from me now. You see, it is not an option, an added adornment at the end of a creation, a finishing touch, an enhancement. No. It is the key: it is the *essence.* Everything turns on this essence. Without it, everything ends, is doomed to failure, is temporary or shortlived. But with *bhakti,* the essence of loving devotion and service, everything is perfect." She paused. "Do not make the mistake of inviting the Lord to simply 'bless' your life, your work, your plans. No. Instead, make him the centre. Make everything you do richly fuelled with loving devotion, to him and for him. He is not a guest; he is the foundation. He is inherent in every activity performed, every function, every ritual, building, celebration, and purpose. It is thus for every form of worship of the Lord. And this is *your* purpose."

Vrinda Devi's words invoked the memory once more of Hanuman's: "*...your own path, Rajendra, it is so strongly impelled by your desire to fulfil your dharma, for this land to once more fulfil its dharma, for those who visit to see it in action, to sense it, to taste it, to take it into their hearts... your Dadaji sent you to me for this purpose. In bhakti, there are nine processes, and I am the representative of the process of dasya, service. Again, this is not my glory, but rather my only purpose. As it is yours. You have met the purpose of your existence, and his name is Kali...*"

The word "purpose" resounded in Raj's heart. Hanuman had said it, Dadaji had said it, and now Vrinda Devi was speaking it: *do not simply build another empire... this is your purpose.*

He looked up at Vrinda Devi. "So my purpose is to destroy Kali, and to do so I must dedicate my life to one of devotional service..."

Vrinda Devi nodded. "Hanumanji told you that this *bhakti* was the one obstacle Kali could not destroy or defeat. Remember, Rajendra: Kali may not appear before you in the form he once did. He will, as Hanuman warned you, be represented by philanthropists, billionaire individuals and corporations, multi-national bodies of power whose sole purpose is to dominate this land and rid the people and country of culture, to rape the earth's resources, to minimise and undermine spirituality, culture, history. You must be armed, and your only weapon is loving devotion."

Vrinda Devi straightened, stepped back, and again

stroked the vivid green feathers of her bird. Raj felt the descending darkness of her impending departure, and suddenly wished he was the parrot who perched so peacefully on the finger of the goddess.

"Now, Rajendra, here in Vrindavan, spend your time wisely. And remember, even though Dadaji has moved on, he has not left you. He will never leave you. He is your eternal guide, your ever well-wisher, and your master and friend always in all things spiritual and material. You are one of the most fortunate people in the world, Rajendra. Do not misuse your fortune. Go now... meditate on all that has been given you by the grace of your beloved Dadaji, and take it with you into the future. That is where it belongs."

She read Raj's thoughts and said, "Yes, Rajendra, I shall leave you now. You have come to the end of your journey." Seeing the alarm in Raj's face, she laughed lightly and said, "Not the end of your life, no. But the end of this part of it. It is over, this adventure you set out on. It has been put to rest with Dadaji in the Yamuna, where for you it all began... on the banks of that sacred river as she flowed through Agra." Although it was less than a year ago, it felt like another time and world to Raj.

"Remember what Dadaji told you: a godly and powerful culture is not a matter of history or geography or birth or caste, but is the nature of the soul. You will be the guardian of millions of souls who take birth in this nation. Ensure it is a godly culture they come to, nothing else. And remember, Rajendra: to meet this Gopal whose mantra you chant, your life must be one of service. Do not simply build another empire."

The air filled with the silence of the approaching

morning. Raj did not want to speak, unsure if there was anything to say. He surprised himself, speaking before the words could be filtered through his intellect, his heart open and its contents flowing freely: "Please don't leave me, Vrinda Devi..."

Tears flowed from his eyes and he bowed his head, unsure of what her response would be to his unchecked emotion. Her voice caressed his ears, "I will never leave you, Rajendra. Simply think of me, and I will be with you..."

The words quenched the thirst of his heart, and he was filled with gratitude. He looked up, sure now that he would not be abandoned.

But she was gone. *As I knew she would be,* Raj thought. But he was not bereft; her presence filled his heart, his mind, his senses. "*I will be with you,*" she had said, and he knew it to be true.

He still sat on the damp, cool earth beneath the tree. Rising, he set off towards the guesthouse. The family would leave soon, and then his next life would begin...

PART

TWO

7

The Emperor's Residence

January 2037

THE sounds of the city waking were distant as morning rolled into Delhi. The light breeze that lifted the curtains was crisp, but carried the sun into the room through the open balcony doors, warming the emperor as he stood barefoot on the butter-soft marble, listening to the fading peal of bells that sounded from the pillars of the palace. His gaze wandered across the expanse of Persian gardens, taking in the bright red jackets of the guards on horseback, the sound of a trumpet call in the distance signalling the change of guard, and the slow rhythm to which the winter morning began to sway.

As the last few drops of sparkling fog were dispersed by the subdued but determined winter sun, the emperor thought of all the years he had woken in another marble-floored room as a young boy, then a teenager, then a young man; of when he had stood in the doorway of another balcony across town on the outskirts of Delhi; of the pre-dawn silence of the same sleeping city of a different time, whose shadows lay one upon the other, shapeshifting from black to grey to daylight.

The scent of the gardens drifted up to the balcony as the sun warmed the flowers and the paths, and avenues were dampened with a spray of rose water, a morning ritual the city embraced: in the hot summer months it was cooling and now, in the dry cold season it settled the dust and soothed the city's grateful residents.

The sound of morning *ragas* caressed Delhi, the music issuing from speakers hidden in walls and rooftops throughout the city, inviting the residents to rise at dawn, easing their work-filled days at noon, welcoming them home in the early evenings, and lulling them to sleep at night.

The emperor had spent the first days of his appointment personally implementing all these changes. It had been almost two hundred years since an emperor had existed in this land, and he intended to make the massive shift in his country's social functioning a positive one. He had changed the face of the city, altered the habits and practices of its residents, encouraged the positive, swiftly removed the negative, and crushed swiftly and decisively the corruption and crime that ran freely through alleys and streets – especially the government laneways and halls of parliament. While it was hardly Utopia, still it was a vast improvement on what it once had been. He was not fully satisfied and doubted it was even possible, but he was content that his appointment to this post was bearing fruit.

It had not been easy. As he turned away from the balcony, Emperor Rajendra Gupta's mind swam with memories of decades before...

* * * *

Over the course of twenty years, Raj's life had become all that Dadaji had said it would, and all that Hanuman had foreseen that morning on the mountainside in Rishikesh. As Raj and his family left Vrindavan, so he had left the remnants of boyhood behind; though too old to still be considered a boy before, now his mind, thoughts, and consciousness had caught up. He was, with Dadaji's passing, firmly planted in the field of manhood. In the years that followed, he carefully constructed the beginnings of a career, working for the government ministry of culture and tourism, his mind fixed on the goal of reestablishing the lost heritage of India. Hanuman's words had come to fruition in exactly the way he had said: "*You will be a leader in these fields. You will work in the international arena, bringing India's past into its present, resurrecting and maintaining culture, making this land's history known to the world, reestablishing the spiritual and cultural traditions it has lost and introducing the world to the beauty this country has to offer. You will find your place in the higher echelons of these elements of the life you so rightly hold so dear. You will become a person of national importance and fame, and your reach will extend beyond this country, across the seas to other lands whose pasts echo this nation's.*"

In time, he had become the Minister of Culture, and

success and fame soon followed; across the world his name became known and he was recognised as the warm and likeable leader whose touch turned everything to gold, while his solitude touched the hearts of all who crossed his path. Ancient traditions again became the norm, sacred sites were restored and preserved under a national heritage protection scheme that Raj had implemented. In schools across India, life was once again breathed into the beauty and art and science of the cultures that had dwindled to nearly nothing in India's rush to become modern: Hindu, Muslim, Persian, Parsi, Buddhist – all the cultures that decorated India's landscape were revived and incorporated into the curriculum of schools, colleges, and universities. Raj became the bearer of the crown of knowledge, culture, art, science, and tradition, and had travelled to countries across Europe and Asia to help them also reestablish their own failing or dwindling origins and heritages.

It had been the shared desire of Raj and the then-Prime Minister to revert the ruling of the land from modern-day political titles and processes to those of India's past: while hardly returning it to a collective of princely states, the government now ruled under the guidance of an emperor, not a prime minister. And the first emperor of this newly-risen Golden Age in India was Raj. He, in turn, had rekindled the duties of royal families across India where it was feasible. Some states were more inclined than others, formerly the most powerful and solid of the princely states, like Rajasthan, Gujarat, Hyderabad, Mysore, Gwalior, Kashmir, Kerala, and Orissa, all whose traditions remained even after the royal structure had been dismantled by the tragic mistake that was the British, and then Indira Gandhi.

Despite there being several generations since the royals had reigned, still it was easy for the people of India to embrace their regal roots, and so the royal families again took up the mantle of monarchy, if only in a symbolic capacity. It was, so far, an amenable partnership of which the people obviously approved. While the royals were often merely frontmen for a collective of administrating state heads, still Raj understood the peoples' need to identify an individual as their leader, as the symbol of their state. Their modern-day version of royalty worked, he thought, because the people *wanted* it to.

Raj's only sadness was that Dadaji was not alive to see all that had been accomplished. Yet he felt his grandfather's presence daily, still. His parents lived with him in the residential wing of what had once been the President's House in central Delhi. It bore the same name, Rasthrapati Bhavan – literally, "the house of the father of the state" – but the domed palace, one of several of Lutyens' beautiful landmarks in Delhi, was now the home of the emperor. Had it not been for his parents, the three hundred-plus rooms of the palace and the surrounding acres of grounds would have echoed with emptiness. Raj had never married, and people now spoke of him sometimes as a modern-day Bhismadeva, a renounced holy man in the position of ruling the land. While he knew he was but a shadow of that great soul, still the peoples' trust in and affection for him, expressed through this comparison, touched his heart.

Dadaji had often spoken of the Golden Age of India and how it lay within reach. Raj knew that the people of India longed for this, and while they spoke of the changes in the country as proof of its arrival, still he understood they were merely on the shores of that great ocean, only wetting their toes. There was still so much to do before they could swim in its nourishing waters.

The political climate had changed in the past twenty years. While India had willingly embarked on its cultural renaissance with Raj, he had simply been at its helm. The entire country had been ready for it, the air was thick with it, the people begging for it, so many elements had combined to bring into being what had for so long hovered in the ether, and hundreds of thousands of hands had worked to bring it to life. It had manifested only two years back, yet it had suffered little to no teething problems, reaffirming for Raj and others that timing was everything. India – the world, in fact – was ready. Other nations watched as India took the bold step back into its past and embraced its heritage. Raj had worked with other government ministers and leaders for many years to eradicate the religious bigotry and prejudice that were obstacles to the nation's renewal, and had been met with surprising cooperation and kindness from all – even more affirmation that this was something for which everyone had so long dreamed.

There was yet so much to be achieved, but Raj felt confident: the foundations had been laid with care and strength, and the world had opened its arms to the hope of a globally peaceful existence.

And tonight would be the icing on the cake: the inaugural Bhavya Mahotsava, or "grand celebration," the first of what he hoped would be an annual event hosted by a different nation each year. This year's hosting was India's privilege, and tonight the world would watch as the

Mahotsava was broadcast across the globe. From the world over, dignitaries were arriving in Delhi: kings and queens, princes and princesses, the noble, titled, rich and poor, famous and unknown, from every realm they would come and unite in an evening of world celebration, an event that would be followed by a week of summit meetings between leaders of nations, philanthropists and idea-*walahs*, artists and culturists, dreamers and doers. It held the promise of a united and rich future, and the world was ready. The evening had taken more than a year to organise and plan, and Raj was thrilled it had finally arrived. Tonight, the rest of his life would begin...

* * * *

Birds adorned the city's sky with song as night crept up on Delhi, decorating the air with notes of varying melodies. Dressed in flashes of streaking colour, they rushed to finish their business before darkness fell. Excited children played on rooftops, anxious to squeeze the last minutes from the day before a mother's voice called them into the house. Long strings reached out from the rooves, guiding colourful kites that flapped in the breeze and competed for space with the bats now venturing into the dusk, freed from their daytime hibernation. The sun had lost its power, the moon tiptoed to the corner of the horizon, ready to pounce, and the air tingled with the excitement of the evening ahead.

A rhythmic hum danced across the colonnaded forecourts of the emperor's palace. Music drifted from the open doors and windows; ankle bells worn by dancers preparing for the night shook with a timeless purpose;

motorcades arrived and delivered guests; and the footfalls of hundreds of attendants and staff – the backbone of the evening's success – sang in time to it all.

From balconies that lined the walls above the Durbar Hall, the world's media discreetly filmed the unfolding evening and sent it in real time across the world, where in every nation huge screens hung in streets and parks, on railway platforms and in sports grounds, broadcasting the grand celebration to millions. It was a much-anticipated event that would be remembered for years to come, an event the likes of which the world had never seen, and Raj marvelled at the phenomenal display before him in the enormous Durbar Hall. India's culture was the star of the show and flitted around the room through the music, costumes, food, and entertainment. The room sparkled with the combination of clothing, jewels, and the movement of people, but even more so with the celebratory energy that filled the air. *This is what I've waited for,* Raj thought, as he noted the truly united mood of the nations who filled the hall and drank in the sights and sounds of India's heritage. *Dadaji, if only you were here...*

"Your Majesty..." Raj's thoughts were saved from entering the vault of melancholy where Dadaji's memories lived as another new arrival was presented, and he did his natural best to make them feel at home. The cameras watched every moment and had recorded the arrival and reception of everyone, but this guest was different. All the media people on the balconies above the hall collectively turned their eyes towards the person who stood before the emperor, and all shared the one thought: *who is she?*

She was beautiful, an elegant and entrancing woman

who, in just moments, had captured the room and held the attention of the emperor. Everyone slowly and unobtrusively turned, their actions not motivated by idle curiosity but instead laced with the same desire the entire nation held: that Emperor Rajendra Gupta – in his mid-forties, handsome, successful, and very, very single – would find his true love and marry… maybe even produce an heir to the realm he had helped steer back onto a course from which it had long ago diverted.

On the balconies above, the press and media scrambled to identify the woman; hushed calls, whispered demands for a name, details, background, information, anything. The room was filled with princesses, dignitaries, business people, ambassadors, politicians, movie stars... so many recognisable, famous faces. But this one… Raj felt a twinge of recognition or familiarity, but it was fleeting. He was conscious of the room's gaze, and politely moved on.

Yet as soon as he walked away he felt a pull – something was drawing him back to her, and that something was unlike anything he had before experienced. He was conscious of his role in India and how his age and single status played on the minds of the nation. He was always touched by the concerns that he should marry, but there had never been a woman upon whom the public's focus rested and with whom they could unite that concern for his single status. Consequently, he was largely unaffected by the topic of his unmarried state, and remained affectionately amused by it.

For his own part, it was rarely something Raj thought of: he had always been conscious of his loneness, which had never tipped into the neighbouring paddock of loneliness. He was content, self-satisfied, and busy in a balanced way.

And since his parents accepted his single status, he was free from the pressure.

In truth, no woman had ever intrigued Raj long enough or deeply enough to "turn his head," as Dadaji had been fond of saying. They hadn't spoken of it at length, and Raj had long realised that Dadaji had known all along how his life would unfold and thus had never felt the need to discuss the details with Raj.

But now... Raj found himself looking across the hall at the woman, drawn by her energy. He would not ask who she was or from where she came. To do so would bring unwanted attention. Regardless, the media was hard at work, as were the minds of all in the room. The small but certain spark between the emperor and this woman had been duly noted, and was quickly becoming the subheading of the evening's agenda: the possibility that the emperor had, at last, met the woman that the world wanted him to meet.

International media agencies buzzed with live feeds and photos of the woman speaking with him, captured her beauty and laughter as she watched the spectacular and colourful dramas, and were entranced with her delight at the mesmerising performances of the bharatanatyam dancers. In just two brief hours, the world began to fall for the mysterious woman who might one day be Empress.

The Durbar Hall shined, pulsed, pounded with rhythm, shook with laughter, and reclined sated after a sumptuous feast, and the world watched and felt the joy of a new era that the emperor had ushered in. Everywhere that the Bhavya Mahotsava was seen, free food was laid out for anyone who arrived, seating provided, and families and individuals encouraged to come out of their homes, fill the cities' public areas, and participate as the world took a new course in international relations. It was considered a global success, and while it would always have its detractors, the positive energy that thrummed from the centre of the Durbar Hall and out to every continent dominated the airwaves with joy.

The evening was in full swing as a few international leaders and delegates prepared to leave, wanting to retire early and rise refreshed for tomorrow's commencement of the summit meetings. Raj stationed himself near the enormous entrance doors with a full view of the hall and of those who were now beginning to make their way toward their rooms in the palace grounds. He was filled with happiness as he watched the celebrations, and knew that the evening would never be forgotten.

As he bade goodnight to an elderly statesman from Budapest, Raj's eye was caught by a quick flash of golden, gossamer-like chiffon that waved through the air like mist as the woman approached, clearly also preparing to make her departure. Raj again felt the pull of familiarity, and a small frown touched his forehead. Although she had been presented to him, he could not for the life of him recall what had been said, nor summon her name – two things that were a first for him, as his memory was swift and sharp and he made a point always to remember such details.

Cameras on the balconies above swung towards the doors, following the woman's path, eager to capture every detail of another exchange with the emperor. The room again crackled, the electricity of the impending union of these two beautiful people – despite how brief it might be – like an intoxicant in the otherwise sober city of Delhi. Guests and media alike watched the sleek back of the mystery woman, and the tall, handsome figure of the beloved emperor as once again they were face to face.

Their exchange was brief, and Raj was aware of all eyes upon him. He was as charmed by the public's affectionate curiosity as he was by the woman's presence, and smiled throughout their brief exchange. As she took her leave, with the world press zooming in, Raj accepted her offered hand, signalling through the formal yet uniquely intimate gesture that this was perhaps not an end at all, but rather a beginning.

As Raj bowed slightly over the woman's extended hand, he could not help but notice that her wrist was draped with a beautiful golden bracelet from which dangled sparkling ornaments.

And he froze.

He felt his blood turn an ice-chill and vault like a striking snake through his veins, exploding in an arctic burst in his mind as he recognised the small golden orb that swung from the jewelled hand of the woman... the same golden orb that he had picked up from the grass in the park on that day so many years ago... the day Kali had appeared with his three attendants – Kama, Krodha, and Lobha. The same golden orb that had fallen from Kama's ankle bell as she had departed, that he had kept all these years and which was hidden in the depths of a safe in his suite of rooms upstairs in the palace, a reminder of all that had happened that day.

And here she was again, thought Raj: *Kama.* What to onlookers was but a moment felt to Raj like an unwinding of decades – ages, even – as he rose, raised his head, and called, "*Guards!*" in a voice that commanded the room and felled it to silence but for the gasps at this sudden outburst from the emperor.

Without hesitation the guards appeared, and Raj and the woman were surrounded, the guardians of the emperor and his realm materialising from covert positions around the room, tense and alert to an unknown, sudden, but very real danger: everyone had heard the tone in the emperor's voice, and it brooked no argument. The shock that enveloped the room deepened at Raj's next words: "*Remove this beast!*"

There was not a moment's hesitation in the guards' minds as they quickly obeyed the instruction. The room erupted, the media's story-hackles rising. *What had happened? What made him do this?*

And then suddenly, they saw.

In front of the entire world, as the collective nations watched live, the woman morphed into a creature of terrifying appearance, its teeth gnashing, saliva splattering the clothes of those who were not quick enough to scramble away in horror at its appearance, its red eyes flashing and its growl terrifying. They watched as the emperor, wearing a similarly terrifying smile, stepped back and glared down at the beast now caught in manacles and chains. The hall was in uproar, but Raj raised his hand high and called, "*Silence*!" and thus it fell.

The low growls of Kama reverberated off the marble walls as Raj looked slowly around the hall, knowing for certain that within its walls a greater enemy than Kama stood, disguised as a guest, his face wearing a surprised and shocked expression but his heart carrying blackness and malice.

With an unearthly volume, Raj's voice boomed around the hall: *"Show yourself, you despicable coward!"*

As in the Durbar Hall, street gatherings across the globe came to a halt as millions turned to the large public screens. The world watched and waited in astonished silence at this most stunning turn of events, chilled even at such great distances by the frightening tone of the emperor's voice.

And then, from the corner of the Durbar Hall, an opulently dressed middle-aged woman began to move forward, her hair coiffed to perfection, her jewels sparkling, her pale gown falling elegantly to her feet. As she crossed the floor, to the horror of all who watched, she, too, began to morph into another form, but not that of a beast. This one was human-like, yet somehow even more terrifying than the last. In but a few steps the woman assumed the dark and menacing form of a man, his black robes billowing in the now-cold air, the atmosphere around him thickening and changing, a chill snaking through the room. His form grew upwards and outwards, expanding as he walked.

This was the agent of evil who would never be satisfied with the arrival of the Golden Age of India that Raj had heralded in and which now, as the Bhavya Mahotsava evidenced, was taking hold worldwide. This personality would do anything in his quite considerable power to stop it from taking hold.

Kali was back.

8

Defeat

EVERYTHING was the same: the stride, the black robes, the pride of his posture, his heavy boots and wide-legged stance dominating the Durbar Hall, assuming ownership of everything, including the ground upon which he stood.

This was no mere harbinger of doom, but Evil himself, in the flesh. Like a pit of snakes let loose from the bowels of hell, the silence and chill that announced his entrance crawled the walls, slithered across the floor, and found its home on the exposed flesh of the guests, rooting them to the spot. Indeed the whole world seemed to screech to a halt, millions of eyes across the globe locked in uncomprehending awe on screens broadcasting the arrival of vileness itself.

Raj's skin hackled as Kali looked down on him, his

salacious eyes unnerving everyone in the room. He threw his head back and laughed, the sound tearing through flesh and snap-freezing the spines of all. Then he spoke, his voice digging the grave of any hope left lingering in the hall, his words the fall of soil upon the coffin of what once had been life and joy and celebration and purpose but which now lay in the ground awaiting its fate.

"Hello, *Rrrrrraj,*" Kali snarled, his eyes raking the hall, his voice dripping with scathing contempt. "Having some security issues, I see..."

Raj felt a fury rising from deep within, a fury not felt since this monster had last stood before him. He had been younger then, so much younger in every way. Two decades had passed, not long in the annals of the universe, but long enough that those seeds of wisdom, depth, knowledge, and destiny that Dadaji had planted within him so long ago – perhaps which he had been born with – and had sprouted so swiftly, delicate and new in Dadaji's presence, had since bloomed, their fragrance permeating his life and settling on those with whom he came into contact, his grace and depth leaving its mark.

And one thought resounded through his being: *I cannot let him leave.*

Kali broke Raj's reverie. "Hmmm? What's that, *Emperor*? You do not want me to leave? Well, well... what a surprising train of thought! And here I was thinking you would call your sleuth-like army to remove me!" His disdainful laugh was filled with venom, and he turned to the crowded hall, his robes swirling and his mood menacing. "Tell me *Emperor* Rajendra, do these people know what impossible flights of imagination dwell in the corridors of your mind and which tell you it is possible to defeat me, the *god of this age, Kali Yuga personified?*"

Half the hall gasped in fear at the revelation. While the international guests shared the horror and fear, they had been unaware of Kali's identity. The Indian guests, however, knew full well that the agent of evil animus of whom they had heard all their lives now stood in the Durbar Hall, challenging the emperor – and what's more, they seemed to know each other.

The media had lost not a moment: around the globe Kali's name was spread across screens and live broadcasts, details of his role in the administration of the universe being fed to every television station and media outlet in the world – no longer a myth from the pages of ancient scripture, not imagination or the product of a creative mind. No. He stood before the world, Kali Yuga, and not a single person the world over doubted it. Internet systems were crashing and rebooting, public parks and streets and sports grounds were filled with silent spectators, their eyes drinking in every word that filtered out from the balcony above the Durbar Hall and into the ether, introducing to the world the person responsible for – the *creator of* – poverty, crime, corruption, greed, violence, and a host of other ill-bred compatriots of his realm.

And they wondered how he could possibly be vanquished.

In the hall, Kali's eyes fell on Kama, still manacled. He frowned, his lip slowly curling in disdain, his black-booted foot reaching out and nudging the beast that she now was with its tip. "And what are *you* doing, my dear? Get up. Have you no pride?"

Raj's voice was low and deep, belying the rage that welled inside him, capable on its own – the world thought as it listened – of splitting the thick walls of the palace. "She is doing your bidding, you loathesome wretch. That is all your blackguards do; they have no other value. Where are they? Elsewhere fouling the air, or did you trawl your abominable offspring with you?" Raj turned and looked around the Durbar Hall, expecting to see the cast of Kali's operatic perversion of family. He knew of Kali's descendants, knew their names and roles in his earthly reign. The first two were Fear and Death, the execrable offspring of Kali's union with his own sister, Harsh Speech. Their equally vile siblings included Falsity, Cheating, Greed, Bluffing, Hell, and a slew of others. Three he had met in the park with Kali that day twenty-plus years ago: Greed, Anger, and the one who lay at his feet, Lust – Lobha, Krodha, and Kama.

The sneer melted from Kali's face at Raj's words; he was caught offguard, expecting shock and awe yet seeing instead in Raj's persona a withering contempt. Raj gave him no time to respond. "What did you come for, Kali? You have no business here." He looked around the hall at the guests, then up at the balcony, where the media were recording every word, every second. His eyes locked on the central camera, and in that moment, he felt not only the eyes of the world upon him, but their fear, their bewilderment, and even more their desperate need to hear the emperor explain this person and his leashed beast on the floor, to soothe the fears of all who were witnessing the most remarkable turn of events, and eventually – though they were not aware of it yet – to watch as Kali and his minions were disembogued from the city, the nation, the planet. He saw in the face of the camera all the work he and thousands of others had done for two decades; how the world had waited and watched and welcomed every step of the way, all of it culminating in tonight, all of it now threatened by Kali's arrival. *I will not allow him to destroy everything I have worked for, everything Dadaji wanted from me, everything all of them wanted from me...*

He turned back to Kali, and everything inside him – the raging, pulsing hatred and anger for this bastard son of Untimely Death gathered within him, fuelling that fury. The words were steel blades slicing the air, and as Raj aimed them at Kali he circled him, taunting him with his fearlessness and rage. "You have no business here at all. You do not rule in this land. You are powerless! There is nothing – *nothing and no one* – over whom you have any influence. Did you come to unsettle me, these people, this land?" His arm swept towards the guests in the hall, and everyone watching felt included. "Are you so deluded by your own evil energy you cannot see that *no one is interested in you here, Kali?*"

As he threw the gauntlet of universal challenge at Kali's feet, Raj's mind and intelligence reeled, his heart silently screamed for mercy to all his mentors, gods, and beloveds, beseeching his silent benefactors to intervene. He had challenged the ruler of the age, the personification of evil, the father of every bad quality in existence, and as he realised he had no idea what he had done, he just as suddenly knew what he had to do next, and the fury inside him towards Kali exploded...

The roar was deafening, consuming every atom of

air and space and sound in the hall, yet welcome; Raj recognised its tone, its voice, its words, but he was frozen – so long had passed since it had caressed his ears. The love rose like a tidal wave from deep within and crashed into his mind and senses:

Dadaji. He is here.

Kali loomed before him, an enormous presence of malicious intent. But Raj was in another world, where the master of ceremonies was his beloved Dadaji. The voice was other-worldly, a roar that could unseat the universe, but only Raj could hear it. He longed to scour the room and find its source, but knew it would not respond to the tangential demands of his senses. It was after something else…

"Harness your mind, Raj! I have given all you need."

And just like that, all that had come before this moment now rolled into place, locking almost audibly into a tangible form, no longer unmanifested, not scheduled for understanding in a future beyond his reach. *This was it, it is now.* And the words of Hanuman surfed the waves of his newborn realisation: "*In time you shall know the full extent of Dadaji's wisdom." And here it is,* he thought. *Here it is. Here he is. And I know, Dadaji, I know…*

The roar engulfed him, turned within, rolled and heaved and gathered itself into a voice that now spilled from him and blasted into the ether, leeching the menace from the air, scorching the unholy aura that spilled from Kali's form, harnessing the viscera of unleashed evil that oozed from his blackness:

"*Klim Krishnaya Govindaya Gopi Jana Ballabaya Swaha…*"

...and once more the universe tipped on its axis, a sufficient degree to alter the malefic influence of the age whose personified form stood before him; these, the words of the mantra Dadaji had given him all those years ago – chanted for decades, morning noon and night, never failing, never leaving, never anything else carving his life-path but these words...

They soared into the air, a storm-force purity of transcendent beauty, the only antidote to this cancer, devouring the disease that was Kali and vanishing to oblivion the ill-effects of his presence. And as Raj roared the words repeatedly, others in the Durbar Hall began to chant the mantra with him, quietly at first, unsure, but emboldened by the pure energy that laced the air and drenched the walls. And as Raj roared and lost himself in the power of the mantra, the world watched in stunned fascination and saw, before Raj did, the death of Kali's power, as before their eyes, under the force of Raj's chant, his form once more changed: no more the cruelly handsome, powerful, large, and dominating figure that had crashed the party. This creature, now wilting and shrinking, began to assume his real identity.

Raj had been lost, absorbed in the energy that was the mantra, in Dadaji; he now lowered his gaze to Kali and saw the mantra, still hanging in the ether, pouring like acid over the hideous form before him. Raj and the world watched as Kali's writhing body became smaller and assumed a crow-like appearance with a face frightening to behold, his tongue red and protruding, a hideous creature equalled only by the foul stench emanating from his body.

The unexpected laugh burst into Raj's consciousness,

the laugh of Dadaji, here in the room. *He is here.* He looked up.

And there he was.

A wave of love so powerful and raw and real, so real, there, right in that moment, swept Raj into its embrace and filled his heart, overflowing and pouring from his eyes in torrents. The beautiful, light-filled form of Dadaji stood before him, and the world around him stopped, everyone in it blind to his Dadaji – a pocket of eternal time in the universe that no one could enter into.

And then one by one they appeared: Devi, her sparkling, jewelled form draped in gossamer-thin red silk; Saraswati, whose ethereal white robes lit up the world; Hanuman, his enormous form contained within the walls of the Durbar Hall, the heady scent of *parijata* surrounding him; and Vrinda Devi, her parrot emitting screeches of victory as she laughed in delight.

And in the middle of them all, his Dadaji.

It was then Raj realised that he had known all along, known that his Dadaji was not just his grandfather but the agent of these exalted beings. He had known and never asked, never dared to enter into a realm of understanding whose borders he felt unqualified to cross, knowing that the question itself barred his entrance to the answer that lay on the other side of those borders. For years, it had teased the edges of his intellect, and he had dismissed it: *in good time,* he had thought.

And now the time was exceptionally good. It was only natural that Saraswati, the goddess of learning, would speak. "Yes, Rajendra, you are right," she said, as her arm waved gracefully towards her associates. "We all mentioned

Dadaji to you, because he is known, and so very dear, to us all." She paused, turning to Hanuman, inviting him to speak with a slight movement of her head. Hanuman bowed his head slightly, his palms together at his chest, honouring the demigoddess before him. He turned to Raj, his face softening, the memory of the loving exchange they had shared suddenly manifesting like a tangible energy between them. "Rajendra… I have missed you," he said, his words surprising the others, and especially Rajendra. They laughed in delight, and he continued, "You are right. Your grandfather was never an ordinary person, and not just in your eyes. He is the living form of the divine energy in your heart, Rajendra. He is your *caitya-guru.* The Lord is eternally situated in the heart of every living being, and when the time comes, he will manifest in person in the form of one's spiritual guide. This is your Dadaji, Rajendra. This is your spiritual master, the Lord from your heart…"

Dadaji came forward then, as did Raj, and they melded into one, their arms holding the other to him with such force. Raj had never experienced the feeling of love he was drowning in now; his arms once again around his Dadaji, once again just a young boy, *chhota pota,* the intervening years since Dadaji's death gone, melted, forgotten. Dadaji stepped back and held Raj's face in his hands, his love emanating in waves and once again drowning Raj. "*Mera pota…*" and everyone laughed, the loving exchange so very powerful, sweet, and fulfilling.

Raj had so much to say but knew his time was brief. Fresh tears sprang forth at the thought, but he checked them, and said, "What now, Dadaji? How can I stay here? What is there to do… will Kali return? What is my purpose..." the words rushed from him in a desperate bid to be spoken before this moment ended.

Devi spoke, her musical voice washing over Raj. "*Ahh*, Rajendra, do you forget so easily for what purpose you came? Not satisfied with your former life as the Imperial Princess Zeb-un-Nissa, you again took birth to fulfil her destiny, your destiny. And it awaits you... it is only the beginning. All that you longed for will come to you, do not doubt it."

Dadaji looked from one to the other, overwhelmed and speechless. He turned back to Dadaji and said, "Dadaji, all these years I have felt you next to me always..."

"*Mera pota,* do not be sad! Yes, I have been with you, and I will always be with you. Do not fear the future; you have accomplished a great feat here today, the whole universe is singing your praise... believe me. And we will always be together, all of us. Do not fear, Emperor Rajendra Gupta. Do not fear..."

And just like that – just as always – they were gone. Raj turned and the Durbar Hall was there once more, the guests all there still, waiting for his next word – only a moment had passed in their eyes, and none had seen his meeting with his lords and Dadaji. *I do not know how I am meant to go on,* he thought.

And as he did so, a roar burst from the hall as the guests erupted in applause and cheering as Raj noticed the once-powerful Kali, now a crumpled, tiny, horrendous being on the floor before him, and his off-shoot, Lust, no longer a snapping and furious beast but an equally insignificant bird-like creature who flapped in distress and lunged in futile desperation towards her master, longing for his once-guaranteed shelter that now lay in the mess of stool and droppings that muddied the floor.

Raj curled his lip and called to the attendants, "Clean this mess up..." and again the crowd cheered, the deafening roar, Raj realised, now coming from the beyond the Durbar Hall, from outside the palace, beyond the gates, and across the city, the nation... the world.

Raj turned to the one thousand guests in the Durbar Hall, and raised his hands in the air in a victory salute as his attendants carried Kali and Kama from the room. He then turned towards the balcony above the hall, his arms still raised, and beamed a smile into the camera that in turn beamed across the world...

We have won, Dadaji... we have won...

9

Interval

IN the ensuing days after Kali's defeat, the world leaders and guests who had attended the Bhavya Mahotsava assembled and listened as the emperor addressed the nation, and the world, from the palace lawns. "While Kali has been defeated, it should be understood that he cannot be confined." The world once again drank in the emperor's words on the same screens and in the same public areas as they had watched him defeat Kali, and Raj did his best to explain what they had witnessed. "Where the mantra of the holy names is sung and heard, Kali cannot survive. He was given dominance only over those areas where the lower qualities of life are prevalent. And so those, too, have been confined; we cannot control the desires of every individual living being, but we can protect those who want to live in a world free of the influence of Kali and his cohorts."

Thus the world accepted readily the power of the spiritual energy over the material, and embraced the changes to their daily lives in much the same way as the people of Delhi, and then the whole nation, had done under Raj's influence and compassionate guidance. Gone was the religious divisiveness, the prejudices and segregations that swamped the world and prevented the unity of spirit and purpose that Raj and so many others had for so long dreamed. There was a long way to go, but Kali had been defeated.

The world had again cheered at Raj's words, and as the weeks unfolded, cities around the world decorated their own skies morning, noon, and night with divine chants from every form of spiritual practice that existed in their countries; sacred mantras emanated from walls and rooftops across the planet, and provided a subtle yet ultimately, far more powerful protection than any number of armed forces had ever achieved. While Kali was trailed always by greed, falsehood, robbery, incivility, treachery, misfortune, cheating and vanity – just the tip of the iceberg of his abhorrent associates – in his defeat they fled. And so the lands flourished as Kali was banished, his attendants shunned, and the vices they so freely distributed renounced.

And as the emperor's words on Kali's demise were listened to internationally, so, too, his words were read the world over on news sites and in magazines, answering the question that arose in everyone's mind of how Kali and his aide, Kama, were able to enter the Bhavya Mahotsava;that one small sparkling orb that had fallen from Kama's ankle bells decades ago, her possession, her energy, all owned by Kali, had been sufficient to allow their entrance, its odious connection to its owners a reminder to Raj how even a glimpse of the energies of the lower qualities in life was enough to bring down an entire nation. It had been retrieved from the safe in his chambers and tied to the neck of Kama as they were banished from the city, both taking a pathetic flight in their weakling states, stumbling through the air, falling repeatedly, but eventually disappearing... to where, no one knew, but all praying that they would never been seen again.

Raj thought now of the history of Delhi and the curse that had been laid at its door: that whomsoever assailed her borders and triumphed would himself one day be defeated. Thus while emperors had ruled for thousands and thousands of years and all had failed to keep evil intruders at bay – especially Kali – so Emperor Rajendra had set out to deepen the spiritually rich impact the culture had in its many forms over the city and its people, protecting them and pleasing them at once. He had no intention of allowing this curse to have power in what he and all within her walls considered *their* city.

Despite the differences in all the forms of spirituality that India hosted, still there was one key element they shared: chanting, praying, and singing the names of the Lord – however that Lord appeared to the individual. The Sufi *qawwalas,* the Vaishnava *maha-mantra*, the Muslim *salat,* the Buddhist *daimoku,* the Christian hymns – these and indeed all the practices shared the element of praise in word and song. And so Raj had taken that element and expanded it to the point that it was the one religious extreme he would tolerate in the land. Thus throughout the country, songs, prayers, mantras, and chants of all forms could be heard all through the day, honouring each and giving favour to none. The country now courted a multi-national, multi-religious, multi-spiritual mood. That was all Raj was interested in.

Now from each pillar of the palace emanated not only the *ragas* commensurate with the time of the day, but also the sound of sacred mantras, duplicated in similar, smaller pillars all across the city. The effect was stunning: imbued with spiritual potency, the sound vibration stood guard to the lower qualities that threatened to disrupt the peaceful lives of all within Delhi's walls, and kept the darker elements at bay. Kali was unable to break through this most powerful of security systems, and those within felt little or no need at all to leave its precincts and seek that which Kali and his consorts had to offer. The city was, at last, safe.

We have been through a lot, this country and me, thought Raj. While it was true that the greatest adventures of his life were behind him, Raj was lured into the trap of thinking that little could surprise him. He was about to be reminded of how wrong he could be...

* * * *

It was dark. The thick, stone walls were cold, and chilled the room. He paced the floor, his boots grinding the dirt and sand on the ground, the crunching the only sound in the vast room. They all watched him pace, too afraid to speak.

Kali knew he had been defeated, and knew there was little he could do in an immediate sense to turn his fate around. It had been written long ago, and while he would never surrender to it, still it would take him some time to set his course straight and again rule this miserable planet.

Just like the days of that foolish emperor, Parikshit, he thought savagely to himself as he paced. While he could attempt to unsettle Raj and his "kingdom," he knew it would be to no avail. Raj ruled, and Kali was subjugated.

The anger in the room pulsed and throbbed, and his attendants cowered, silent and fearful, waiting.

My time will come again, he thought. *And you will feel my wrath and bear the suffering due to you for usurping my reign, 'Emperor' Rajendra...*

Kali continued to pace, his anger building, as his attendants continued their fearful, silent vigil.

10

The Jewel of the Empire

ALL was well in the land.

It has been a year since the Bhavya Mahotsava, and much had transpired.

As in the days of Zeb-un-Nissa, now once again grand events of song, poetry, and music, exchanges of literary, philosophical, and spiritual depth, readings and performances, dramas and soliloquys were the ornaments of the evening, and the diamond-like stars that studded the sky were merely observers. The birds sang in appreciation, flowers bloomed in support, and thousands gathered around the palace grounds to hear and watch. Daily the city resounded with these jewels of all the cultures of the land. Raj loved the rich atmosphere that prevailed in the heady dusk air, and was always in attendance: it was his favourite time of day.

He was still unmarried: no woman had ever breached the wall of his resolve to dedicate his life to the service of his Lord. While he had never taken a vow of celibacy or renunciation, he was seen as something of a monk. Yet, while the nation's hearts held nothing but respect for that order of life, they still felt pained at Raj's aloneness and prayed that his heart find love... as his parents did, still. They all felt the futility of their hope, however; especially since the evening of the Bhavya Mahotsava, which Raj would never forget. A woman had captured his mind and lowered his defense, and it had almost cost him everything. He had to remind himself often that it was lust personified, Kama herself, who had been the only woman ever to almost storm the ramparts of his single life. *I will not allow that to happen again,* he thought.

As the autumn day turned its burned-orange leaves to night, Raj's thoughts were gently interrupted as a woman entered the grounds and took a seat at the edge of the gathering. She was dressed in white, her face partially veiled with a thin chiffon cloth that draped delicately below her eyes from one ear to the other. *The unmistakeable beauty of chastity,* Raj thought, as his forehead frowned slightly in concentration. He wondered who she was and from where she hailed. Distracted by the entry of other guests, Raj turned from the woman and played host to the latest arrivals. As he spoke quietly and affably to all, suddenly a sound tore through the ether and entered his... *heart?* he wondered.

Turning to its source, he saw her: the woman in white, singing a Persian *ghazal,* now a *qawwali* – the poem-turned-song style of Sufi singers, decorating the air with lyrical string notes.

Her head-dress and robes were of the Sufi tradition, and as the night's cultural performance continued, she read poetry and sang again. As the evening drew to a close, Raj bid his his guests goodbye, and as he turned back to where the woman sat, he was sorry to see that she had left. He discreetly asked his attendant who she was; all knew her, as she frequented the cultural evenings around the city and in neighbouring towns, and she was admired by *brahmins* and *muezzins* alike, though no one knew of her background – at these events, the anonymity of the night and the open door to all was part of the magic. She was, apparently, always attended by a tall man, a servant who accompanied her and was clearly her guardian.

The next evening, however, she returned, and Raj watched with quiet fascination as she again lifted her lilting voice to the skies, and recited the most beautiful *ghazals,* some classics, some her own. She was in her late thirties, he guessed, and was surprised to note his relief that she was not just a young girl. He smiled to himself, watching his enamoured attraction as though a third party. It took him only two audiences with her to realise that despite his new resolve to actively avoid female companionship, this woman had captured his heart, although they had not yet met. As he watched her from the Emperor's Terrace this second night, he suddenly understood that in her sat all the things he had dreamed of, the elements of culture and beauty and language and song and art and history and literature and spirituality that he longed for and to which he gave shelter in his city – all of it came to fruition in this woman.

And he knew it was futile to postpone the inevitable. Rising from the soft cushions of the white wicker chair on his terrace, he walked down the low-slung steps into the gathering, the people on the lawns clearing a path for their emperor, his own white robes flowing behind him. He was a vision of regal stature, his enigmatic smile gracing everyone who looked or nodded, who acknowledged or spoke to him. He was truly a king among men, and those around him warmed to his physical presence.

He reached the area where the woman was seated, and she rose to greet the emperor and offer her respects. And as she raised her head, he looked into her eyes and knew *I did not know I was hiding, and yet she found me...*

Raj turned to her male attendant, who had discreetly indicated his presence. He was dressed in the clothes of an imperial court, and Raj was surprised to note the regal detail of his bearing. The attendant bowed and addressed Raj in a voice that glowed with the polish of faraway land. Raj was intrigued.

"Your Majesty. I am Colonel Surindar Singh of the Rajasthan Court."

"Welcome, Colonel Singh. I am honoured by the appearance of the noble Court at our evening *soiree*. Forgive me for not recognising the presence of royalty..." Raj said, his eyes moving to the woman, the question lingering in the air.

Colonel Singh reassured Raj. "Please, Your Majesty. There is no apology required. For so long my charge has remained unknown. In her youth, her parents longed to give her an international education, an anonymous schooling with all the benefits yet none of the burdens of her upbringing." He paused, and with a hint of pride continued, "Her true love is literature and art, poetry and song, and she has avoided society so that her love of these things would not be hindered by the pursuance of those who longed only for her kingdom and wealth through the dubious disguise of love and marriage."

Raj was surprised and said, "I'm sorry... her 'kingdom'? Please... who is this fine lady?"

"Your Majesty, I present to you Her Highess Rajputani Radhabai Veera Jodhamala, the jewel of the Rajput Empire, the Imperial Princess of the Rajasthan Court, the daughter of Maharaja Singh and Queen Gayatri." He bowed again and then rose, stayed silent, and waited.

Raj was confused. He had never known that the Rajputs had a daughter, an heiress to her father's throne. Why did he not know this? Seeing the questioning frown of confusion on Raj's brow, the attendant said, "It was the parents' desire, Your Majesty. They wanted their heiress to have as broad and balanced an upbringing as possible. Her schooling – indeed her life – has been a truly international yet rather covert operation." He smiled in obvious glee at the mysterious drama that had been her life. "Her pale complexion and green eyes have given her entrance to nations who are ignorant of her true background. She has been the Rajput Court's best secret." He paused, a quiet and solemn tone entering his voice: "And since the death of her mother, the queen, she has remained in-state; it has weakened and saddened her..." his voice trailed off, and Raj silently absorbed the revelations of this princess's existence.

While the royal families had been prominently returned to their former grace for almost two decades, it was a different kind of rule that shunned the glitz, fame, and wastrel mood of former princely ruling. It was hardly surprising, then, that this princess's early years could be kept a secret to most. The families were private, their noble blood now stronger from years of adjustment to a changed world, their inherent skills sharpened in banking and business circles, and their associates able businessmen whose influence could benefit their states.

The colonel smiled at Raj's silence, detecting a pleasure in his eyes that satisfied him. He hesitated, but decided that His Majesty the Emperor should know the full story; he had spoken this much, why not tell him the last detail?

"The truth is, Your Majesty, the king and queen never expected their daughter's identity to remain secret for so long, but to their delight it has. To aid in this harmless, but what they felt necessary, 'deception,' they never referred to Her Highness as a member of a royal family, or addressed her by her full regal name."

Raj was intrigued. "Then perhaps you would be so kind as to tell me how Her Highness is addressed?" he said, smiling at the silent, bowed head of the Imperial Rajput Princess who stood before him.

The attendant smiled. "Her Highness has, all her life, been affectionately called by the name another emperor's daughter was once known by long ago, a girl who also sang *ghazals* and penned poetry. Her Highness's nickname is the pen name of the Mughal Imperial Princess Zeb-un-Nissa: Makhfi, the Hidden One..."

...and the world once more tilted on its axis as Raj's mind trembled, then stilled. Memories from decades before surged to the forefront of his thoughts, not decades old at all but fresh, born only moments ago, new and meaningful and ever-present and eternal. One by one they came: first the laughing voice of Dadaji eddied and swayed like the rising and falling ocean tides; then Devi, as she had appeared in the sparkling waters of the Yamuna at dusk in Agra, her gossamer robes splashed with the sparkling drops of the river's waters; then Saraswati, her purity and clarity cutting through all his illusions in the crisp dawn in the Ganges; Hanuman in Rishikesh, and his warmth, love, affection, and wisdom; and Vrinda Devi, the goddess of the eternal playground of Krishna and Radha in Vrindavan. All of them appeared before him suddenly, and he was uncertain if it were memory or whether, if he reached out to touch them, they would disappear. His heart soared in gratitude at their appearing once again before him, so many years of separation now evaporating as his eyes drank in their forms, his heart dancing in joy at their scent, sound, and vision.

And he especially remembered Saraswati's revelations of his former birth as the imperial princess of the Mughal Empire, Zeb-un-Nissa, whose life was driven by a longing for union of all forms of spirituality and tradition, who had died untimely in prison at the hands of her father Aurangzeb, her wishes unfulfilled yet powerful enough to dictate her future birth in the form of Rajendra Gupta, who would one day be Emperor, and who now stood before this woman who reminded him of who he once had been, and who called herself the name he, as Zeb-un-Nissa, had been known: Makhfi, The Hidden One...

...and somewhere in Vrindavan a parrot screeched, and the world kept turning...

Epilogue

Gopal

IT was dark, the heavy blinds lowered to just a few inches above the mirror-like marble floors. From the pillars beyond the balconies the notes of *ragas* and *mantras* drifted across the city that sat still and quiet outside the palace gates as its beloved lay dying within.

The suite was large and open; wide spaces and clean lines, smoothness and polish, uncluttered simplicity, refined elegance. The exquisitely carved marble platform in the centre bore the softest of mattresses and pillows in muted tones; a stage set for the evening performance, slightly raised, still yet ready.

And upon the crisp white sheets lay Emperor Rajendra Gupta, his breathing slow and quiet, his life nearing its end, his eighty eight years drawing to a close...

While his body laboured, his mind was yet sharp; peaceful, resigned, and ready. *It is nearly time,* he thought. *Not long now...*

* * * *

Decades had past since the night of the Bhavya Mahotsava, and the defeat of Kali. In so many ways it had all been about that night: though he had not known it then, that was his legacy, his service, his purpose. So much had ended that night, but another lifetime had begun. Radhabhai: the impossibly beautiful love that had been his Radhabhai. Their marriage, their years together, and the love they had shared.

Gone... just one week before she had breathed her last, taking with her Raj's one remaining reason for staying in this world.

They had spent over four wondrous decades together, every moment more blissful than the last. There were no regrets; his sadness was soul-deep, yet while he could express it to no one, it fuelled his internal spiritual meditations, a life no one saw or knew of, could ever understand – only his Dadaji, and then Radhabai. *They are all within: Dadaji, Radhabhai, Mammi and Bapi... the love was not of this world, not confined by this world... they gave me everything, materially, physically, and spiritually... Dadaji... he gave me my life and my Lord, my meditation and meaning, my purpose and life breath. What would I have become had I not been born into Dadaji's family?*

* * * *

Briefly his eyes opened, then the eyelids dropped shut as he reminded himself there was nothing to see... nothing without, only within. Raj drew himself back into his own depths; he remembered his long-ago descent into the dark, cool waters of the Ganga on his pre-dawn visit to her shores in Patna; the soothing possibility of absolute silence and intoxicating stillness as the waters rolled velvety over his body.

...descend lower, descend only into the world of perpetual solitude...

But it is not like that, he thought now, as the world closed around him. *I was so young and... nothing, nothing... there was so much to love and know and hear and taste and do... just do...*

More and more he heard Dadaji's voice, an echo in his heart that rang in his mind, over and over, beckoning like Ganga's waters, luring him to the edge and wanting, wanting to pull him over.

And this is death, Raj thought. *This, at the end of it all, is death. I have no energy to speak, I hear the words of my Dadaji, the poetry of my beloved Radhabai, the ghazals by my own hand as Zeb-un-Nissa... what does it matter, my name, now? It is over. I wait now not for the taunts of my next birth, but for the call of that one voice...*

All through his life Dadaji had given, encouraged, taught, reminded, and returned to force him when needed, only ever to rely on that *mantra*, that name. *This is what it was all leading to. This...*

Again, still, he heard the voice of Dadaji, did not know what he was saying though the words were constant, loving, and there, always there, just there, though they were a blur... but it did not matter; it was all given, all known, all done and said and spoken and experienced. There was nothing to say. *This... only this...*

The Gopal mantra flooded his mind, a dervish dance in the transcendental drunken state of being he occupied, the words flowing and flowing, whirling faster and louder, a rush that drew him and pulled him and would not let go, would never ever ever let go...

...and amidst the noise and movement and silence and absolute nothingness and everythingness of his private, most private moment, suddenly he appeared, more beautiful than Raj could take, promising to press the life airs from his body with sheer beauty, the scent and sound and sight enough to release him from the universe, and he rose breathless and followed the form, dark like a monsoon cloud and draped in golden-yellow, the form whose flute-song drew him closer and closer and the taste, oh the taste of Gopal, Gopal, his Gopal...

Acknowledgements

I once thought, many years ago, that the Acknowledgements page in a book was an author's personal note to an expected few, a somewhat private exchange made public – formal, required, but not something anyone was really so interested to read. I was wrong.

I started reading them, and found that they were like a doorway into a warm, all-embracing, formerly private club whose membership was now open. And I loved them. They drew me in, shared things I would never otherwise have known, broadened the field of exchange and personalism, and tied up the entire book with a shiny new irresistible ribbon that one simply cannot help tugging at, unravelling the deliciousness within.

So here are my acknowledgements...

Before the book even began, it was given wings by my friend and favourite writer since the '80s, William Dalrymple. A few years ago, as we wandered around his farm after lunch, surveying his kingdom of goats (peace be to Gilbert), he encouraged me to "write from the heart... write what you know." And so I did. *Of Noble Blood* is the direct result of that day, which for so many reasons remains a very dear memory. I am grateful and indebted for the loving ease with which William and his beloved Olivia share themselves so often and with so many. Thank you.

While *Of Noble Blood* found its wings on that farm in Delhi's outskirts, it found its feet and formed its foundation on another farm: this one in Hungary, two hours from Budapest, in the breathtakingly beautiful valleys of Somogyvámos, at a most special and unique place called New Vraja-dhama, known across Europe and beyond as Krishna Valley. In 500 acres of rolling green hills, next to rivers and trickling brooks, under the shade of the pink-sweet cherry trees, I was given a cottage, a home, guidance, shelter, advice, and so much love and encouragement from the devotees of Krishna who live in that idyllic setting. Especially, Sivarama Swami: a prolific author of Vaishnava literature, my guide and mentor, my dear friend, the person who is my writing "partner" in so many ways. I serve as editor to him, but find it impossible to clearly explain what I am given in return. Although I only stayed there for a few months, he helped daily as the beginnings of this book started to unfold, gave me ideas, storylines, and helped in so many ways over the years it took to bring this book to fruition. To him, and everyone at New Vraja-dhama, I am, always, grateful and indebted. Thank you.

To my agent, the wonderful Kanishka Gupta from Writer's Side Agency in New Delhi, who thought that one book was obviously too easy a deal, and so secured me a publishing contract for another, almost simultaneously; who shared with me, throughout the process, of bringing both books to publishing readiness, his own unique, marvellous, deep, hilarious, and thoroughly entertaining self through his own writings, for which he has also found a publisher. It is no surprise that he is considered by Publishers Marketplace (NYC) to be "the number one dealmaker in publishing." He is definitely my #1 Dealmaker, my Rockstar Agent. Thank you, Kan... and here's to many more... for us both.

To my husband, Jahnu, who believed in this book, and all the others, long before I ever did, whose encouragement is the backbone of my writer's life, whose support means that all I need do is write, and nothing more...yet I cannot find the words to express what a gift my life is because of that support and encouragement, the no-expectation ease that is his nature, the space he gives that allows me simply to write, the ideas, thoughts, depths, philosophy, and explanations that pour from him like water from a tap. I am, again, grateful and indebted. Thank you.

In the Vaishnava tradition, the best is saved for last. And so it is that I come to the end with an acknowledgement that will never be read by the one for whom it is written. My spiritual master and dearest friend, Tamal Krishna Goswami (1946-2002), my inspiration and rock, whose last letter to me read, "Just write...", and so I did. He is the reason I came to India, the reason I live here still, the reason I write, the reason for most things practical, spiritual, and most deeply heartfelt, heart-changing, and heart-born with me. He would have loved *Of Noble Blood,* and indeed he is within its very pages, his unique and remarkable personality woven through the character of Dadaji, a character who is a combination of him, of the person to whom the book is dedicated, A. C. Bhaktivedanta Swami, and of Sivarama Swami. In Dadaji, all three are present. In me, I pray all three are ever present...